G.D.

**ON THE FRONT LINES OF
THE WORLD'S LAST WAR:**

FRANCISCO MARTINEZ, U.S. SPECIAL FORCES:
He's a highly trained, highly disciplined, multilethal Green
Beret captain. He got the go-ahead for a daring prisoner
snatch and rescue mission in the Nicaragua jungle. Then
he got permission to lead his twelve men out again—into
a jungle full of enemies.

MORRIS REISMAN: The experienced,war-tested journalist saw a savage Chinese atrocity in a Nepalese village
twelve hundred feet in the mountains. But the world was
too busy to listen to his story, and another conflict, halfway around the globe, was waiting to be exposed.

SANDI PAULDING: The former university instructor had
been called into active reserve during Operation Desert
Storm. Now, as chief of intelligence, she tried to warn the
top brass that Mexico was the number-one powder keg—
and that Cuba was the fuse ready to ignite it.

WILLIAM JOSEPH DANIELS: He called himself commander of the Defenders of the Texas Revolution. With his
ragtag army of fanatics, he would stage a raid on an American auto factory in Mexico—and then make a bloody
stand against a U.S. military siege.

MAJOR JOHN FRANKOWSKI: As hard and sharp as
steel, he was flying a crucial air patrol over the U.S.-
Mexican border. In a matter of hours, the conflict had spun
out of contro⸏⸏⸏⸏⸏⸏⸏⸏⸏⸏⸏⸏⸏⸏ng machine
down the thr⸏⸏⸏

D0963741

Bantam Books by Capt. Kevin D. Randle, USAFR
Ask your bookseller for the books you have missed

DAWN OF CONFLICT
BORDER WINDS

GLOBAL WAR

Book

—————— II ——————

BORDER WINDS

Capt. Kevin D. Randle, USAFR

BANTAM BOOKS
NEW YORK • TORONTO • LONDON • SYDNEY • AUCKLAND

BORDER WINDS

A Bantam Falcon Book / November 1992

FALCON and the portrayal of a boxed "f" are trademarks of
Bantam Books,
a division of Bantam Doubleday Dell Publishing Group, Inc.

All right reserved.
Copyright © 1992 by Kevin Randle.
Cover art copyright © 1992 by Alan Ayers.
No part of this book may be reproduced or transmitted in any form
or by any means, electronic or mechanical, including photocopying,
recording, or by any information storage and retrieval system,
without permission in writing from the publisher.
For information address: Bantam Books.

ISBN 0-553-29820-8

Published Simultaneously in the United States and Canada

Bantam Books are published by Bantam Books, a division of Bantam
Doubleday Dell Publishing Group, Inc. Its trademark, consisting of the
words "Bantam Books"-and the portrayal of a rooster, is Registered in
U.S. Patent and Trademark Office and in other countries. Marca
Registrada. Bantam Books, 666 Fifth Avenue, New York, New York
10103.

PRINTED IN THE UNITED STATES OF AMERICA

RAD 0 9 8 7 6 5 4 3 2 1

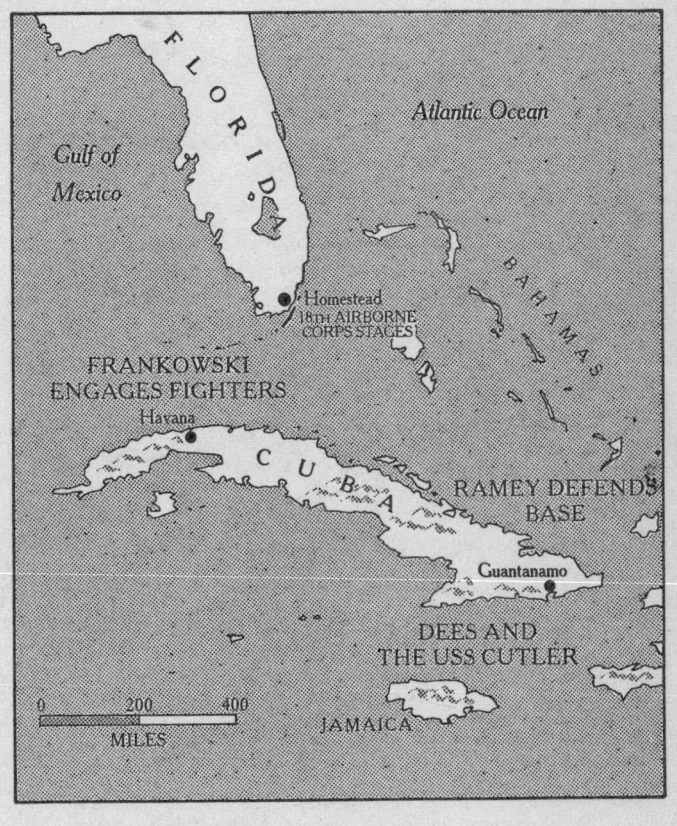

FLORIDA

Atlantic Ocean

Gulf of Mexico

BAHAMAS

Homestead
18TH AIRBORNE
CORPS STAGES

FRANKOWSKI
ENGAGES FIGHTERS

Havana

C U B A

RAMEY DEFENDS
BASE

Guantanamo

DEES AND
THE USS CUTLER

0   200   400
MILES

JAMAICA

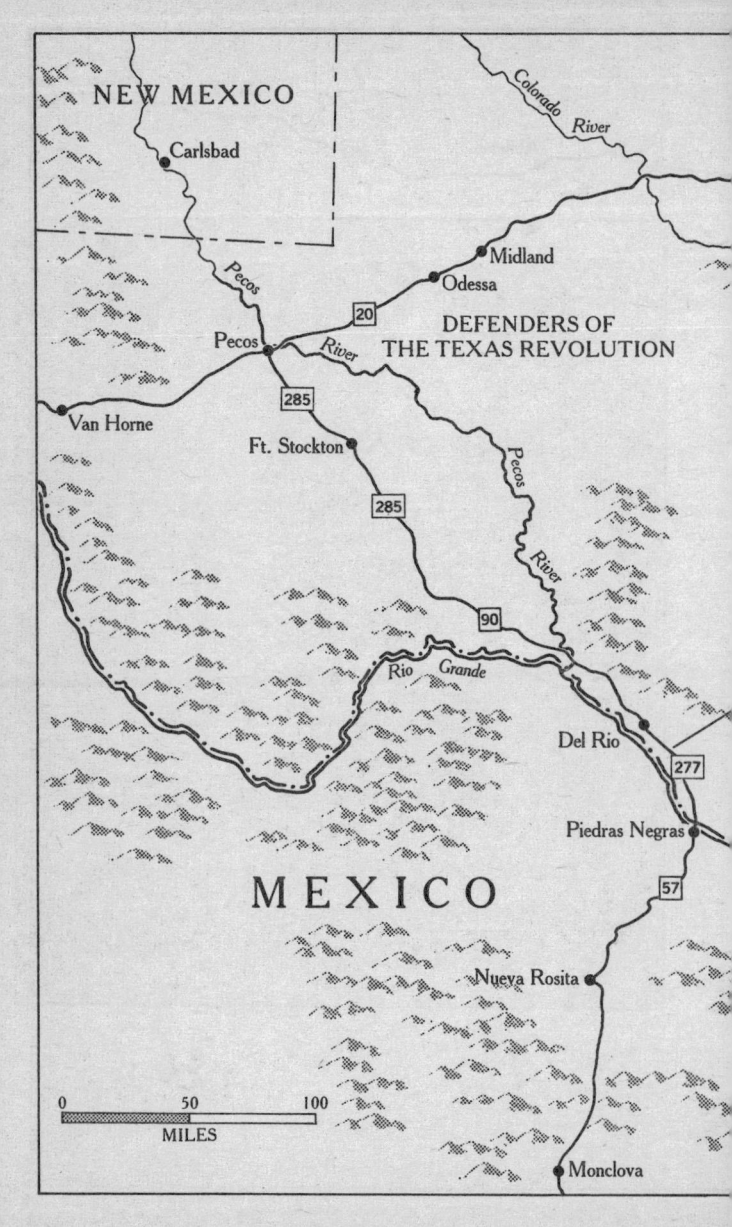

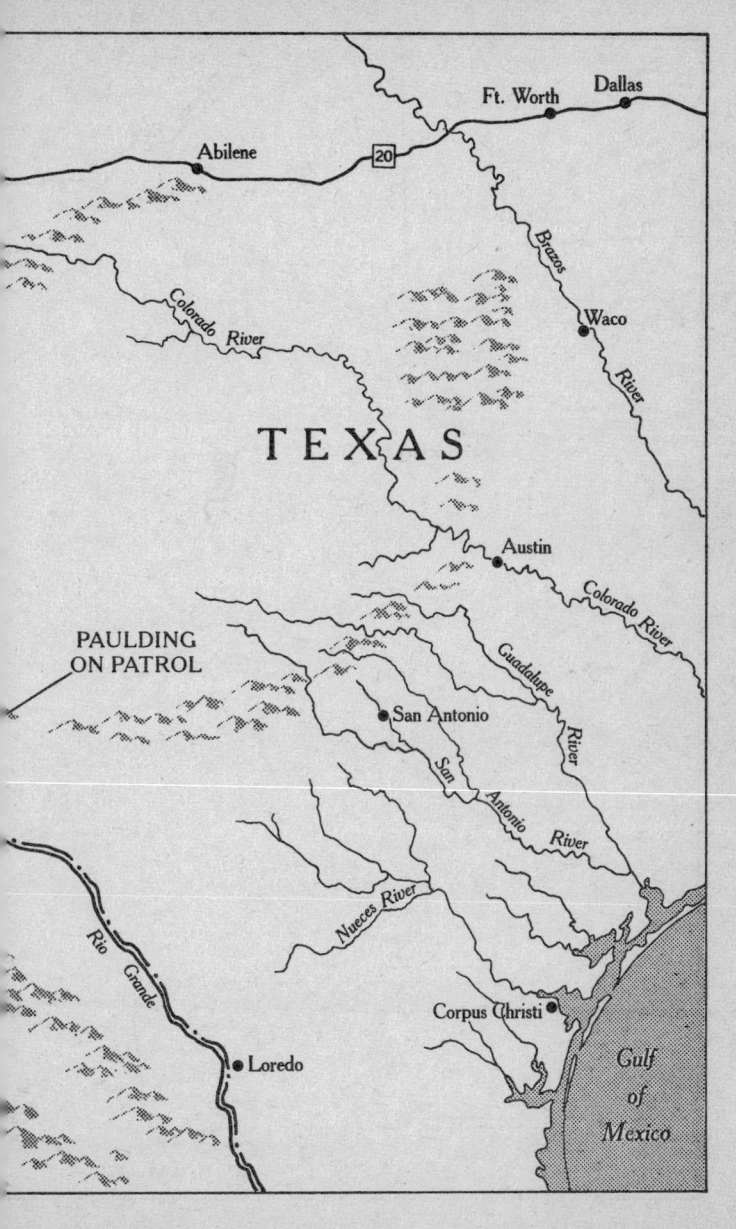

THE JUNGLE OUTSIDE MANAGUA, NICARAGUA

There was one last chance to pull it off, and if it failed, Jesus Castillo along with his men in the jungle and those who supported him in Managua would forfeit their lives. He slipped back from the edge of the jungle, hiding himself in the deep shadows. Even with the sun high in the morning sky, the jungle was dim and damp and protective.

"We are ready," said Julio Llanca.

Castillo lifted a hand and wiped the sweat from his face. He pulled the soft, camouflaged hat from his head and ran a hand through his soaked hair. He rubbed his palm on the front of his fatigue shirt, leaving a wet, ragged stain. "Another few minutes. We must wait for the signal."

"Certainly, sir."

Castillo watched Llanca move off, crouching near a sergeant and then disappearing into the thick foliage. He checked his weapon, an old AK-47 that had been given to him twenty years earlier when the Sandinistas had been courting the Soviets, who were supplying military and economic aid.

It was a reliable weapon. Parts of the stock had been worn thin and shrapnel scars showed on the receiver group. But the weapon was sound and as reliable today as it had been when new. Not a spot of rust on it.

"Colonel," said a voice behind him. "They're beginning the move now."

"Thank you, Sergeant." Castillo thumbed the selector switch on his AK to single shot and then back to safe. He was never sure if it was better to move through the jungle with the weapon ready to fire or not. A wrong step, a vine or branch, and the rifle would discharge. But in the beginning of a firefight, in case of an ambush, it was better to be able to shoot back. A fraction of a second could mean the difference between life and death.

Again he moved to the very edge of the jungle. The trees, bushes, vines, ferns, and flowers stopped abruptly, as if they had been hacked clean with a giant knife. The ground dropped away gently to a camp occupied by government soldiers. Normally they stayed behind their barbed-wire fences, but in the last three weeks, as rumors of coups had ripped through the capital, the members of the elite Managua Freedom Brigade had quietly moved to the camp. They were waiting to see if they'd be needed to put down a revolt.

For the last two weeks Castillo and his men had waited in the jungle, watching. They had kept moving, patrolling, searching the enemy position, but the commanders in the camp had decided it was best to stay put. Let the people think the soldiers were content to sit back.

"First radio message is in," said a man standing close to Castillo. "They're going to move."

Castillo looked at his watch, though it told him nothing. The attack signal would be broadcast. It was not timed. He nodded but kept his eyes on the enemy camp.

There was movement behind the wire. A soldier, his rifle shouldered, marched inside the perimeter. It was for show and nothing more. A real guard would not be so easy to watch. He would be hidden where he would be able to fire at an approaching enemy. This soldier with the rifle was an ornament.

The radio operator, an earphone of the headset pressed against his ear, reached down and twisted a knob. He sat back, glanced at Castillo. "We are ordered to attack."

Castillo knew what that meant. Other soldiers, in other areas, in the small cities far from Managua, would begin their assault, everyone moving at once so that no one could alert the government stooges.

The single guard had moved off. It would be ten or twelve minutes before his path brought him around so that he would see Castillo and his soldiers attacking.

Without a word Castillo rose to his feet. He glanced right and left, watching as the line of soldiers stood with him, each wearing camouflaged fatigues and carrying the weapons supplied by the Russians, and later by the Cubans. Waving a hand, Castillo left the cover of the jungle and stepped out into the sunlight.

He hesitated and then began to run down the hill toward the enemy camp. His eyes swept the fence line and the structures behind it, including the guard towers and protective bunkers, though they were unmanned.

There was no indication from the base that anyone saw them coming. Castillo knew that he had the advantage of complete surprise. There had been no hostilities for months and the government soldiers had slipped into apathy. They were unprepared for any type of military action. Before they could react, the fight should be over.

In less than a minute Castillo was crouched at the base of the chain-link fence. Sweat was dripping down his face and sides. His breathing was rapid, but the short run downhill hadn't taxed him.

Two men with bolt cutters were snipping at the fence

near the post. They would take out a twenty-foot-wide section. The rest of the assault team had fanned out in a semi-circle, protecting the rear. The second wave was at the edge of the jungle, waiting for the fence to fall.

As it did so the single guard appeared again. He stopped, looked at the assembled, armed men, and tried to pull his rifle off his soldier. Castillo fired once from the hip. The bullet slammed into the guard's chest, driving him back. He dropped his rifle, fell, and rolled. Blood spurted from the hole in his chest, first a fountain, then a bubbling, and finally nothing.

The men rushed through the fence, spreading out, filtering through the camp. Castillo and a squad ran toward the headquarters building. It was close to the front gate, with three flagpoles in front of it. A howitzer, probably for display rather than combat, sat pointing at the road leading to the camp.

Castillo reached it as two men came out the door. Both were dressed in pressed uniforms, one with a pistol holstered at his side and the other holding a rifle. A single shot on a military reservation was not an uncommon occurrence. It had alerted no one.

But the man with the rifle saw the armed soldiers running at him and recognized none of them. He swung his rifle around, but before he could fire, a burst hit him, stitching him from the throat to the groin. He was pushed back to the wall and fell to the ground, his blood splattering the grass.

Castillo fired at the other man. The round hit his shoulder and spun him. As he slipped to a knee he tried to draw his weapon, but a dozen shots were fired at him. A window behind his head exploded, and bits of wood from the building flew. He tried to dive for cover and was hit a second then a third time.

The rebels ran to the steps, jumped up them, and then Castillo stood aside as one of his men kicked in the door. They burst through. Two men inside scrambled for an exit, but were cut down. Another stood up slowly, his hands raised above his head. Castillo didn't care. He killed the man with a shot to the heart.

"Upstairs," yelled Castillo. He pointed to the rear of the office.

Two men broke from the main group and ran up the stairs. There was a shout and then a burst of fire. Something hit the floor.

Castillo snapped his fingers and pointed at the main door. A man spun to guard it. Before Castillo could point to the rear, a couple of his soldiers ran through the office, kicked open another door, and took up positions.

"Let's clear the building," ordered Castillo.

The rest of the soldiers began searching for anyone hiding. They dragged one man from a closet and pushed him to the floor in front of Castillo. Without hesitation Castillo put the barrel of his rifle against the man's head. When he pulled the trigger, the man flipped to his back. Blood poured from the wound, gray-green brain splattered the floor as the man drummed his hands and feet on the wood before dying.

Another group of soldiers appeared, pushing a lone woman. She was dressed in a short skirt, blouse, and sandals. She fell to her knees in front of Castillo and refused to look up at him.

A man ran into the room and stopped in front of Castillo. He began to lift his hand in salute and then remembered soldiers didn't salute in the field. "We have taken the main barracks. The soldiers have surrendered."

"Good."

"We hold the armory as well. The weapons are locked in there. We don't have the key."

Castillo waved a hand. "It doesn't matter now. We'll open it later."

"Yes, sir."

"Where is Major Fontes?"

"He is with the men who stormed the motor pool."

"Casualties?"

"No, sir. They surrendered without a fight. They had no weapons."

Castillo couldn't help grinning. That was what happened when bureaucrats and bean counters ran military operations. Rifles and pistols were dangerous, so they were locked up to prevent accidents. Then, when the soldiers needed them, their weapons were locked away where they were of no use.

Castillo turned and walked to the window. Shards of glass lay on the floor, sparkling in the afternoon sun. Clouds were building to the west, but that wouldn't matter now. His soldiers had shelter.

He noticed that three of his men were standing near the gate. They had moved a machine gun, which looked to be a 12.7mm antiaircraft weapon of Soviet design, to a point where it could guard the approaches. He turned and looked at the man who had joined them. "We hold the camp?"

"Yes, sir."

Castillo glanced at the radio operator, who had stayed close during the assault. "You may radio the code for success."

"Yes, sir."

"Do we have guards out in the whole camp?"

"Yes, sir. Guards on the captured soldiers, the motor pool, and the arms lockers."

"We get the radio room in time?"

"I don't think they managed to get off a distress signal. We knocked down the antenna farm before anything could be broadcast."

Castillo kicked his way into the commander's office. A chair had been knocked over and one pane of glass had been broken, but there was no real damage. He righted the chair, pushed it behind the desk, and sat down. He reached out, rubbing his hand across the desk, almost as if caressing it. He felt a sharp pain in his hand and jerked it back. A sliver of glass was embedded in his flesh, a drop of blood around it.

He pulled the glass from his finger and sucked off the blood. The first steps had been taken. The road to total control of Nicaragua was now before him.

The door opened then and Castillo looked up. The soldier standing in front of him wore a dirty uniform with one sleeve ripped. "Looks like you ran into it," said Castillo.

"Yes, sir, but we were able to overcome them easily. Major Cruz wants to know what to do with the prisoners."

Castillo took a deep breath. "All right. I think we'll shoot the senior officers, captains and above, the senior NCOs, and hold the others." Standing, he said, "Let's go find Major Cruz and take care of it."

"Yes, sir."

Castillo walked toward the door. It had been easy to take the camp. The question was, could they hold it? But that was always the question.

THE SPECIAL FORCES ISOLATION AREA, PANAMA

Army Special Forces captain Francisco Martinez sat in the air-conditioned briefing room listening to José Espinoza, one of the communications NCOs, give a lecture on first aid and snakebite during the briefback. That was the thing about the briefback, the FOB commander and his team asked everyone every question they could think of. The commo man might have to answer medical questions, the demolitions man might have to describe how to field-strip the light weapons, and the medic might have to explain the techniques of dropping a bridge.

Martinez was only five nine, with a slender build, but he was surprisingly strong, wiry and hard. He had short black hair, brown eyes, and an olive skin that was sun-darkened, so that he looked as if he had been born in Panama or one of the surrounding countries. He spoke fluent

Spanish, though those in the know could tell it was Texas Spanish, heavily accented with the inflections of the region.

He glanced to the right, where Colonel Cameron Boyce sat. The Special Forces officer was listening intently to what Espinoza was saying. Now pushing fifty, Cameron was an old man to be in the Special Forces, but he had done three tours in Vietnam, had run quiet operations into Latin America to eliminate guerrilla bands and drug lords, had survived the beginning of Desert Storm, when Special Forces teams had dropped into Iraq before the air war had been launched, and was as knowledgeable about SF operations and Latin America as anyone in Panama, the CIA, or the Pentagon.

Boyce leaned over and whispered something to Major Kirby Lombard, who then said, "Sergeant Gibson, what are the check-in times for net control?"

Gibson, who had been sitting to one side, looking uninterested, stood up and provided a comprehensive list of times and frequencies.

Martinez looked at his watch and realized they'd been at it for nearly four hours. They had been over everything, from the moment of insertion to the reasons for extraction, locations for extraction, emergency procedures, and limitations dictated by the Department of State. Every aspect of the operation had been considered, analyzed, and then integrated into the overall plan.

Boyce sat up in his chair and looked at the assembled officers and men. Speaking to his team, he asked, "Are there any additional questions or comments?"

Lombard said, "You have made arrangements for resupply?"

Martinez took the question. "Yes, sir. There are four sites close to our base where aerial resupply would be possible with little or no exposure of the flight crews to hostile fire." Grinning, he added, "Not to mention easy access into a couple of local villages where *we* could resupply if necessary."

"Okay," said Lombard. "I'm happy."

Boyce looked at the rest of the staff, but none of them said a thing. Standing, he walked to the map that was held against the easel by a couple of large silver clips. His back to the assembled soldiers, he studied the map, the acetate overlay showing the projected drop zones and the best location for the forward operating base.

"Captain Martinez?"

"Yes, sir."

"It's a good plan," Boyce said. "A solid plan that protects the secrecy and limits the involvement, or the suspected involvement, of the United States if something goes wrong. I think you're a go."

Martinez was standing. A thrill passed through him. It was as if he'd just passed his orals for a Ph.D., won the most coveted role in a major film, been told that his lottery ticket matched the winning numbers, or had quarter-backed a winning Super Bowl team. He wanted to leap and shout but knew that Army officers did not leap and shout. He stuck out his hand instead and said, "Thank you, Colonel."

"Air assets are available from this moment on. Coordinate with Colonel Curt Jacobs, the air-force operations officer."

"Yes, sir."

Boyce stood for a moment, studying the younger officer. Finally he said, "I wish I was going with you. This"—he waved a hand—"being cooped up to push papers for the bureaucrats is not soldiering."

"Yes, sir," said Martinez. "I understand."

"When I was younger, a newly minted second lieutenant, I was standing in the club talking to a full bull. Man was about to retire and pick up his star. I was envying his position. He had the power. He had the money. I was a slave to the orders of everyone, including the senior NCOs. But he had it all. And he looked at me over his beer and said, 'I'd trade places with you in a minute.' "

Boyce scratched the side of his face. His fingernails made a light sound. "Of course I didn't believe him. He was at the top of his career, at the top of the hill, and I was in a valley looking to climb out. Now I understand what he was saying. He couldn't get into the action. For a soldier that's what it's all about. Rank and power don't matter. It's getting into the field and getting the job done."

"I wouldn't want to be locked up in an office all day," said Martinez, "but the paperwork is important." He realized that the words sounded strange to his own ears.

"To a point," said Boyce. "In the final analysis it isn't the paperwork or the plan but what happens in the field."

"Yes, sir."

"Good luck to you and your men. It's a good plan. A very good one."

"Thank you, Colonel."

Then, pointing to Sergeant Arturo Chavez, Boyce said, "Have him trim that mustache."

Martinez nodded. It wasn't the first time that his operations NCO had gotten into trouble over his pistolero mustache. Chavez, like most of the team, was a small dark man with black hair and brown eyes. A stocky, heavily muscled man, he had been in the army for over fifteen years. The only regulation that he willfully and consistently violated was the one concerning his mustache. He thought it made him look so much like a bandit that no one would suspect that he was a soldier.

Without another word Boyce opened the door and stepped into the hallway. His staff followed him, leaving Martinez and his team in the briefing room. As soon as they shut the door, Espinoza let out a whoop.

Martinez fell back into a chair. He looked first at Chavez and then at his deputy, First Lieutenant Esteban Alvarez. "I don't know why I'm so happy about this," he said. "It just means that we're about to go live in the jungle for the next several weeks."

"That's what it's all about," said Chavez.

"What we train to do," added Alvarez.

"We should be able to hit the field by six in the morning. Boyce said the aviation assets were in place for us."

"Time for a steak dinner," Chavez said. "Equipment, gear, and weapons are all ready to go."

"Okay," said Martinez. "Let's get ready to move."

Chavez turned. "Gentlemen, the celebration is now over. We've a little more work to do."

"Someone going to buy beer?" asked Leroy Jones, one of the medics.

"Nope," said Chavez.

"Shit."

Martinez laughed. "I'll buy the beer once we get back."

"Yeah!" said Jones. "I can live with that."

Several hours later Martinez and the team were sitting in the darkened fuselage of a C-130, orbiting over the Pacific Ocean, waiting to head inbound to the IP and then the DZ. They were using a C-130 rather than one of the newer C-17s. The newer aircraft would have been more comfortable, but the C-130 was in the inventories of nearly every Latin American country. In the dark, with the unit insignia painted in small, flat black letters and numbers, no one would be able to tell who owned the aircraft.

Martinez sat in the red webbing that was strung along the fuselage for the troops. Lined up in the center of the aircraft, tied down with thick gray cargo straps, were cylinders that held the spare equipment, batteries for the radios, extra rations and ammunition, including some heavy weapons in case they needed to defend their camp.

Martinez studied the men who sat in the aircraft with him. His team exec, Alvarez, had been born in California but raised in New Mexico, taking some training at the New Mexico Military Institute in Roswell. Like Martinez, he was a young man with black hair and olive skin. He could speak Spanish like a native of Mexico or Spain, depending on assignment, Italian like a resident of Rome, and strangely, was as fluent in Chinese as a man from Hong Kong.

Next to him was Chavez, the team sergeant. Chavez knew everything there was to know about military tactics and military life. If there was a question to be asked, Chavez was the man to answer it. While the rest of the team sat in the darkened C-130 waiting to jump into the night, Chavez was using his flashlight to study his map, making sure that everything was wired before they hit the ground.

Gibson, the intelligence NCO, the man with the specific knowledge of the locals, the terrain, and the military forces they would be engaging was sitting opposite him. Gibson was one of the three remaining Anglos on the team. The fourth, Banse, was killed as they exfiltrated during a rescue in Saudi Arabia.

Next to him was Leroy Jones, the only black. He had been selected because his diminutive size and his ability to speak Spanish made him appear to be a native of Panama. Although he was the senior medical specialist, he was also an expert with explosives and light weapons.

The rest of the team, lost in the darkness of the aircraft, was Hispanic. The team had been assembled for missions into Latin America, where they had operated almost exclusively, except for a brief run into the Middle East because no one else had been available for that critical mission.

It was a good team, thought Martinez. Well trained, used to working with one another, and disciplined. Each man knew he could rely on the others; if one was in trouble, the others would come to his assistance. No one would be left flapping in the breeze.

Martinez took a deep breath and closed his eyes. For a moment he could visualize the beginning to the mission. The men lined up to exit the troop door on the left side of the aircraft. First the equipment pods and then the men. One by one they'd jump into the night, using the glow of the stars and the charcoal line of the horizon to guide them.

And then he forced his mind away. He's spent five days in isolation, living and breathing the planning of the mission until the briefback. Suddenly the mission was alive. They were on the aircraft, heading into the DZ. Now it was time to let go of it for a moment. Martinez was afraid that he would be overprepared, overrehearsed, so that the first unexpected complication would set him off. It was time to relax. At least momentarily.

It seemed that only a minute had passed. Martinez wasn't aware that he had been asleep. But he felt a hand on his shoulder and opened his eyes to see Chavez grinning at him. The master sergeant had smeared greasepaint on his face in a nightmarish pattern designed to mimic the lights and darks of the jungle.

"We're within thirty minutes, Captain." Chavez had to shout over the roar of the four turboprops.

Martinez blinked and tried to focus on his wristwatch, rubbing his eyes with the heels of his hands. "Everyone ready to go?"

"Ready as we'll ever be," shouted Chavez. He retreated, dropping onto the troopseat.

The loadmaster, an air-force NCO dressed in a gray Nomex flight suit, unhooked and wrapped up the cargo straps, storing them so that they wouldn't be in the way.

Martinez had watched it done dozens of times, but it always sent chills through him. It marked the real beginning of the mission. The last of the waiting was over and it was time to prepare to leap into space.

Michael Brown and Raoul Munyo were already checking each other's equipment. Robert Cline and Juan Ortega were doing the same thing. Martin Davis was crouched on the deck, examining the seals on the equipment pods a final time.

Martinez stood up and moved toward the troop door in the rear. He stepped close and looked out the porthole. The silvery landscape of the ocean was gone; they were over land. There were no artificial lights, no cities, no signs of life. They could be flying over the jungle that had been there a thousand years earlier. Or a million.

He turned and Alvarez was standing behind him. Without a word they began to check each other, making sure that all straps were pulled tight, all snaps fastened, all equipment tied or taped down.

"Ready?" yelled Martinez.

"Never ready. Don't like jumping out of perfectly good airplanes."

"This is a C-130."

"Good point."

The jumpmaster moved forward and yelled at Martinez, "We're about ten minutes out now."

Martinez turned to his team. "Ten minutes to drop," he shouted over the roar of the engines. "Everyone up and check your equipment."

Once again they ran through the ritual, each man making sure that his equipment was properly strapped and buckled and that the quick releases on the parachute were secure. Then he checked the gear of the man in front of him, finally turning to complete the check on the man behind him. Chavez, who would be first, and Martinez, who would be last, checked each other. As they all finished, each man handed the other's static line to him, and they placed the nylon webbing between their teeth to signal completion and that they were ready to jump.

Chavez studied the men behind him. Finally he ordered, "Hook up." Each of the men snapped the metal hook over the metal cable and then yanked on them to show that they were properly fastened and that the cover was properly secured.

The jumpmaster moved forward, grabbed the latch for the troop door, twisted it, pulled in, and then pushed up, out of the way. The rush of the slipstream and the roar of the engines filled the interior of the aircraft. Cold air rushed into the cargo compartment.

"Two minutes," he said, holding up two fingers. A tiny red light came on near the hatch.

Chavez glanced over his shoulder and yelled, "Move to the door."

As the men shuffled forward, the equipment pods in front of them, the jumpmaster leaned forward slightly, staring into the darkness in front of the aircraft. The unbroken jungle stretched below him.

The light at the side of the door began to blink and the jumpmaster dragged the equipment pods forward, ready to push them out.

The red flashing light suddenly changed to a bright steady green. Shoving the bundles out, the jumpmaster looked up at Chavez and yelled, "Go! *Go!*"

Chavez moved forward and jumped. Martinez, at the end of the line, shuffled forward as one man after the other leaped into the night. At the door himself, he brought his feet together on the edge, tucked his chin in, and then put his hands on the framework on either side of the hatch.

An instant later Martinez was falling, though he didn't sense it; instead it was as if the plane had suddenly leaped into the air over him. He could just make out the black outline and the tiny blue flames from the rear of the turboprops.

There was a rustle behind him as the main container opened and the chute was dragged out. A quiet crack told him the chute had opened, and he glanced up to make sure that he had a full round canopy with no holes or blown panels.

Down and to the left Martinez could make out a string of chutes, though he couldn't see the men or the equipment pods hanging under them. With the aircraft disappearing over the horizon, there was almost no sound. Had he shouted, the men would have been able to hear him easily. Of course, the shout would alert anyone on the ground, if the enemy was there, waiting.

Below him was a break in the solid black of the jungle canopy. The DZ was more than a mile long and about half a mile wide. A ribbon of silver wound its way through the center of it.

At three hundred feet, according to the altimeter on his reserve chute, Martinez brought his feet and knees together. A moment later he hit the ground and rolled easily. The vegetation under him was soft. He scrambled to his feet and hit the quick release on his chest, dropping harness. Unzipping the coveralls, he grabbed his pistol, though he had no reason to suspect that the enemy was anywhere near or that anyone had been alerted to their sudden arrival.

Around him he could see the charcoal shadows of his men as they moved to clear the DZ. Rolling his chute into a ball, he moved toward the center of the drop zone.

Chavez reported, "I think everyone is down safely, though I haven't heard from Cline."

"Cline was the second man out?"

"Yes, sir."

"Let's get clear of the DZ. If we don't hear from him, we'll have to search."

Chavez moved off into the dark. Martinez slipped to his right, where Jones was bent over one of the equipment pods. He was tugging at the quick-release catch on it.

Sensing someone near him, Jones glanced up. "Jammed. Don't think the chute fully deployed."

Martinez suddenly had an uneasy feeling. Everything had gone smoothly; the mission planning, the briefback, loading the aircraft, everything had gone like clockwork. The aging C-130, older than most of the men on it, had performed flawlessly. But now one man was missing and an equipment pod was jammed shut.

Martinez crouched next to Jones and held the main part of the cylinder. Jones tried again, then used his combat knife, trying to get the proper leverage, but the latch wouldn't release.

"Damn," Jones said quietly.

Chavez appeared and leaned close to Martinez.

"Munyo reports movement in the jungle. Four, maybe five men, coming in this direction."

"ID?"

"No, sir. We've no clue, but I don't like the idea of people moving around at this time of night. Anyone out now is probably up to no good."

Martinez stood up. "Let's get going. Anyone find Cline?"

"Not yet."

Martinez turned slowly, surveying the DZ. He could pick out the shapes of four or five of his men. Another was hurrying toward him.

"They're at the edge of the jungle," the man reported.

Martinez dropped to his knee, his pistol in his right hand. The problem was that they couldn't just open fire. It wasn't like Vietnam or Iraq, where anyone moving around them could be considered the enemy. There might be farmers, or hunters out searching for game. He had no reason to believe the men coming were enemy soldiers, even if the odds said they were.

Before he could react, one of the men stumbled out of the jungle, stopped abruptly, and shouted in Spanish, "Who are you?"

One of Martinez's men, holding his hand up as if in greeting, responded, "Juan Ortega." He began walking toward the newcomer.

Chavez was down on his belly, crawling away rapidly. Martinez raised his pistol but didn't aim it. He was watching the jungle to see if the other men appeared.

"Juan Ortega, what are you doing here?"

"Setting traps."

"You have a permit?"

Ortega laughed. "Permit to catch food for my family? Why do I need a permit?"

Jones was on the move, to the right. He was crouching low, moving rapidly, his rifle in his hands. He disappeared into the dark.

Two more men appeared at the edge of the jungle,

talking. One laughed out loud and then said, "Juan Ortega, you are under arrest."

"Arrest? Why?"

One of the new men raised his rifle and snapped, "Because we said so."

Martinez knew that there was no way to talk their way out of it. A group of armed men couldn't be explained. And the newcomers were also armed. They were either soldiers or bandits or both, and either way they were the enemy.

Martinez was too far away to be sure of hitting anyone if he fired. But those closer weren't going to fire until he ordered it.

Aiming at the closest man, Martinez slowly squeezed the trigger. The pistol jumped in his hand as it fired. There was a bright muzzle flash.

"Take them," yelled Chavez in English.

Firing erupted. One weapon on full auto. The strobing of the flash showed the men in the clearing. One man staggered and fell. Another dropped to a knee and tried to return fire. He was cut down.

"In the jungle," shouted Chavez. He broke from the group, ran to the trees, and leaped over a bush. The stuttering of his weapon cut through the night. The trees masked the muzzle flashes.

Martinez was up and running. He dodged right and then dropped to the ground, his pistol pointed at the enemy. The firing had tapered off rapidly and then died. A final shot punctuated the night.

"Four down," said Espinoza.

"Five," corrected Chavez. "I'm coming out."

"Come ahead."

Chavez appeared, dragging the body of a man. He dropped him at the edge of the jungle. As Martinez moved toward him Chavez said, "Soldier. Irregular, though. Not very well trained."

"We get them all?"

"Yes, sir, I believe we did."

"Then we better get the hell out of here."

"What about the bodies?"

"Leave them. There's no way that we can be tied to this." He hesitated, then asked, "What about Cline?"

There was a rustling and another man appeared. He held his hands up, but he was too burly to be one of the locals. Cline stopped a few feet away. "Sorry. Got tangled and then heard those bandits. Had to lay low."

"Right," said Martinez. "It's getting close to dawn. We've got to hurry."

"Yes, sir."

THE PERMION BASIN NORTH OF
ODESSA, TEXAS

The black silhouette pop-up targets lined the bullet-riddled berm. Standing on the firing line were half a dozen men and two women, each holding a weapon that was illegal to own in the state of Texas. To the rear was a white tower that stood thirty feet high, and from the top was a bloodred banner that announced that the range was active.

Standing in the tower was Commander William Joseph Daniels, a rotund man of forty-seven who had started the Defenders of the Texas Revolution, a paramilitary organization that allowed him to wear general's stars and a khaki uniform. Daniels had volunteered for the army during the Vietnam War but had been rejected; his eyes were too poor, his health too bad, and he had failed to complete high school.

Daniels picked up the microphone of the PA system, whipped the cord behind him like a lounge singer in a second-rate club, and stepped to the window. Pressing the button, he said, "Ready on the right. Ready on the left. Ready on the firing line."

Below him the men and women lowered their weapons and aimed at the silhouettes. Bright sunlight highlighted the targets. The deep blue sky and the puffy white clouds made it look festive. Daniels put the thought out of his mind because they were there for deadly reasons.

Daniels squeezed the microphone tightly and yelled, "Open fire!"

There was a single stuttering as one weapon began to shoot, but an instant later everyone was firing, the detonations combining into one long explosion. The dirt behind the targets and along the top of the berm erupted under the impact of the 9mm and .30-caliber slugs.

One of the men emptied his weapon, hit the release, and dropped the magazine to the ground. He slammed a fresh one home and opened up again.

The center target was shredded by the impact of the rounds. The target's head fell forward and then the center disappeared. Another was cut in half and fell back.

Daniels used his microphone again. "Cease firing. Cease firing. Cease firing on the firing line." He turned and handed the mike to the second man in the tower. "Looks like they've got the feel of the weapons."

"Yes, Commander."

Daniels moved to the trapdoor and ladder that led down from the tower. When he reached the ground, he hurried toward the firing line. Two of the men were kneeling, picking up the brass that had been expended, throwing the used rounds into coffee cans.

"Looked good," said Daniels.

One of the women, Cheryl Gannon, stepped up, cradling her weapon in her arms. Her slightly dirty face was beginning to burn. "How'd that look, Commander?"

"Pretty as can be," said Daniels. "Hardly any wasted rounds at all."

"I thought so, too."

Daniels looked at one of the men standing near a wooden table, his weapon set on it. "About ready to begin the briefing. As soon as the brass is all collected and turned over to Sergeant Amos."

"Certainly, Commander."

Daniels walked across the compound to a square cinder-block building. It stood by itself, had no windows, a single metal door, and a rooftop air conditioner that was more than adequate to keep the interior pleasant in the hottest July or August.

As Daniels entered he acknowledged the corporal sitting in a lawn chair next to the door and continued to the raised platform that served as a stage. In one corner was the American flag and in the other was a Confederate battle flag. Daniels claimed that it had been carried by a Confederate regiment at Gettysburg as they reached the Angle during Pickett's Charge on the third day of fighting. In reality he had bought it in a shop in the Austin Centralplex a couple of years earlier.

The slide tray was in place and the projector was sitting on the table. The cable for the remote was strung out and set on the lectern. Everything was ready for the briefing, including the cold beers set out for his top staff. Daniels wished that they had a rear projection booth like that available on some military bases, but there hadn't been the budget when they had built the briefing room.

A single fan stood to one side, blowing the air around. There was a bar angled into a corner that had a small refrigerator under it. If they needed something larger, they brought it in for a day or two.

As he reached the lectern the door opened again and the first of his soldiers entered. All wore a pistol in a holster and carried a larger weapon, all of them automatic. The man walked to the front of the room and plopped into one of the metal chairs.

"This going to take long?"

"As long as it takes." Daniels hesitated for a beat and then added, "And let's remember the chain of command."

"Sorry, Commander."

The rest straggled in. One of the women sat behind the projector so that she could turn it on and off or change the slide trays. The other, Gannon, took a seat in the rear, using one of the chairs that had an arm designed to hold a notebook. She would take the minutes of the meeting. The men spread out, finding beers and then seats. No one spoke.

Sergeant Amos, a big man with thick black hair, tiny blue eyes, and a perpetually sunburned face, closed the door, locked it, and then walked rapidly to the stage. He stepped to the center and said, "Attention."

When everyone was standing, he said, "Ladies and gentlemen, I give you our commander."

Daniels waited for a moment, watching the men and women, and then walked purposefully to the lectern. "Please be seated."

After the momentary commotion as the people followed the order Daniels pointed at the woman behind the slide projector and she turned it on. The screen brightened and Amos turned off the overhead lights.

The first slide appeared, a homemade logo that pictured the flag of the Defenders of the Texas Revolution: a drawing of the chapel at the Alamo and crossed muskets to represent the infantry.

Glancing down at his prepared speech, Daniels said, "In the last ten years American manufacturers have closed factories in the continental United States and moved their operations into Latin America."

There were mumbled agreements from the people in the briefing room.

"Hundreds of thousands of Americans have been put out of work. Families have been disrupted and destroyed.

People have lost their houses, their savings, everything they ever owned. They have lost their future."

Daniels's voice rose slightly, taking on the pitch of an evangelist talking of sinners and eternal damnation. He slammed a fist into the lectern and the echo reverberated throughout the briefing room.

"Those jobs, those opportunities, and that future have been exported south of the border. Economic policies designed in Washington by men and women whose futures are assured are destroying the American way of life. Why should the laws of this country provide all the advantages to those outside the country? We work to build and then those in Washington rip it away from us, hand it on a platter to others, and expect us to sit back and take it."

Daniels hit the button on the remote and the slides began to flash. Scenes of Flint, Michigan, looking like a ghost town. Closed car plants that led to closed stores and shops and businesses, and blocks of boarded-up houses. Attempts to revitalize the town failed as more money was thrown into a problem that could have been cured if jobs had not migrated south of the border.

The scenes were repeated elsewhere. Towns that had thrived on the business brought by a major military installation were suddenly abandoned as those installations were closed. Other towns, with economies based on a single major employer, slowly died.

"Why?" shouted Daniels. "Because it is to the advantage of corporations to build cars, tractors, TVs, everything outside the United States. Taxes and tariffs that would protect our people have been legislated out of existence while similar tariffs are reinforced in other countries. A Chevrolet, because of import taxes and tariffs, costs fifty thousand dollars in Korea, but we allow the importation of their cars without similar tariffs applied."

"There a point to this?" asked one of the men.

Daniels put down the remote and moved to the edge of the stage. He looked down at the man and said, "You have a problem, Phil. You got a big mouth, Phil."

"Yes, sir. But we know this. Hell, Commander, we see it in our own newspaper. We see the gov'mint spendin' billions for some stupid atom smasher for the scientists to play with while our folks are starvin'."

Phil Rogers—small, balding, with a protruding belly, and a ferret's face—had been one of the first to join the Defenders, and it was his money, inherited from his father, that had bought the land for the installation. Like Daniels, Rogers had tried to join the army but had failed. Unlike Daniels, he had then tried the National Guard and found a slot there. Rogers had been a good clerk typist who failed to qualify with either the M-14 or the M-16 until the company commander had looked the other way and one of the sergeants had pencil-whipped the scorecard.

"You be patient, and you'll see, Phil." Daniels retreated to the lectern and flipped through the pages of his text. He picked up the remote and rushed through more slides showing the decline of dozens of American neighborhoods. Finally he stopped at one showing the interior of a modern factory. The latest equipment, shiny and new, was spread out along the assembly line, surrounded by hundreds of workers.

"This is the plant built six months ago in Nueva Rosita. You see that all the workers here are Mexican. They are building cars that will be transported north and sold in this country. Cars built by American corporations in Mexico. That is the reason that so many of our fellow countrymen are out of work."

Daniels looked up at his audience. They were sitting quietly, staring at him, waiting for his next words.

"What would happen," he asked quietly, "if that plant was suddenly shut down? What would happen if it was badly damaged in . . . say, an earthquake?"

He waited, but no one volunteered an answer. "You can turn off the projector." As the lights came back on, Daniels moved to the side of the lectern. He leaned an elbow on it. "Seems to me," he said, "that the car manufacturer would have to find a way to pick up the slack. Seems to me that he would be scrambling to find another place to build his cars."

"He could build a new plant," said Phil.

"Take too long," said Daniels. "He'd want to get back into business as quickly as possible. Building a new plant would take a year or more. Not the quickest way to get back into business."

Daniels grinned. "But reopening one of his closed factories would do it. Retool quickly, easily—hell, they used to shut down in August to retool for the new model year and be up and running in four to six weeks."

"You all prayin' for an earthquake?" asked Phil.

"Nope. We could pray for years and not get that quake. But God helps those who help themselves. I say we help ourselves. I think it's time that we create an earthquake."

"How?"

"For the last five years we have been training. We have created a defense force of more than six hundred men and women. We have built a camp that contains everything we need to survive for more than a year after the collapse of the federal government and our society. Economic factors are pushing us in that direction faster and faster. But like most of you, I don't want to see the end of our society any sooner than it has to happen. So, I propose that we take some positive action."

"What?"

Daniels turned to Cheryl Gannon. "Why don't you forget about taking notes for the next few minutes? I don't want a written record of what I'm about to say."

Gannon closed her notebook. "Certainly, Commander."

"What I'm about to say cannot leave this room. Right now talking about it breaks no laws. But once the planning starts, then we could be arrested for conspiracy, if any of us ever talks. I want nothing written about this."

Amos said, "Door's locked, Commander. Corporal Barker will make sure that no one approaches the center here. I swept it this morning and found no evidence of transmitters, recording equipment, or bugs."

"Thank you, Sergeant." Daniels moved closer to his audience and sat down on the edge of the stage. "I propose that we, using our knowledge and talents, eliminate that plant in Nueva Rosita. That we destroy it completely to force the car company to reopen one of the plants in this country. That we take those jobs away from the beaners and give them back to good Americans who deserve them."

"I don't know," said Phil, standing up. "That's illegal. Hell, Commander, we're talkin' about attackin' and destroyin' property."

"We're taking jobs away from Mexicans and giving them back to Americans. We're doing something for ourselves."

"Still . . ."

Daniels angrily waved him to silence. "Any of the rest of you have anything to say?"

"I want to hear more about this," said Gannon, looking at the others. "I'm not going to reject the plan until I have all the facts."

Daniels waited, but no one else seemed inclined to comment. "Okay," he said. "Just the rough preliminaries."

For the next ten minutes he sketched the plan that he had created. No more than two dozen of their most trusted soldiers carrying the weapons that they had worked so hard to purchase, including the one 3.5-inch rocket launcher and a half-dozen LAW rockets in their disposable sleeves. Daniels thought they could leave the plant a smoking ruin that would take two to three years to rebuild, if the car company decided that it was worth the effort.

Finished, he dropped from the stage, walked slowly to the bar, and got himself a beer. He popped the top and took a long, deep pull. Wiping the foam from his lips with the back of his hand, he said, "Well?"

Rogers was the first to speak. "I don't like it. Not into Mexico and not to help people we don't even know."

Amos hesitated, wanting all the officers to speak before him, but when no one said anything, he jumped in. "I like it because it is something that we can do. We sit around and complain about the government and all the jobs being sucked out of the States, but that's all we do. Now someone has come up with a plan that could bring a couple of thousand of those jobs back into this country."

John Thorsen, a tall, skinny man with a thatch of blond hair that was still unruly after more than forty years of training, said, "I think that we can go ahead, at least into the planning. Nothing committed for the moment, but with the plans under way. Hell, we can stop it at any point if we run into problems."

Gannon, who had been sitting quietly, her notebook on her lap, spoke up. "Too many groups sit around and complain, but they never do a damned thing. They claim they're going to right wrongs, but in the end they drink beer, shoot holes in cardboard, and then complain some more. This might not be the right plan for us, I don't know. But it is a plan."

Daniels turned his attention back to Rogers. "You're either with us or not."

"Hell, Commander, I'm with you all if I can't talk you all out of it. I just don't want us to make a mistake that's going to ruin everything we've built here."

Daniels finished the beer, crushing the can. He tossed it over the bar at the wastebasket, but missed. He didn't bother to pick it up. One of the enlisted Defenders would take care of it.

He returned to the stage and looked at the assembled officers. "Everyone agree that we should continue to move forward with this?"

"With the stipulation," said Rogers, "that there will be a final, unanimous agreement before any of our troops are sent into the field."

"I can live with that," said Daniels.

"And that we do not engage forces of the United States," said Thorsen.

"Who said anything about attacking American soldiers?" asked Daniels. "Hell, I'm just trying to get some of the jobs that the politicians have given away."

"Okay," said Thorsen. "I'm for it."

"Good. In the next couple of days I'll provide a breakdown of specific assignments and areas of responsibility." Daniels hesitated for a moment and then added, "We are moving into an area that is not completely legal. It would be wise if we kept as few notes as possible. The smaller the paper trail, the better we're going to be."

"What's the target date for the operation?" asked Thorsen.

Daniels scratched the side of his jaw with his thumbnail, thinking. "I don't see any reason that we can't hit the field within two weeks. It's not a complex operation, we have the equipment on hand. It's merely a question of working out all the details."

Thorsen was suddenly on his feet. "To the success of our first major operation!"

The others joined him. "To our success!"

Daniels looked at the men and women and knew that they couldn't fail. Not with the attitude they had. In less than a month the world would see that Americans were not weak. And that was the real reason for the exercise.

SAN ANTONIO, TEXAS

The office was not air-conditioned and the building was of World War II vintage. The furniture—an old desk, a chair that squeaked constantly, and a battered bookcase that held a series of black binders—seemed to be of the same era. The only new items were the computer with its external disk drive and impact printer and a heavy file cabinet containing the classified documents Sandi Paulding needed to prepare the daily intel briefs that the general demanded.

Paulding was a university instructor who had been sucked into the army reserve with a promise of extra pay and a suggestion that there wouldn't be a massive call-up of reserves and National Guard. Desert Shield a few years earlier showed that the military would call them up, though now there was constant argument against massive activations.

Paulding, believing that she would not be drawn into the active service and whose unit had avoided Desert Shield and Desert Storm, had stayed in the reserves. Now she found herself on active duty while someone else taught her classes.

She was a fairly young woman who had stayed in good shape because of the military and her heavy teaching schedule. Her blond hair, which she had worn long, had been cut because of military requirements. She was a tall but delicate woman with almost tiny hands. They had caused her trouble when she tried to hold the new automatic pistols that the military used instead of the old revolvers.

She shifted through the folders on her desk, searching for the latest intelligence reports from Mexico and Central America. It was funny: everyone had assumed that with the death of Castro there would be a reduction in the number of people's revolutions. Castro's Cuba had been exporting unrest for over thirty years. There had been those who claimed that the world had rocketed past Castro, but the man had been too old and too narrow-minded to see it.

But Latin America was more turbulent than ever before. Weapons and money were pouring in from somewhere. Anti-American demonstrations were being held in the capitals of countries that had been the best friends of the United States. There was even talk of an expedition against the Great Satan, though no one took that kind of thing seriously. Since the United States military machine had rolled over Saddam Hussein's "elite" forces in a matter of hours, almost no one believed there was any danger from an outside power.

Paulding pulled a folder from the center of the pile, opened it, and shook her head at the latest pictures. Hundreds of people rioting in Tegucigalpa and San Salvador. Government troops were standing by as the mobs attacked the American embassies. The marine guards, reinforced because of the trouble, had kept the people out of the embassies for the moment.

The real problem was in Nicaragua, where the government was badly pressed. Rebel forces were operating in a half-dozen areas. Government spokespeople were denying reports that the regime was in trouble, but rebel leader Jesus Castillo was claiming that his forces would invade the capital in a matter of weeks.

The thing that bothered Paulding was that no one ever attacked the Soviet embassy or the Cuban embassy or even the British embassy. It was always the American embassy. She was never sure if it was because the United States was the richest or because it had the news media that would make sure that pictures of the assault would be broadcast throughout the world.

Captain Jim Wheeler, the commanding general's aide, knocked on the door and then stuck his head in. "You about ready for the staff meeting?"

"Got to gather up the classified and get it locked away."

Wheeler centered himself in the door. He was wearing desert-camo BDUs, including the tan boots that required no polish. He had lost weight since the call-up and was looking thin, with dark circles under his eyes. His thick hair had been neatly shaved, so that there was a dark shadow on his skull. "What's the main thrust for today?"

Paulding shrugged. "Just as the general wanted. I'll be concentrating on the unrest in Mexico, though there's plenty brewing in Central America."

"Thought Mexico was in Central America."

"Nope," said Paulding. "North America, along with us and Canada. Christ, didn't they teach you anything in school when you were young."

"Not trivia like that," said Wheeler.

Paulding stood up, a number of file folders in her hands. She straightened the edges, tapped them together, and then stuffed them in the safe.

"Inspectors would write you up for that," said Wheeler.

"I'm well aware of what inspectors would do, but there are no inspectors, and in the interest of saving a few minutes I'll put them there. I'll fix it later if it bothers you."

"Sorry," said Wheeler.

Paulding pushed the drawer of the safe closed and spun the combination lock. Looking at Wheeler, she said, "I'm ready."

They left her office and she closed the door but didn't bother to lock it. They walked down a long corridor covered with red linoleum. It had been polished by soldiers for nearly fifty years so that it was worn to the base in a few places. The recently painted walls were an ivory color. There were no pictures hanging on them yet.

They reached the conference room. It was too small for a complete general's staff, but the briefing was only for the top officers in each position and the brigade commanders. Later they would brief the battalion officers and their staffs.

Paulding entered, but Wheeler diverted, heading toward the general's office. She sat down in one of the chairs, ignoring the other officers who were engaged in conversation.

Since joining the unit a number of years earlier, she had felt like an outsider. It seemed that almost everyone had started his or her career with the division and had stayed with it. They had selected those who would move up. It was like the regiments of the Civil War. The leaders were elected by popular vote from among the soldiers. Everyone knew everyone else. They had grown up in the same town, gone to the same schools, and attended the same churches. While the division didn't elect the officers, those who held the staff positions had come in as second lieutenants and worked their way up the chain of command. During the push to bring women in Paulding had secured her position as the chief of intelligence. Most resented her because she'd moved into the intelligence slot as a major. They didn't believe she'd earned the position, which they believed should have gone to someone already assigned to the division.

Wheeler entered the conference room and announced, "Ladies and gentlemen, the commanding general."

The assembled officers came to attention. The general entered, sat down, and said, "Be seated."

A short man with short gray hair, the general wore a khaki uniform that held only his combat decorations, a combat infantryman's badge, and jump wings. He was the only one in khaki; everyone else wore BDUs.

He waited until it was completely quiet in the conference room, opened the leather folder that Wheeler set in front of him, and then glanced at his watch. "The purpose of this briefing is to get an update on the situation in Mexico." He looked directly at Paulding. "Major?"

Paulding stood, recalling that one of her instructors had told her never to brief without some kind of visual aid. But the conference room wasn't set up for slides and the single vu-graph projector had broken down. Her attitude was that no aids were better than poor-quality ones. Good visuals made a good briefing great and poor ones could ruin an otherwise good briefing. She didn't even have the rough map her instructor recommended.

Looking at the commander, she said, "Much of this information is classified secret. It is not to be discussed with those who do not have the proper clearances or in unsecured locations."

Satisfied with that, she moved a step back and opened the folder she had brought with her. Glancing at the other officers, she began. "Although moves toward a trading partnership throughout the North American continent have been made in the past, it seems that the leaders in Mexico believe that equality has not been reached. Feelings—and these are reinforced during their speeches in Mexico City—throughout the country, and in many of their Latin American partners, are that they are the poor cousins, that the Canadians, and especially the Americans, or the North Americans as they call us, do not wish to acknowledge them."

She flipped the page and stole a glance at the audience. They didn't realize the importance of the information. They were probably thinking that they could read the same thing in *Time* or watch it on CNN.

"During the last six months, and since the death of Fidel Castro, there have been outbreaks of anti-American activity in a number of cities, including—"

"Major," interrupted the general, "we've all seen the riots on the television. Are you suggesting that they are Cuban-inspired?"

"Yes, sir, I believe that we can draw that conclusion." She glanced at her prepared text and then ignored it. "It had been thought that the death of Castro would allow the moderates to come to power, that with the erosion of the communist base in Eastern Europe, the splintering of the Soviet republics, and the move toward a capitalistic economy, Cuba would follow suit. But it seems that the opposite has taken place. The hard-liners, believing that they are now the cradle of communism, are trying to export their system to the rest of the world."

"Are they having any luck?"

Paulding laughed and waved a hand. "You've all seen the riots on CNN. The history of Latin America, and Mexico, is filled with revolutions. Santa Anna rose to power and was toppled a number of times. The instability of the region is legendary."

"Major," said the general.

"Yes, sir. Anyone promising reform . . . anyone with a proper forum, is able to find a base in the population. These people have been exploited by everyone. Each is as bad as the last, but the people hope for a change. Given the proper financing, the proper popular appeal, and Cubans, because they are fellow Latins, they could make a great deal of trouble for us."

"Ha!" said one of the colonels. "Everyone learned his lesson when we rolled over the Iraqis."

"They learned"—Paulding flared—"that they can't win a straight-on fight. They learned that fixed defenses and forts are a thing of the past. The lesson is not from the Middle East, but from Vietnam: a guerrilla war to sap our strength and our national will."

"If we allow ourselves to be sucked into such a conflict," said the colonel.

Paulding waved a hand. "I think we learned lessons in Vietnam, too. We learned not to allow ourselves to be drawn into a conflict without the will to win it. How long would the North Vietnamese have held out if there had been the kind of bombing of Hanoi that there was of Baghdad? How long would they have held out if Haiphong Harbor had been blockaded? But that's not important. What is are the attitudes of the people of Latin America."

The general interrupted again. "And what are those attitudes?"

"They look at us and see us consuming the future. They see us with wealth that is undreamed of in their countries. They see us satisfy our every desire, and it seems to them, or it is told to them, that we are crushing them underfoot. The Cubans, who see themselves as the keeper of the Marxist flame, are in there telling everyone that it is the United States, through its manipulation of the world markets, that is holding them down. Hell, they even blamed a hurricane on us, claiming that we had the power to divert it into Mexico so that it wouldn't hit the United States."

"They can't believe that?"

"Why not? When you're hungry and poor and someone gives you hope by telling you that the United States will fall and you'll gain the reward when it happens, you don't think in rational terms. You let yourself believe."

"Is there anything else that you want to add, Major?"

Paulding glanced at her notes. The briefing ran to

nine pages and she had spent two days on it. She had gathered information from a dozen sources including secret CIA daily briefs and assessments. She wanted her opportunity to shine.

But there was nothing new in the briefing. The poor were still poor and the powerful were still attempting to exploit them.

"No, sir. Just documentation and some interpretation of the data."

"Anything special in that interpretation?"

Paulding was about to say that there wasn't and then changed her mind. She decided to take a chance. "There are indications that certain factions in the Mexican government, with assistance of the Cubans and others in Latin America, might raid into the United States. Quick raids into the border towns—"

"Oh, for Christ's sake," snapped a colonel. "That is the most ridiculous thing I have heard in the last year."

"Pancho Villa did it in 1916," said Paulding.

"In a time when the telephone was a novelty, the telegram was haphazard at best, and there weren't satellites circling the world that could pinpoint the enemy to his street address. Villa could raid into the southwestern United States then. Today such a raid is impossible."

Paulding closed her folder. "A lightning raid, into one of the border towns, shoot a few Americans and get the hell out, would gain a great deal of world press at a very small risk to the attackers. I'm not suggesting an invasion. Just the possibility of a raid."

With that she closed her folder and sat down. She refused to look up because she knew that no one believed her. But she had gotten their attention.

Now the general spoke. "I'm not sure how much weight to attach to Major Paulding's assessment, but I will say this: Washington is concerned about the growing unrest south of us. They are concerned about the possibility of violence directed at American holdings in Mexico and American tourists throughout Latin America. And for

those global thinkers, there is the big target: the Panama
Canal. Well-placed conventional explosions could damage
it and take it out of commission for a year or more."

The general signaled to Wheeler, who passed out an
agenda. When each of the officers had one, the general
said, "We are to deploy one brigade to the border area
south of here. They are to be in place inside a week." He
looked at Paulding. "Your assessment of trouble along the
border seems to have been accurate, though a raid into
Texas seems a bit unlikely. Anyway, good job, Major."

"Thank you, General."

"I'll be giving the specific instructions to the appro-
priate commanders in the next couple of hours. The specif-
ics of the deployment, which units will move first and the
ultimate destinations, will be worked out then. For those of
you not involved in this deployment, don't think you're
getting out of this. I wouldn't be surprised to learn that the
remainder of the division will be ordered to the border in
the next few days."

"How long?" asked an officer.

"No more than a year," said the general. "But what
the hell, we're still going to be home in Texas. Not bad
duty."

"No, sir."

NEPAL

Morris Reisman thought that it should be warmer this close to the equator. The problem was that he was at twelve thousand feet, where the air was so thin that walking half a block caused him to breathe as if he had just sprinted a quarter mile. His breath was visible and the snow crunched under his boots. It was too cold and too hard to breathe.

Reisman was a reporter who had served with the army in Vietnam and wished that he could have served with the army in Saudi Arabia. He had, as a reporter, been in Saudi Arabia as Desert Shield became Desert Storm, but that wasn't the same thing. He watched, night after night, as soldiers who had spent three or four months in the desert came home to heroes' welcomes, while he remembered that on the night he got back, he couldn't even convince the people in line at the airport to let him move forward to catch the last plane home.

Reisman considered himself a young man: he'd just turned forty-five. One good thing that had come out of the Saudi Arabian war was that among the soldiers thousands were in their forties. Although he'd felt old when he had returned from Vietnam, he no longer felt that way. Lying in the snow at the top of a rocky ridge swept by a wind that had to be blowing at more than forty miles an hour, he not only felt young, he felt extremely cold.

The man next to him, a British journalist named Colin Evers, tapped his shoulder and handed him a pair of Zeiss binoculars. "Right down there. At the edge of the village."

Focusing, Reisman saw what Evers wanted him to see. The village was made of stone huts with small windows and wooden doors. Smoke poured from the chimneys, blown along the rooftops.

"On the eastern end," said Evers.

"Yes," said Reisman. There was a narrow road that led out of a valley. With the wind blowing in the wrong direction he couldn't hear the sounds of the engines, but he knew a tank when it appeared. "Chinese?"

"Of course."

A line of men walked behind it, each carrying a weapon. It was too far to see the weapons easily, but from the shape Reisman knew that there were AKs. Maybe not the AK-47 of the Vietman War but the newer AK-74. They were Kalashnikovs, of that he had no doubt.

The tank clanked up the road, stopped, and pivoted, aiming its barrel into the town. The soldiers spread out on line and then halted. Searching the town, Reisman could see no sign of life other than the smoke.

"Looks like your information was good," said Reisman.

"Of course, old boy. I've been doing this for twenty years."

"Still, getting the movements of the Chinese military . . ."

Evers laughed. "People just don't realize how much information can be gathered by listening. Or watching. Changes in the routine operations. More lights on at night, more people at the front gate."

"Yeah." Reisman remembered mornings in Vietnam when they expected mortar attacks because none of the Vietnamese workers showed up. It wasn't that they were sympathetic to the Viet Cong, it was that someone in the VC would tell a friend or relative to be late for work and that person would tell a couple of other people, and within an hour everyone knew what was going to happen. Of course, when the Vietnamese didn't arrive for work, the Americans knew what was going to happen, too.

The Chinese stood at the edge of the village, the tank coughing black clouds of diesel smoke. The soldiers knelt on the windswept plain, watching.

"What are they going to do?" Now that Reisman had seen the Chinese, he wanted to get the hell out. It was too cold to be lying in the snow. It was too cold to be sitting still.

"Wait," said Evers. "The Chinese are deliberate. They have patience, something you Americans seem to have little of. Patience can be useful."

"Sure." Reisman realized that Evers would sit there until he froze solid if the Chinese didn't move.

Using the binoculars, Reisman scanned the village again. An ox cart without an ox was parked next to one of the huts. A double-decker bus that looked as if it should be in London was parked near the center of the village. The red paint was fading, making the bus look old. One windshield was broken.

A flash of movement caught his attention: a man was running along one of the streets carrying a weapon that could have been mistaken for a Kentucky long rifle, a gun that belonged in another era and another place.

Touching Evers's shoulder, Reisman pointed out the man. Evers said, "Now we should get some action."

The man reached the end of the village and crouched behind a stone wall. He crawled along it, reached the side of a house, and hoisted himself up onto the roof. Carefully he eased his way forward until he reached the peak.

Reisman knew exactly what the man was going to do. For a moment he wondered about the ethics of lying there doing nothing. He remembered two reporters who had watched and videotaped a man who dumped gasoline on himself and then set himself on fire. Neither the reporter nor the cameraman ran for help. They stood by, filming the event.

As a newsman, Reisman had a horror of becoming part of the story. Yet the line "We must never forget that we are the story" kept running through his head. With a shout he could alert the soldiers to the danger. And he could make sure that the man didn't get the shot off, probably saving his life as well. If the man knew the soldiers were alert, he'd run away instead of committing certain suicide by firing his old rifle.

But Reisman didn't move. He watched as his photographer, using a lens that looked as big as a mortar tube, shot pictures of the scene below.

The man on the roof poked the barrel of his rifle over the crown of the house and aimed. A moment later, as the Chinese dived for cover, one of them fell to the ground. The man scrambled to the edge of the roof, dropped to the ground, and ran back into the village.

The sharp crack of the rifle reached them seconds later. There was a burst of automatic weapons fire. The roof erupted. The heavy machine gun on the tank began to chug, ripping into the building, tearing great chunks from the roof.

The soldiers, under the covering fire, advanced on the house. They hit the wall and took cover, popping up to fire their AKs at the windows and the doors.

The tank rumbled forward and the main gun swung

slowly. The soldiers dropped back and the tank fired, point-blank, into the hut. The round punched through the wall. An instant later the windows and door blew out in a boiling, rolling cloud of smoke and fire. The roof seemed to leap up and then fall back as one of the walls collapsed.

Half a dozen soldiers leaped the wall and ran forward, firing into the rubble. They kicked at the debris, firing down in short bursts.

Finished, the soldiers dragged two people from the rubble. Both were obviously dead, though a Chinese fired his weapon at the bodies as his fellows scattered.

Now the tank turned and centered itself on the road at the edge of the village. The turret moved slowly, like the head of an elephant, until it was looking down the street. An instant later there was a flash from the barrel and an explosion in the street. The tank aimed again and fired again, and this time one of the houses exploded.

"Christ!" Reisman wanted to do something, but the Chinese had a tank and were all armed with automatic weapons. He was with a British reporter, a photographer, and two local men who were serving as guides. There was nothing they could do.

The soldiers, lined up along the stone fence, began shooting into the village. The rattling of their weapons, along with the rhythmic booms of the tank's cannon, drifted to them.

A man ran from a house, bullets licking at his heels. The snow around him splashed under the deadly fire like the water of a lake. It looked, for a moment, as if the man would escape, but then, suddenly, he stumbled. He fell to his face, struggled to stand, and staggered on for another few steps before pitching into the snow. Slowly, around him, the snow turned from white to crimson.

"I got all that," said the photographer, but his voice held no joy.

"We'd better get out of here, old boy," said Evers.

"No!" said Reisman.

The scene below held him fascinated, though he'd

witnessed similar scenes before. Viet Cong destroying a village because someone had given an American soldier a cup of water. Saddam Hussein pounding villages into rubble because the people had wanted a taste of freedom.

And he'd seen it on the news. The Russians in Afghanistan, leveling a town where the rebels had been holed up, bodies of poison-gas victims scattered in the streets.

It was an old story. The government, wanting to retain its power, rolled over those who opposed it. The deaths of a hundred, two hundred, a thousand, weren't important. The message was. The people were powerless against the might of a mechanized military. People with Kentucky long rifles could do nothing against tanks and automatic weapons. That was the message.

The Chinese were moving through the village, shooting at individual houses. Fires had sprung up and a few of the buildings were in flames. Black smoke rose and was blown along the rooftops by the wind.

"You seen enough?" asked Evers. He was no longer looking down at the village.

Reisman kept watching as the Chinese began forcing the people out into the street, shooting a few as they tried to run. Men, women, children, it didn't matter. All were cut down as they tried to escape across the frozen ground.

The tank moved, rolled over part of the stone wall, and crushed a house into rubble beneath its tracks. It stopped, the turret swung right and left, but it didn't fire again.

"What'll happen to the people?" asked Reisman.

Evers shrugged.

But Reisman didn't really need the answer. He thought of the pictures that they'd taken and could imagine the color spread in *Time* or *Newsweek* after they had been printed in his newspaper. People would be outraged until they turned the page and sat down to dinner. Nothing ever changed.

"We'd better go," said Evers.

This time Reisman nodded. He'd seen more than

enough. Firing from the village was tapering off as the Chinese finished rounding up the last of the inhabitants.

Slipping to the rear, Reisman finally stood and brushed the caked snow from the front of his clothes. With the others he started down the hill, sliding in the knee deep snow. Waiting at the bottom of it was their Jeep.

When they reached it, Reisman asked the photographer, "How many pictures did you shoot?"

"Couple of hundred. I got everything, from that man shooting the Chinese soldier right through them gunning down the people as they tried to run."

To Evers Reisman said, "How long until we reach your office?"

Evers pulled back the sleeve of his parka and looked at his watch. "About dark."

"What time will that be in New York?"

"Morning. Early morning."

"Maybe early enough to get something on one of the news shows?"

"We could get it on CNN right away. Without having to wait," the photographer said.

Reisman nodded. "Have to be careful because we owe some loyalty to the newspaper."

"Hell, no one's going to fault us for dropping this at CNN first. Give them a taste and then let the paper break the whole story a couple of hours later on the West Coast."

Reisman opened the rear door of the Jeep and climbed in. He'd thought that it would be warmer inside, but it wasn't. The driver started the engine, but the blower was putting out cold air.

"Let's get going," Evers said, "before the Chinese decide to check the high ground for spies."

"Right," said Reisman.

The driver dropped it into gear, let the tires spin and the rear fishtail until they burned through the snow for traction. They hit the pavement and rocketed forward, heading downhill.

"Couple of hours," Evers said again.

All that Reisman could think of was that at the height of the Persian Gulf War a couple of hours would have meant the end of the story. Yet here, at the top of the world, no one knew that anything was happening.

...

NICARAGUA

Martinez, along with Chavez and four other men, lay in the jungle and watched the maneuvering of the rebel soldiers as they drilled in their small camp. The soldiers were there to make sure that the people of the region stayed on the rebel side and provided the raw food supplies they were tasked to produce.

It was a small camp with a fence around it. Two gates led to a number of low buildings that had been built from mud and straw and a little refined lumber. The exceptions were the arms locker, an ammo dump, and a cinder-block building that had to be a radio shack because of the antenna array on the top of it.

As a military installation, it wasn't well designed. There was a good approach from the left that would provide an attacking force with excellent concealment. On the right the jungle had been cut back to about a hundred yards, but it was growing up again. An assault force, if it had the time, could crawl nearly to the wire before anyone saw them.

All the equipment had been stacked or parked in the center of the camp where it was the farthest from the fence, but where it would make an excellent target for mortarmen. A single soldier with a few well-placed grenades or a little C-4 explosive could destroy a great deal of the equipment.

Chavez crawled forward and whispered, "We going to take them out?"

"Not yet," said Martinez.

A moment later a truck appeared on the road. It was followed by a car. At the gate it stopped. A man got out of the passenger's side of the truck, opened the gate, and waited as both vehicles drove through.

The car went toward the headquarters building and stopped again. The driver leaped from behind the wheel, hurried around, and opened the rear door. A tall man got out, stood, and surveyed the area. He then walked up the steps and disappeared into the building.

Chavez, leaning close, asked, "That looked like what's-his-name. The rebel leader?"

"Castillo," said Martinez quietly. "One of the rebel leaders."

"Be great if we could take him out now," said Chavez.

Martinez thought about it. "Not our job now."

"Target of opportunity," said Chavez.

Martinez didn't respond immediately. He watched the headquarters, waiting. Finally he said, "We are not going to change our battle plan now. If he gets in the way, we take him, but right now we stay clear."

"That's a mistake, Captain," said Chavez. "It's going to come back to haunt us."

"Maybe," said Martinez. "But the decision is made."

The radio crackled and Espinoza leaned close. He listened and then slipped closer to Martinez. "The lieutenant said that they're in place and ready to move."

"Ten minutes." Martinez looked toward Chavez. "You got the guards spotted?"

"Only two that we need to worry about. I'll take one and Ortega will get the other."

Martinez nodded and slipped to the rear. Jones was crouched near a tree, leaning against the trunk. His medical gear was spread out as he checked through it quickly, storing it into his ruck as he did. "We're going in ten minutes."

"I'll be ready."

Martinez returned to the edge of the jungle. He knew that Alvarez and the rest of the team were concealed across the clearing, ready to move on the rebel camp. He could see no sign that they were in position, but if Alvarez had done his job right, there shouldn't be any.

The lights in the compound were beginning to come on. Three of them were aimed at the road, lighting it. The rest were in the buildings in the camp. Martinez could hear the whine of a generator.

There were no lights from the village beyond the camp, other than the flickering of a fire. The village didn't seem to have any electricity.

Martinez checked the time, surprised that the ten minutes were already gone. He checked the safety of his weapon, pulled the bolt back slightly, and checked to see that the round was seated properly in the chamber. "Let's go."

Chavez led the way, inching from the cover of the jungle, but staying in the long, deep grass. Martinez, crouching near a tree, watched the sergeant work his way toward the enemy camp.

This was what it was all about. Heading out to attack the enemy. It was what he had trained and practiced for and it made no difference that the war was undeclared and that he was operating under special orders from the Office of the President.

Chavez was about ten or twelve meters in front of him now. Martinez stretched out and began to pull himself through the grass, carefully setting his hands and feet down, listening to the sounds around him, trying to pick up a change in the environment signaling that the enemy had detected him.

He concentrated on getting through the thick, tall grass. He reached out, pushed it to the side, and pulled himself forward. He stopped behind a large rock for a moment, using it for cover. He closed his eyes and listened, but only the hum of the generator and buzz of the insects could be heard. Nothing from the enemy camp.

To his right he saw Espinoza crawl over a log and disappear into the grass again. Had it not been for that, he would never have known he was there.

Martinez reached a point about a hundred meters from the jungle and only fifty or sixty from the camp. He stopped and rested. Around him he could hear nothing new. The insects still hovered, flitting in and out, trying to get at the salt from sweat at the corner of his eyes. The generator was still making enough noise to cover any sound that the assault team might create.

Before he could move again, the front gate opened and two men ran out. They separated, one of them heading to the east and one to the west. It looked as if one had spotted Chavez because he was running straight for the master sergeant.

There was nothing Martinez could do. He was too far from both the enemy soldier and Chavez. Anything he did would alert the rebels.

But Chavez didn't seem to know. He had stopped moving and had turned his head toward the right. Then, suddenly, as the man was about to reach him, Chavez stood up directly in front of the running man. His right hand flashed, striking at the solar plexus of the soldier; with his left he grabbed, and then fell back, into the protection of the grass.

Martinez hurried forward. Chavez was lying next to

the dead soldier, going through the man's pockets. Moving closer, he saw blood on Chavez, but the master sergeant shook his head.

Quietly he said, "Not mine."

Martinez nodded toward the camp. "We've got to get going."

Chavez pulled the dead man's weapon closer, released the magazine, and then field-stripped it. He scattered the parts, knowing the tropical environment would rust them in a matter of days.

Chavez then moved around a bush toward the fence guarding the camp. He reached it and then hesitated, looking back over his shoulder.

Martinez crawled to within a couple of meters but stopped short. He pulled his weapon around and aimed it at the interior of the camp.

Espinoza reached the wire. Using the bolt cutters, he snipped at the fence, creating a hole. He pushed the wire aside and slipped through.

As soon as he was inside, Chavez followed him, as did Martinez and Cline. Jones remained outside, with the medical kit, and to act as a rear guard. He'd cover the extraction, if they needed the cover.

Now, inside the camp, crouched in the darkness in the shadow of the unmanned guard tower, Chavez whispered, "Prison facilities are there and there. Barracks there. Armory there."

Martinez agreed with Chavez's assessment of the camp. "Let's move it."

They were up and running a second later. They rounded one barracks and stopped as the door opened, spilling light. A man stepped out, almost like a home owner on a lazy summer evening. A last breath of fresh air before retiring for the night. The man groaned, stretched, and laughed. He answered someone inside the barracks and then turned to join them.

As soon as the man was gone, Martinez moved again.

He rounded the corner, saw that the door was closed, and headed toward the prison compound.

Chavez held back, studying the barracks. Using a short length of wire and a hand grenade, he fashioned a booby trap quickly. The first or second man out the door would trip it, and three seconds later the grenade would detonate. If there was a general alarm, the explosion might slow the rest of the soldiers. They would hesitate, not wanting to run into the next grenade.

Chavez joined Martinez, and they reached the prison compound. It was little more than a fenced-in area with a couple of tents for shelter. A dozen people were milling around with another group sitting near the tent. A guard was watching the prisoners.

"Don't see anyone else on this side," Chavez said.

Martinez pointed at Espinoza and motioned him around so that he could kill the guard. Espinoza nodded his understanding and slipped to the rear.

Glancing at his watch, Martinez said, "Alvarez and his team should be inside by now."

Lieutenant Alvarez, along with the remainder of the team, had no trouble reaching the wire or cutting their way through it. They saw no guards. They saw movement inside the camp, but that was normal.

Once inside, they spread out, heading for the motor pool, where the trucks, Jeeps, and cars were parked. One of them was up on blocks, the wheels pulled from it and a puddle of oil under it.

Without a word from the lieutenant, the men scattered among the vehicles, disabling them. They used knives to puncture the tires and the gas tanks; opening the hoods, they ripped the wires from the distributors and the spark plugs. In moments they had ruined all the vehicles.

As they swept by, Davis placed a couple of simple booby traps. He set thermite grenades so that the pins were nearly out of them. The enemy, rushing to grab their trucks or cars, would inadvertently pull the pins, ignite the spilled gas, and in seconds the motor pool would be in flames.

That finished, he joined the rest of the team as they headed toward the prison compound. They reached it and spread out, searching for the guards.

Holding his silenced pistol, Alvarez spotted a guard about twenty meters away. He aimed and fired. The sound of the shot was lost in the humming of the generator. Even the quiet clicking of the bolt was covered.

The guard fell forward without a sound. Alvarez hesitated, watching for a response from the camp, but there was none. He surveyed the area, spotted no other guards, and waved his men forward.

As they reached the fence of the internal compound, another group emerged from the darkness. Alvarez whirled, but recognized them immediately as the other half of the team. One man detached himself and attacked the wire with bolt cutters.

In seconds the man had cut through the fence and peeled it back. Alvarez and his team entered while the others remained on guard.

Inside, the men spread out again. Alvarez rushed forward and, speaking quietly in Spanish, said, "Everyone out. Quickly."

A man appeared in the flap of the tent and stared. He glanced to the rear and then ran out, wanting to hug the Americans.

Alvarez ducked and pointed the man at one of his soldiers. In English he said, "Get them moving out."

"Yes, sir."

Now others were appearing, forming a line. Alvarez and Davies were trying to get them moving, away from the center of the prison compound and toward the gap in the wire that would lead to safety.

A man appeared outside, his hands on his hips, looking as if he was trying to figure out what was happening. Finally he moved forward waving a hand. "Hey!"

Alvarez raised the silenced pistol and fired. The first

shot was wide, but it stopped the rebel soldier. He stood, frozen, as if not understanding. Alvarez fired again and the man spun to the right, falling. He didn't make a sound.

"Go!" yelled Alvarez. "Hurry!"

The prisoners, men, women, and children, reached the hole in the wire and ducked through it. Alvarez ran to the closest tent, looked in, then searched the rest of them quickly. Satisfied that they had freed all the prisoners, he whirled and ran toward the wire.

"We clear?"

"We've got everyone."

"Then let's go."

Martinez watched as the last of the people ducked through the fence. Espinoza and Gibson led them off into the dark. Martinez, along with Chavez and two others, held back, forming a rear guard.

Once the prisoners were freed, Martinez turned, crouched, and searched for the enemy. He felt a slap on his shoulder and saw Chavez standing next to him, gesturing toward the rear.

"Right." He stood, took a single step back and then spun, hurrying after the rest of the team.

For a moment it looked as if they would get clear easily. Then a siren began to wail. At first it was a quiet cry, like a small child, but it built until it sounded like a banshee.

Martinez looked back and saw the first of the enemy soldiers spilling from the barracks. He flipped his selector switch to full auto and raised his rifle.

One of the soldiers hit the booby trap at the barracks door. White-hot shrapnel ripped through the night. There were screams from the injured. Firing erupted from the barracks, but no one had a target. They were shooting at anything that moved, including the shadows.

Martinez didn't return the fire; there was no sense in giving away his position with a muzzle flash.

He turned to run. Behind him were shouts; officers were trying to get the soldiers to act, but having no luck.

Then, from the motor pool came another explosion. White phosphorus erupted and gasoline burst into flame; it went up quickly, the vehicles engulfed in fire.

Martinez reached the fence and threw himself to the ground. He rolled to his belly and watched the camp. A half-dozen enemy soldiers sprinted from their barracks, firing their rifles. Martinez aimed and pulled the trigger. Two fell; the others scattered.

A moment later half his men opened fire. The ruby-colored tracers flashed, some hitting the ground and tumbling into the night sky.

"We're clear," yelled one of the men.

"Everyone out," Martinez ordered.

Chavez was up and moving. He emptied his weapon and then spun, diving through the hole in the fence. An instant later he was firing again, providing cover.

Martinez was the last out of the camp. He saw the shadowy shapes of the prisoners as they rushed for the safety of the jungle. More of the enemy reached the wire and a few of them began to shoot. Martinez shot back, hosing down the area, aiming at the muzzle flashes.

Chavez was next to him, but was throwing grenades. The explosions dotted the landscape, ripping at the wire of the fence. In the flashes of the fountaining explosions Chavez could see the enemy soldiers diving for cover.

When firing from the camp died, Martinez leaped to his feet. "Let's go!"

Together they fled, running through the waist-high grass. Martinez veered to the right, his foot catching on something. He pitched forward, his hands outstretched. As he landed he lost his grip on his rifle.

Chavez slid to a stop and dropped to a knee. "You hit?"

Martinez struggled to come to his hands and knees. The breath had been knocked out of him. He shook his head, but Chavez couldn't see it.

"You hit?"

"Hah . . . Rifle."

Chavez leaned forward and reached out, feeling with his fingers. He found the weapon and held on to it. "I've got it."

Behind them was growing bedlam. There was more firing now, a wide variety of weapons. The arms locker detonated with an earth-pounding explosion, the cooking-off ammo shooting into the air like a mad fireworks display designed by a modern artist.

Martinez sucked in the warm air and said, "Let's move." He got shakily to his feet. The jungle was only twenty yards ahead.

Chavez handed over the rifle and the men jogged forward, ignoring the sounds behind them. The enemy had lost track of the attackers and were now firing wildly into the night. The tracers, white, red, and green, were flashing high overhead.

Reaching the jungle, Martinez whirled and crouched. The camp was a sea of fire. Flames had spread from the burning motor pool and were racing across the barracks. Men were firing their weapons into the air as if they were being bombed, though there were no fighters overhead. Explosions erupted, sending boiling gouts of flame into the night sky. Shadows appeared in front of the fires, but there was no attempt at pursuit.

"Everyone clear?" asked Martinez.

"Yes, sir."

"Casualties?"

Jones appeared from the darkness of the jungle. "Couple of the prisoners are going to need treatment for injuries received during interrogation, but nothing we need to worry about now."

"Have Alvarez and his team move out now. We'll follow in about ten minutes."

"Yes, sir," said Jones.

Martinez turned his attention back toward the camp, searching for a sign that someone was coming. The firing was tapering off again and none of it was directed into the jungle. The enemy soldiers were just shooting, probably out of rage and frustration.

Martinez stood up. Chavez was standing near him. "Guess that one caught them by surprise."

"Next time might not be so easy."

"If there is a next time." He pointed at the jungle. "Let's get going and get these people home. We've got a ways to go before sunup."

"Yes, sir."

From the moment of the first shot Castillo was standing at the window of the headquarters. He could see the movement of the raiders as they swarmed into the camp. He heard a sound behind him, but refused to look to see who it was.

"They've hit the prison compound and released the prisoners."

Castillo continued to stare out the window. "Let them go. Gives them the problem of feeding and housing them."

"We look weak."

Now Castillo turned and walked away from the window. He sat down at the desk and leaned forward, his elbows on the edge. "It makes no difference to us here. The prisoners tell of their treatment by our guards and that scares others. We let them go for the propaganda."

"We should hunt them down and kill them. A perfect object lesson."

"Our plans are bigger than that. This is a small raid and means nothing. We shouldn't waste our time on this trivia."

"Yes, Colonel."

"Have my car readied. I am ready to leave."

"Yes, sir." The aide didn't move.

"You have a question?"

"Ah . . . the raiders?"

Castillo smiled. "You must look at the bigger picture.

This will not be reported. We must not concern ourselves with it, unless we can find them easily."

"Yes, sir. I'll alert the scouts."

Castillo ignored that. "Get the car."

"Yes, sir."

PIEDRAS NEGRAS, NEAR
THE TEXAS–MEXICO BORDER

Jerry Rider, of the U.S. Border Patrol—and the Defenders of the Texas Revolution—had told Daniels where the border patrols would be and when they would be there. He had also mentioned that the officers would not be worried about people trying to sneak into Mexico; their concern was those going the other way. The border patrol wasn't all that worried about drugs, either; that was the problem of the DEA.

Daniels, with the patrol map spread out on the hood of his Chevy Blazer, looked at the landmarks that led to the ford in the Rio Grande and at Mexico on the other side of the river. The closest town was twenty miles away. No people were in sight, no man-made structures, and no sign that people had ever seen that section of Texas.

Pointing, he said, "Cross the river, travel about three

miles over land, and then we should turn to the east and we'll hit pavement."

Rogers came around the front of the Blazer and leaned over the map, moving so that his shadow wasn't on the truck. He studied the map. "Put us into town about midnight?"

"Depending on how fast we drive. Then I think we'd better retreat along here and hit this road, driving north. If we're in the clear, we cross back in the daylight."

Rogers looked at his watch. "We'd better hit the trail."

"Weapons concealed?"

"If we're stopped and searched, they're going to find them. If we're stopped and just questioned, I doubt they'll spot anything."

Daniels nodded and turned. The second Blazer was filled with men, three in the front and three in the back. Behind it was a Ford Bronco with another nine men, and behind that was a pickup holding the last of the raiding party.

With the four men and two women in his Blazer, Daniels had a raiding force of about half a platoon, or two squads, though they were more heavily armed than a regular army squad. In addition to the personal weapons, some of them hunting rifles, and some of the AR-15s modified so they would fire on full auto, they had a case of grenades and a few LAW rockets. Even without the 3.5-inch rocket launcher, they would be able to create quite a mess.

Daniels laughed. "Don't think our regular army hits the field in air-conditioned trucks with tape and CD players."

"With the amount of money they spend, I wouldn't be surprised," said Rogers.

"Let's get going." Daniels folded the map and stuck it in the pocket along the thigh of Desert Storm surplus camouflage fatigues. He pulled the boonie hat lower, as if to hide his eyes.

He opened the passenger door and climbed into the truck. He put a foot up on the dashboard and leaned his elbow against it. To the driver, Sergeant Amos, he said, "Forward slowly. Down the hill and to the river. We'll stop on the bank to make sure that we can ford it."

"Yes, sir."

The engine ground and sputtered to life. With it cold air began to spill from the vents. Daniels reached over and turned on the radio. He searched the dial, stopping first at a Mexican station. Daniels liked to think that he could speak Spanish, but the rapid-fire chatter from the radio shot past him. Instead he searched until he found a soft-rock station in Laredo that was only occasionally interrupted by bursts of static.

From the backseat one of the men asked, "Should we be listening to that crap?"

Daniels turned in the seat and looked at Ralph Hyatt, a burly man who had been rejected by the army because of asthma and who didn't want to be a marine or a sailor. He had a shock of red hair and a red beard that annoyed Daniels, who told him to shave it. He was an intense man with bright blue eyes that seemed to blaze at all times and who never forgot how he had scored the winning touchdown in a game over twenty years ago. It was his single claim to fame, one that he brought up at least once a week.

"I don't remember taking a vote," said Daniels. "I don't remember opening the floor to discussion."

"Don't hand me that parliment—that parli—that procedure bullshit."

Before Daniels could respond, the truck slowed and then stopped. They were parked in a copse of cottonwoods on the bank of the Rio Grande.

Daniels reached out and opened the door, but didn't exit. He sat for a moment, feeling a sense of history. This had to be how the Texans felt in 1836 before the ill-fated Matamoros expedition. They were taking the war to their enemy. Times had changed and the enemies had become friends, except in the economic arena. Mexico was still the enemy, sucking jobs away from good Texans. Time to invade again and steal back that which belonged in Texas and the United States.

Amos climbed out, walked down the bank to the river, and stared at the other side. Mexico looked just like Texas. Had it not been for the river, he wouldn't be able to tell the difference.

He took a step into the river and then stopped. His foot sank slightly into the mud. The water had a rusty color to it, as if there had been heavy rains upstream. The red earth of the Big Bend area filled the Rio Grande.

Daniels climbed out and walked slowly to the river's edge. "What do you think?"

"Looks like it's a little deeper than we planned on."

"That going to be a problem?"

"I don't think so. Water shouldn't be up over the hubs. Just put it in four-wheel drive and keep the power to the wheels. We stop we could be fucked."

Daniels turned and saw that the others were getting out of the trucks. They came forward and surrounded him. He was tempted to tell them that a single well-placed grenade would kill them all, but knew it would sound like a line from a war movie. Besides, no one was going to be throwing grenades at them.

"Sergeant Amos," said Daniels, "brief the other drivers on the procedure to cross the river."

"Yes, sir." Amos waved the drivers over and then crouched at the base of a giant cottonwood.

As Amos talked to the drivers Daniels asked the others, "Everyone square on what we're going to do?"

Rogers said, "We destroy the factory, but we give the people a chance to get out."

"Right. We have no quarrel with the people. They were offered the jobs and they took them. If the situation was reversed, we'd do the same thing. No, we just want to destroy the factory and the equipment."

"What about the inventory of cars?" asked one of the men.

"If they've got finished product sitting out and vulnerable, I think we'd be remiss if we didn't destroy it."

"Armed guards?"

Daniels shot a look at the man. These same questions came up at the briefings. It seemed that there was always someone who hadn't heard, had forgotten, or wanted to be absolutely sure. "We take no chances. If the guard attempts to draw, you shoot. If you've got him cold, I don't want him murdered. Roll with the situation."

The drivers joined the rest of the party. Daniels looked at them and wanted to give them a pep talk like a football coach before the big game, but he couldn't think of the right words. Finally he settled for a repeat of the instructions. If they got separated, they should run for the border. If anyone got injured or killed, they were to be helped away. There should be nothing left behind to identify the raiders as Americans.

"Brass from the weapons will tell them that," said Hyatt.

"Good Christ, Ralph, I've told you a hundred times. The government sold so many of those rifles, gave so many of them away, that they're untraceable. Even the Vietnamese, if they could get here, might be using the same rifles." He looked at the people. "Anything else?"

No one said a word.

"Good," said Daniels. "Couple of hours and this will all be over. We'll have the party on this side of the river." He waited for a whoop of excitement, but none came. The men and women stood looking at him dully, as if they didn't understand what was about to happen.

"Let's get mounted and move out."

The group turned and began to walk toward their vehicles. Daniels caught Rogers and said, "Damn quiet group."

"I think everyone's a little nervous about tonight."

"I suppose."

"Once we're clear, you wait to see the excitement. You won't be able to hold them down."

Morris Reisman sat in the warm glow of an old potbellied stove. He'd heard, as he grew up, how families sat around the stoves in the winter, and how they would reach a fiery, cherry glow as the evening wore on, but he hadn't believed it. Now he could see it for himself.

The story and pictures that he'd submitted had caused a stir in Hong Kong and the Far East, but the wheels in New York had decided that it wasn't significant. There had been too many pictures of the oppressed being kept that way. Scenes from Afghanistan, Iraq, Iran, South Africa, and Argentina were not of interest to the people trying to find day care for the kids, trying to advance in their jobs, and trying to live their lives. The people of the United States couldn't see how the Chinese army rolling over a village in Tibet had anything to do with their lives. Unfortunately, they were probably right. The flap, minor as it was, died in a matter of hours.

Reisman had climbed another mountain and seen more villages. He'd seen more Chinese soldiers, but there had been no more incidents.

Evers, the British correspondent, sat with his feet up, a cup of tea near his right hand and a pipe clenched between his teeth. "When do you have to leave, old boy?"

"In the morning. I've been told that the lack of good copy coming out of here has required a reassessment of my job. Money."

Evers nodded. "Maybe it's time to punch out. Go free-lance. Not as lucrative, but at least you don't have some corporate putz telling you how to write your story."

Reisman leaned forward and held his hands out to the warmth of the stove. "I'm not sure that what you're doing here is that important."

"Of course. A few villagers in the hills fighting for religious freedom. Not much of a story."

"Not compared to what else is happening in the world. But I guess the question is what *is* news. Is it what we think is important, or is it what affects the most people? A house fire might make good pictures, but in the long run does it really make a difference?"

Evers sipped his tea and set it on the table near his hand. "No, I suppose it doesn't."

"If the Chinese declare war on the United States, does that affect the people? If they have a way to attack the United States, I would guess it would."

"A fairly narrow view," said Evers.

Reisman shrugged. "It was the information explosion. CNN is live, on the air, twenty-four hours a day. It used to be that you had to wait weeks to learn what was happening, now you can know as it happens. There's so much of it that people finally decide the importance by how it affects their lives. Period. And maybe that is the only criterion that is important."

"But—"

Reisman cut him off. "But nothing. News isn't important because there are spectacular pictures, but too often that was the reason for going with the story. It was visually rich. We ignore important stories because there aren't good pictures to go with it. So who's to say what is important?"

"Where do you go from here?"

"Well, it's going to be much warmer," said Reisman, "and that makes it better. But I'm returning to the United States. Some activity along the border that might have an effect on that young man or woman in New York."

"How's that?" asked Evers.

"It's the growing number of Latin Americans crossing the border from Mexico into the United States. Hundreds of thousands of people, from all over Latin America, get into the country and then require food, shelter, clothing, money, and jobs. If they can't have jobs, they end up on welfare, creating havoc on the system. If they get jobs, they take them away from American workers. So that poor guy in New York ends up having to pay higher taxes, or he loses his job because there is a man or woman in Texas or New Mexico who'll do it for less money."

"It's a lousy way to determine the importance of a story," said Evers, puffing on his pipe. The blue cloud of smoke circled his head.

"Might be, but it's the way they're running the show in New York."

Evers nodded grimly. "Could you do something for me? Could you try to convince them of the importance of what is happening here?"

"I can try," said Reisman, "but they're not going to see it. The Chinese could kill millions. Probably have, and no one is going to get too worked up."

"Show them the pictures and tell them that it could be happening in their own country someday."

"Won't work. They know that the government would never level a village because the people didn't agree. Even if someone shot at them, they wouldn't level the place. Might burn a neighborhood, but they wouldn't level a village."

"No, I suppose not."

Reisman stood. "Got an early-morning car ride so that I can catch the plane."

Evers held out a hand. "It was nice working with you."

"Same. You sure know the territory. Know the people. It was impressive."

"That's what happens when you live in a place for twenty years and keep your eyes open."

"I'll do what I can," said Reisman. "I'll try to get someone interested in New York." He shook Evers's hand.

"Thanks."

Reisman turned and headed for his room. He noticed that it was cold in the hallway. It was as if the potbellied stove stripped the heat from the rest of the house.

•   •   •

The facilities that they had found for them had been less than adequate. The old army post, built for the thousands of soldiers who had been drafted for World War II, had been closed for years. Now it was up to the engineers assigned to the First Brigade to get the place ready.

Sandi Paulding was getting tired of moving from one abandoned fort to the next. It did no good to tell herself that they finally had a mission; it wasn't part of the original mission of the division. And it made no sense to assign an armored division to border-guard duty.

Because the facilities were bad, and because she was getting bored, she decided that she wanted to go out on patrol. It wasn't one of those where the soldier walked over enemy territory with the possibility of ambush and firefight. It was in a Humvee, with an NCO, driving along an assigned area of the Rio Grande, searching for people trying to sneak into the United States, or for evidence that they had succeeded at an earlier time. It wasn't very exciting, either.

They stopped on a hilltop and Paulding climbed stiffly from the passenger's side and pulled the binoculars from the case she wore. She scanned the horizon and saw nothing of interest. With the coming of night there wasn't much to see. Ranch-house lights, the glow of a city far away, and the bouncing of a Jeep's headlights far to the north.

"Can't we go get something to eat, Major?" asked the driver for the ninth time in thirty minutes.

"We're not cleared from here for another hour. Grab one of the MREs."

"They're shit, Major. They're inedible."

"Then you should have brought something." She glanced at the driver, sitting behind the wheel. He was hanging on to the wheel as if he was dangling from a cliff. Paulding lifted the binoculars again and scanned the landscape. There was nothing to see with the exception of a flash of light to the left. That marked the edge of the patrol zone. The other patrol had reached the limit and was turning back.

She lowered the binoculars and then sat down in the passenger's seat of the Humvee. She was quiet for a moment, listening to the sounds of the south Texas evening.

"We going now, Major?"

Paulding had to laugh. "Got a one-track mind, don't you?"

"No reason to stay out here. Nobody crosses the border here. Too far from the towns and roads, and the hills are too steep."

"Which means that we might see something. Besides, it's our job."

"Yeah, but nobody would know."

"Christ, Sergeant, what in the hell are you doing in the army?"

"I keep asking myself that question. I was a mechanic. Good one. Next thing I know I'm called to active duty. I didn't think it would happen that way. Not after all that trouble with that Desert Storm."

Paulding knew the feeling. She could still hear the recruiter telling her that the army wouldn't be calling people to active duty in the massive way they had done during Desert Shield and later Desert Storm. Congress had changed the rules. And there was no real threat to the American continent, so that she could make the drills, a two-week tour, and there would be lots of extra money.

"We're in the same boat, Sergeant."

"So let's go get something to eat. We'd be back in about an hour."

"Let's just do our job," said Paulding. "We'll be here a little longer and then we can get some food."

"Yes, ma'am."

Paulding stood up and turned slowly, scanning the horizon. She understood the sergeant because she was bored, too. There was nothing happening out here and there probably wouldn't be.

Sitting back into the Humvee, Paulding said, "Okay. Let's drive on to post number four."

"Yes, ma'am."

PANAMA

Boyce was in the radio room, a cinder-block building that had a steel vault door on the front and a huge group of antennae on the roof. From it they could maintain contact with teams in the field, Special Forces headquarters at Fort Bragg, North Carolina, the War Room in the Pentagon, and even the White House. They could monitor, through relays, satellites, and microwave, the radio traffic of the entire world. If they wanted, and had a Russian-language expert handy, they could intercept and interpret the orders issued by the Kremlin to the Spetsnaz.

When the NCOIC saw Boyce, he leaped to his feet and asked, "Would you like a chair, sir?"

"No. I was just wondering if you've made contact with the various teams in the field."

"Yes, sir. Everyone made the check. All are functioning normally."

Boyce nodded and looked at the display of radios, every kind from commercially available shortwave sets to military-use VHF and UHF. In front of each was an operator. Some wore headsets and had keypads. Others had microphones. There was notepaper, pencils, message forms, and loose-leaf notebooks for each of the operators.

The interior of the building was extremely cold, to keep the radios operating at their maximum efficiency. Boyce, fresh from the humidity and heat outside, shivered.

"Coffee, Colonel?" asked the NCOIC.

"No, thank you, Sergeant. How is it going?"

"Fine, sir. No problems. Smooth as silk."

"Well, good," said Boyce. He stood for a moment, feeling the eyes of the NCO on him. The sergeant didn't want to do anything that would offend a colonel, didn't want to leave him alone, but did want to get back to work.

Boyce, on the other hand, had the information that he wanted. The teams had all checked in. The mission in Nicaragua was proceeding smoothly. "Well, Sergeant, I appreciate the look around."

"Yes, sir. Thank you, sir."

Boyce sauntered to the vault door and let the corporal there open it for him. Outside, in the humid night, he walked down to the waiting Jeep. Lombard sat behind the wheel. When he saw the colonel approaching, he asked, "You learn anything?"

"All teams have reported in. Doesn't seem that anyone's having any trouble."

"Then we're a go?"

"I think we'll try to get the B-team headquarters in sometime in the next forty-eight hours. Then we can start coordinating the activity around Managua."

Lombard started the engine and then leaned forward on the wheel. "You still planning to go, Colonel?"

"Of course. No reason not to."

"Yes, sir."

"Let's head back to the office."

Lombard dropped the Jeep into gear, glanced over his shoulder, and then pulled out onto the street. He fell in behind a large truck that was belching diesel fumes.

"You want to go?" asked Boyce.

Lombard was quiet for so long that Boyce began to wonder if he'd heard the question.

"I don't know, Colonel. Seems to me that only an idiot would volunteer to jump into hostile territory and give up the comfort of an air-conditioned apartment here for a roof made of jungle vegetation."

"Uh-huh."

"I mean, we've got willing women here. Beer so cold that it'll crack your teeth. Clubs, hot food, movies. Everything that you can imagine."

"Uh-huh."

They slowed, turned a corner, and then accelerated. Lombard continued. "I can't see any reason for going into the jungle."

"Takeoff is at midnight."

"I'll be there."

"I thought as much."

Cesar Castro was no relation to the dictator that had ruled his country for so very long. He had been a farmer for most of his life, ignoring the politics of the world, wanting only to make sure that his family had the food they needed, a shelter, and when times were good, a few luxuries that included a radio, and once he had believed they would someday own a television. That dream had not come true.

Although still a young man of thirty-two, Castro already had a dozen kids. His education had stopped when he impregnated a neighbor's daughter and both families decided that the two should be together throughout eternity. Castro never regretted the forced wedding.

Now, however, the family was left behind, at the

small farm, and he was crouched in the deep grass at the edge of the tree line that overlooked part of the American base at Guantanamo. That was a blot on all of Cuba. An American base, American territory on his soil, without the permission of the Cubans. No one had been able to force the Americans to abandon it.

Although he had never seen the base until he arrived there, and had never heard of it until he was asked to help rid their island of it, it enraged him. He wanted to see the Americans pushed off his homeland.

Their sergeant, a large swarthy man with thick eyebrows that met over the bridge of a nose that looked to have been broken several times, stopped nearby. In a voice that was surprisingly loud he said, "We will do nothing tonight. Let the American dogs lie. Let them think they are safe behind their barriers of wire and bright lights."

Castro looked up at the sergeant but didn't speak. He'd learned in the last few weeks that one didn't address the sergeant without good cause. To do so meant that the sergeant would reach out to smack the offender. If there was a good question, or the sergeant had asked one, that was different.

"We will withdraw and make our camp. No fires and no noise." With that the sergeant slipped off into the darkness.

Carefully Castro crawled to the rear, using the grass and then the trees for cover until he was sure that he wouldn't be seen by the Americans if they were looking at him. He walked forward, a hand out in front of him like a blind man who had lost his cane.

Another of the soldiers moved close and whispered, "I thought we'd attack tonight."

"So did I." Castro grinned and thought of the television. They had been promised the spoils once the base was taken and he'd search for a TV. He might never make enough money to buy one, but he would be able to find one on the base. Americans had everything.

"Always it is the same," grumbled the soldier. "Hurry

up. Run. Faster. And then wait. We must wait. I see no reason to wait."

"The officers must have a reason."

"They're all old women, afraid of the Americans. They see the Americans in the news and fear them like children afraid of the creatures that come in the night. Old women and children."

Castro nodded but said nothing. He was sure that those at the top must have a reason for delay. There were many things about being a soldier that he did not understand. It was not unlike being a farmer. Those who lived in the cities did not understand how to make the crops grow. They didn't know how to coax the seedlings from the ground, how to care for them and nurture them until they were ripe for the harvest. City dwellers couldn't even understand when to harvest. It was a special knowledge. He was sure that soldiers also had special knowledge. He was sure there was a good reason not to attack.

They reached a clearing with ankle-high grass that stretched like a carpet in front of them. As Castro dropped to the ground the sergeant was there, shouting, "No. The enemy can spot us too easily here. We continue on."

Climbing to his feet, Castro was approached by the soldier again. "Dumb sergeant. The Americans won't see us here because they won't be looking for us here."

There was a loud smack and the soldier tumbled to the ground. He rolled over quickly and leaped to his feet, pulling his knife. He crouched, the rifle strapped across his back forgotten. Through clenched teeth he said, "I will kill you."

The sergeant stood flat-footed, looking as if he didn't have a care in the world. He held his hands out, palm down, his eyes on the dark shape of the soldier with the knife.

"Hey," said Castro. "Hey."

"Shut up," snapped the sergeant. Looking at the other man, he said, "Come on, dog. Kill me."

For a moment everything hung there, like a dusky

painting by a man with only blacks and grays on his palette. There was no movement by either man. Then the knife fighter took a step forward, holding his weapon out.

The sergeant moved quickly, stepping forward and not back as expected. He swung one arm out to block the hand with the knife. He kicked with his right foot, aiming for the crotch. With a piercing scream the soldier fell to the ground. He lost his knife as he folded himself into a ball, groaning quietly.

Spinning, the sergeant demanded, "Does anyone else have objections?"

The small circle of men suddenly scattered. They began moving across the clearing toward the jungle. No one had anything to say.

"You help that man," said the sergeant.

Castro crouched and reached out. He touched the soldier, trying to lift him to his feet, but the man moaned and rolled away, turning his face to the ground.

"Get him to his feet or I'll kill him."

Castro got his hand under the man's arm and pulled. Slowly the man got to his knees. He made a sound low in his throat and then looked up. The sergeant was standing there watching.

"You have a big mouth. You will keep it shut." He turned and joined the rest of the company.

Castro lifted the man to his feet and stepped away. He saw the man walking hunched over, one hand between his legs. He had nothing else to say.

Commander Kelly Raymond Dees left the bridge of his ship and headed down to the wardroom. As he entered, the officers slowly came to their feet. Dees waved at them and said, "Keep your seats, gentlemen." Moving toward the coffeepot, he poured himself a cup and then turned. Pulling out the chair, he dropped into it, looked into the faces of his fellow officers. Sipping the coffee, he asked, "Where's Drummond?"

"He'll be along in a moment," said Henry Randolph, the exec officer.

Dees sat for a moment, letting the situation around him evolve. It was like high school. The boys and girls were having fun and then a teacher arrived. Now they had to be on their best behavior, so they all sat quietly, waiting. Dees had tried to break through that barrier but had failed. A captaincy was the only position of absolute power left in the military. A ship at sea was a world unto itself with the captain as the ruler. Although it was now connected to the shore by radios and helicopters, the captain still had the power. Those on the shore, having passed through the system, were reluctant to second-guess the captain of a ship at sea.

Drummond entered, looked at the assembled officers, and grinned sheepishly. "Sorry," he said.

Unlike most of the officers, Drummond had never before been to sea. Assigned to the ship when it was at Norfolk, he had moved into his cabin the day before they sailed. He didn't know the officers or the ship. He was a thin, nervous man who had been unnecessarily afraid that he'd be seasick most of the time.

"You have the latest intelligence data?" asked Dees.

"Certainly, Captain. Good to about four hours ago. I just got the decrypted versions."

"Let's have it."

"Yes, sir." He set the file folder on the table and extracted the typed sheets with the large red secret stamps at the top and bottom. "This briefing is secret and is not to be discussed in unsecured locations or with those not cleared or not authorized to hear the contents."

There was a bark of laughter and one of the officers asked, "Just who do you think we'd share it with?"

"It is a necessary part of COMSEC. I am required, regardless of the circumstances, to issue the warning."

"Carry on, Mr. Drummond," said the captain.

"Yes, sir. Most of the traffic is related to tensions in the Middle East and the Far East. We have learned that the

Iraqi incursion into Saudi Arabia has been turned back. Iraqi forces are retreating, claiming that they have obtained their objectives, and that they have no further designs on Saudi territory. They characterize the invasion as a punitive strike brought on by Saudi action since the end of Desert Storm."

"They can't believe that anyone will accept that, can they?" asked Dees.

Drummond shrugged. "The Iraqis seem to have an amazing capacity for self-delusion. Given the Saudis' internal struggle and the guerrilla activity, they saw an opportunity to get even for Desert Storm, create some trouble for the Saudis. But given the response of the United States and the coalition forces of Desert Storm, I think they realized that they would never be able to hold anything they gained. Therefore, once they had inflicted as much punishment as they could, they got the hell out.

"Anyway, there are continuing border clashes and the Iraqis are using a technique they developed in Kuwait. They've tried to fire the oil fields and destroy the storage facilities with limited success. The things we learned in Kuwait about putting out fires are being used effectively in Saudia Arabia."

"Let's move on," said Dees.

"China has been accused of destroying a village in Tibet near the Nepal border. World reaction, including an attempted United Nations resolution, has been nearly non-existent. No one cares, though estimates put the body count at nearly one hundred."

"Let's move on," said Dees.

Drummond glanced at the captain as if he didn't understand.

"This is not a news broadcast, Mr. Drummond. We have no interest in what the Chinese are doing far inland. It does not directly affect us, and since we have a limited time, we don't need, nor do I desire, a worldview. Just what is happening in our section of the world and might impact on our mission."

"Yes, Captain." Drummond flipped through his papers, turning a number of them facedown on the table. "Since the assassination of Castro, there has been turmoil inside Cuba. The moderates, who are advocating a modified return to the free-market society, have been moving toward the top. However, there are indications, these manifested by riots, that the moderates are not in favor. Whether the riots and protests have been orchestrated by the hard-liners or are spontaneous doesn't seem to matter. There have been riots and protests. The hard-liners might be gaining the upper hand. Normal monitoring of Radio Havana suggests that the hard-liners are not only trying to create problems with the warming relations between the Russians and the United States, but they are advocating action against our base at Guantanamo."

"Is it serious?"

Drummond shrugged. "There has been trouble before, but it was more mob action than anything definitive. Castro, for all his posturing and his bluster, knew that nothing could be done, so he attempted nothing."

"Move on."

"Central America is a powder keg at the moment," said Drummond. "Fighting between government forces and insurgents has taken place in a number of countries." He grinned. "In one country it is the communist-influenced government against the so-called freedom fighters, and in another it is the Western-aligned government fighting the communist terrorists."

"Do I detect a political overtone to your statement, Lieutenant?" asked Dees.

"No, Captain. I'm merely using the labels applied by our State Department. I just . . ." Drummond suddenly realized that he had better not articulate his opinions because no one present was interested and some might be offended.

"Continue."

"The real hot spot is Nicaragua." He looked at the assembled officers, wondering what he should say to them about the activities. Then he realized that everyone at the table had top-secret clearances, were loyal American sailors, and had as much right to the information as he did.

"We've deployed a number of Special Forces teams, under the auspices of the United Nations, into Nicaragua, where a civil war is brewing. One of the rebel leaders, Colonel Jesus Castillo, is claiming to have popular support. It's reminiscent of our involvement in Vietnam before the Gulf of Tonkin in 1965. No overt military intervention; training programs to assist the locals."

"Maps or charts?" asked the captain.

Drummond pulled a sheet of paper from the folder and pushed it toward Dees. "I've marked the reported locations of the camps established by our forces. You'll see that all are in the interior or toward the western coast of Nicaragua. No way for us to support them."

Dees pulled the map forward and examined it closely. Given the locations of the rebel camps, it was obvious that he and his men would have to move to the Pacific Ocean to be of any use. Looking up from the map, he asked, "Is there anything else that you'd like to tell us?"

"Just one thing, Captain, and I confess I don't understand the significance of it. We've got an armored division, a reserve division, redeploying from the middle of Texas to the border area. I happened to pick up some of the orders issued. They were misdirected to us, or rather, Atlantic Fleet."

"I can't see where that'll bother us," said Dees. He looked at his officers. "Any one have any additional questions for Mr. Drummond?"

"The whole division?" asked Randolph.

"I don't know, sir. We only have part of the orders. I know one brigade has been moved and that they're operating around Laredo. I don't know if they're down there to assist in border patrol or if it is some kind of special maneuvers to test their capability to respond to a rapid deployment. I just know that they're down there."

"I don't attach any significance to it," said Dees. "Again, they're far enough inland that it won't impact on our operations." He raised his cup and finished his coffee, signaling the end to the briefing. "If no one else has any questions? No? Then let's get back to work. Thank you, Mr. Drummond."

"Yes, Captain. I remind each of you that everything discussed here is classified as secret."

JUST SOUTH OF THE TEXAS BORDER

Crossing into Mexico had been easy. The river rose to the hubs, but the bottom had been solid, and after they roared up the other bank and into Mexico, Daniels ordered his driver to stop. He turned, watched as the other vehicles splashed through the Rio Grande and onto the solid ground of Mexico. Once they were out, Daniels pointed to the east and they started off cross-country.

Once the map let them down. The floor of a valley had been smooth, looking as if it had been graded at some point. Daniels ordered them to follow it, and a couple of miles later they'd driven into a box canyon with walls too steep for the Blazers, Bronco, or pickup to climb. They were forced to turn around.

They raced out of the canyon as the moon came up over the landscape, but then slowed. This wasn't like driving on an ordinary highway or road; they were bouncing over broken ground where a ravine might not be visible until the front tires fell off the edge. A boulder, dark and camouflaged, could be hidden in the grass, ready to smash a radiator or break an axle.

Using a flashlight without a red lens cover, Daniels studied the map. "Shouldn't be another ten miles back to the road. We hit that and turn to the south."

"Fence line," said Amos as he slowed the Blazer.

Daniels looked up and saw the old twisted logs that had been used for poles and the strings of wire between them. It was a makeshift fence, designed to show property boundaries and to stop wandering cattle.

"Punch on through it."

Amos glanced to the left with a raised eyebrow, but said, "Of course."

They slowed to a crawl. When the nose of the Blazer was against the wire, Amos added gas and the vehicle inched forward. The middle strand parted first with a sudden snap that sounded like a pistol shot. The other two held firm as the posts on both sides tilted toward the middle. Then one snapped off.

"Back it up," said Daniels.

Amos stopped and reversed. As he did so the wire sagged until it touched the ground.

"Let's go."

They pushed on, climbing a gentle hill covered with thick, tough grass. When they reached the top, they looked out on a huge valley. On the floor was a road that led, more or less, to the south.

"There it is," said Daniels.

Amos dropped into low and they rolled down the hill, braking so that they didn't pick up speed. They bounced across a dry streambed and then reached the valley floor. Amos accelerated and then slowed as he pulled up on the road that would lead them to the highway.

"Now we'll make some time."

"Go," said Daniels.

They accelerated until they were leaving a huge cloud of dust behind them. The headlights of the following Blazer were barely visible.

Looking over the backseat, Daniels said, "We're on our way now." He stopped and wanted to ask, again, if anyone wished to back out, but decided this wasn't the smartest thing to do. They'd had their chance. And they'd all been briefed on the situation a dozen times. Talking about it more wouldn't do anyone any good.

"How long?" asked Gannon. Her voice was high and tight as if she realized she was about to do something that wasn't terribly bright.

"Couple of hours. We'll want to scope the plant before we move. Make sure that nothing has been added that we don't understand or didn't plan for."

"And nobody gets hurt?"

"We're here to destroy the factory, not hurt people, but we're not going to let them hurt us, either."

Gannon nodded solemnly and fell silent.

"Let's check the weapons one last time," said Daniels. "No one loads them yet, but let's make sure that everything is in good shape."

Hyatt turned in the seat and reached over into the rear. He pushed a blanket to the side and shoved a cardboard box filled with beer cans out of the way. He found the first of the gun cases and slowly extracted it. Handing it to Gannon, he reached for the next one.

"Got lights on the road in front of us," said Amos.

Hyatt whirled around and sat down. He put the gun case he held on the floor. Gannon, without a word, did the same thing.

The approaching vehicle, in the center of the road, slipped to the right. As it passed they could see colorful splashes of paint: white, yellow, blue, and a green so bright that it hurt the eyes. And then it was gone except for a single tiny taillight blinking red in the dust.

"Bus," said Amos.

"Right."

They continued for a few moments. Daniels leaned forward and opened the glove compartment and, taking out the mike for the CB radio, turned to Channel Fifteen. "Routine. I need a check."

"We're right behind you."

"And us."

"Truck is at the rear. No trouble and no lights anywhere to the rear."

"Roger. Out." He put the mike back and closed the glove box. If a message came in, he'd be able to hear it, but no one outside the truck would know that they had a radio.

"Highway coming up," said Amos.

"Take it slow, Henry," said Daniels.

They approached the highway, but there was no traffic. Although the map showed that it was paved, that was a generous appraisal. The pavement was rough, potholed, and nonexistent in places. But there were wide shoulders and signs and even mile—or now, kilometer markers.

"I make it about an hour," said Daniels.

"Maybe less," said Amos.

They all rode in silence for a few minutes. In his mind Daniels could see the flames consuming the factory as the dazed workers stood by helplessly. He could see the walls falling in, creating fountains of orange sparks that gushed into the night.

He closed his eyes for a moment, and the next thing he knew Amos was saying, "We're maybe five miles out."

"Slow it down." Sitting up straight in the seat, Daniels took out the hand-drawn map. It showed the route to the factory. "Take the first right after we reach the town."

"Okay."

A few moments later they came to the turn. The road here was in better shape than the highway. On either side of it were adobe shacks. A few seemed to have electric lights. Lanterns burned in others. Through an open doorway a color television was playing.

"Go slow. We'll climb that hill and then pull over. I'll check the factory."

"Got it."

Daniels used the radio again. "We're getting close. Let's get ready."

They reached the top of the hill and Amos slipped to the side of the road. Through the windshield he could see the massive plant with its parking lot filled with new cars ready to be shipped. There was a twelve-foot-high chain-link fence around it with a guard shack and gate. Taking the guard shack would be simple. Drive up and order the guard to come with them. No time for him to raise the alarm. Nothing he could do but comply or die.

Nothing had changed since the preliminary recon a few days earlier. No one knew they were coming, so no one could take precautions against them.

"To the front gate," said Daniels.

"On the move," said Amos.

"Guard will be on your side, Ralph. When we get close and he starts toward us, you roll down the window."

"I know what to do," said Hyatt.

Turning around, Daniels saw that they were getting close. Keeping his voice low, he said, "This is it."

As they approached the gate and slowed the guard exited. He was dressed in khaki with a black leather holster on his hip. He had a peaked cap, and a glint on his chest showed the badge he wore.

Amos braked and rolled down his window. In Spanish the guard asked, "What do you want?"

"We're here to see the factory."

"It is not possible," said the guard in remarkably good, almost accentless English.

Leaning to the left slightly, his hand out the window, Hyatt screamed, "Hands up. Don't move."

But the guard didn't obey. Instead his hand shot down and he grabbed at the flap on his holster.

"Hold *it*!" shouted Hyatt.

"Don't," ordered Amos.

Backing up, the guard tried to raise his weapon. Hyatt fired once. The bullet smashed into the guard's chest, driving him into the shack. He hit the wall and fell to the side, reaching for the phone on the table. He failed to get it and pulled the table over as he fell, his blood pooling under him.

"Christ," said Daniels. "Jesus Christ."

Amos kept his eyes on the fallen guard. "You check the body," he ordered. "And hang up the phone." When Hyatt didn't move, Amos shouted, "Do it *now*!"

Hyatt leaned his shoulder into the door, forcing it open. He climbed out slowly and stood at the side of the truck, flat-footed, his pistol in both hands, pointed down at the guard. The odor of hot copper and bowel was heavy in the air.

"Check him," said Amos.

Slowly, carefully, Hyatt moved forward. He crouched near the body, the barrel of his pistol against the man's head. He reached out to the throat but couldn't find a pulse. He saw the spreading red stain that soaked the man's khaki shirt and the rough plywood of the floor.

"Come on," said Amos.

Hyatt picked up the phone, heard the dial tone, and hung up. He saw a locked box and pulled on the padlock, but it refused to open.

"Get in," yelled Amos.

Hyatt backed up and then, his eyes still on the body, climbed into the rear of the Blazer. "There was nothing I could do."

"Let's roll," said Daniels.

They drove through the gate and into the employees' parking lot. Beyond it were the low, lighted buildings of the factory.

Pointing, Daniels said, "We'll stop there, near that door."

When they stopped, he climbed out and then waved the others on. Each of the groups had their own targets.

They would spread out so they could destroy more of the factory.

As Daniels headed toward the door the others joined him. He touched the door and said, "Okay. We protect ourselves. Somebody runs, we let them go. They attack and we kill them."

"Like the guard," said Gannon, her voice angry.

"Just like the guard." Daniels opened the door and entered.

Inside was a long, narrow corridor. On the right was an unmanned reception desk. A guard, unarmed, came forward, pointing and speaking. Daniels pointed his pistol at the man's face. He came to a halt and didn't move.

"Go," said Daniels.

Hyatt and Amos rushed past him to the second set of doors. When they opened them, everyone could see part of the factory beyond. The noise rolled out, making it difficult to hear voices. There were flashes of light as the workers spot-welded the unfinished cars.

Daniels gestured and the guard turned, walking toward the factory. As they passed through the doors Hyatt yelled, "I got a switch over here."

"Shut it down," said Daniels.

Hyatt hit the switch and the line stopped immediately. Lights began to flash and a siren wailed. The workers leaped back, waiting to learn what the problem was.

A man in a white coat ran from an office, coming to a halt when he saw the armed intruders. He whirled, as if to run, and then thought better of it. He turned slowly, his hands up. He walked toward them.

"Go," said Daniels. "Amos, you've got twelve minutes to get your charges placed. Set the fusing for twenty minutes."

Hyatt, Gannon, and Amos took off. They fanned out, opening the rucksacks they carried, placing the charges.

"What's going on?" asked the man in the white coat.

"Nothing to concern you. If there is a way to announce it, I think you'd better evacuate the plant."

"What are you going to do?"

"Just get the people out of here."

A burst of gunfire was followed by a scream that cut through the plant and overwhelmed the siren. Daniels glanced in the direction of the sound and said, "Get the people clear."

Rogers and his team—Thorsen, Roberts, and José Cortez—entered through one of the backdoors. It was locked and guarded, but the guard had the key, and under the threat of death he opened the door.

Once he had done so, the guard turned and ran toward the parking lot. Rogers raised his pistol and fired. The single shot hit the man in the back and knocked him down. Rogers turned and joined the others as they entered the rear of the factory.

Alarms went off as they rushed in. Rogers dropped to a knee, his back against the wall, but saw that the workers were not concerned; the siren, the lights, the alarm were simply ignored.

But then, from the left, a group of men ran toward them. Rogers didn't wait. He lowered his rifle, flipped it to full auto, and pulled the trigger. Roberts, hearing the shots, did the same thing, shooting at the running men.

They all went down under the hail of bullets, sprawling, rolling, blood splattering. One of the men, hit in the leg, tried to stand and flee, but was hit again. He collapsed.

"Cease firing," said Rogers calmly.

For a moment the workers, watching, sat quietly. They looked at the invaders and at the dead men, and suddenly panic erupted. A single scream of pure terror filled the air, and then all of them were scrambling to get out.

The small radio crackled. "All units. Report."

Rogers lifted his radio and said, "We had some trouble but have eliminated it. We are proceeding."

"Roger."

Rogers waved to the men with him. "Let's get the charges in place. We've got a little more than ten minutes."

The team spread out. Rogers moved along the line, opening valves, spilling anything that he could find, ripping at wires, and smashing everything else. There was a flash of movement to the right. He turned toward it, saw a worker, and fired. The round whined off a steel post. Rogers laughed as the man tried to get away. He shot again and again. The last round hit the man in the back of the head. It exploded in a crimson cloud as the body pitched to the concrete. The dead man's feet drummed on the floor.

Cortez appeared and said, "Finished."

"Cover the door."

"Yes, sir."

Rogers turned slowly. There was a cloud of smoke in the center of the factory, a dense black cloud that reached the low ceiling and spread out along the corrugated metal, obscuring the lights.

"Five minutes," yelled Rogers.

There was another burst of fire. Rogers turned toward it and saw two men running, blood spreading down one's side. He staggered and then slipped, running into a post. He fell to the floor.

Grinning, Rogers aimed at the second man. The worker spotted Rogers and stopped. He raised his hands to surrender, but Rogers didn't care. He shot the man in the face.

Roberts returned then. He was smiling broadly. "I'm all set."

"Then let's get the hell out of here."

"We've got two minutes," said Daniels.

Amos tapped him on the shoulders. There was sweat on his face and his hair was hanging down in strings. It looked as if he was fresh from the shower . . . and smelled as if he hadn't seen one in weeks.

"Ready."

"Get to the truck and make sure that we're ready to roll."

"Hell of a lot of shooting going on out there," said Amos.

"Can't worry about it now. Get out to the truck."

There was an explosion near them and both men ducked instinctively. Debris rained down, pattering on the concrete.

"What in the hell was that?"

"I don't know," said Amos.

"That's it," said Daniels. "We're getting the hell out of here now." He pulled his radio. "All units. Time has expired. Everyone out. Hit the rally points." Turning, he yelled, "Let's go. Everyone."

Daniels backed up, still watching the half-dozen men he was covering. Gannon appeared and ran by him, heading for the truck. Hyatt was right behind her.

When everyone was clear, Daniels said, "You men had better get out. This place is going to be rubble in a few minutes."

Daniels ran for the door. He stopped, turned, and looked back. There was a flickering in the factory. Smoke was pouring from a burning car body. Two men in white coats, using large red extinguishers, were trying to kill the flames. They had been warned, but they remained in the building.

Daniels burst through the door and ran to the Blazer. Amos was sitting in the driver's seat with the engine running. The others had already climbed in.

Daniels leaped into the passenger's seat and yelled, "Go! Go!"

Amos dropped it into gear, spun the wheel, and mashed the accelerator. He dodged around the few people milling around in the parking lot as he headed for the front gate. He roared through it and headed up the hill.

"Pull over," said Daniels.

Amos did as he was told, and when the Blazer rolled to a stop, Daniels turned around. "Let's watch this."

Nothing happened right away. There was nothing to see below them. The factory looked peaceful, though there was some movement in the parking lot. In the distance was the wail of a siren, probably an emergency vehicle responding to a call.

The sudden flash of light surprised Daniels. Part of the roof shot up and disintegrated. A ball of fire erupted and the solid boom drifted to them.

"Got it," yelled Daniels.

There was a series of smaller flashes as flames spread along the top of the factory. Part of the roof fell in, revealing the flaming inferno inside.

"Yeah," yelled Amos. "They won't be using that sucker again very soon."

"Let's get out of here," said Daniels.

Before Amos could react, a police car, the lights on top flashing, roared over the crest of the hill. It slowed momentarily as it passed the Blazer, but then accelerated down the hill, toward the burning rubble of the factory.

"They'll be too busy with that mess to worry about us," said Daniels. He pointed up the road. "Nice and easy and we'll get out of here just fine."

"What about the others?" asked Gannon.

"Radio silence until we hit the rally point. We don't want to tip our hand."

Amos slammed the wheel, grinning broadly. "Like clockwork," he said. "Like fucking clockwork."

JUST NORTH OF THE MEXICAN BORDER

Jerry Rider, of the U.S. Border Patrol, was now on overtime. His shift should have ended an hour earlier, but he wanted to stay on, to make sure that Daniels and his raiders got back across the border easily, that no one stopped them, or if they were stopped, that he would be in a position to assist them.

Driving slowly over the broken ground north of the border, he listened to the radio calls as the agents rounded up the Mexicans and others who were trying to slip into the United States. Had to keep them out because of the overcrowding in the country. That's what he had been told.

But driving along the border, over ground that saw little in the way of rainfall during the year, where little grew and no one lived, he wondered about the overcrowding. It seemed to him that there was lots of room for expansion in the country. Not everyone could live in New York, or the Dallas–Fort Worth metroplex, and there was a lot of land and a lot of space.

A helicopter passed overhead, banked, and came back, hovering above him, the searchlight on his truck. He knew that the pilot had identified him as border patrol, but the helicopter hung there, slowly descending, creating a whirling dust cloud. Rider slowed and then stopped, letting the pilot play his game.

From the loudspeakers came the warning, "This is the border patrol. You are righteously and truly fucked, my man."

Rider laughed out loud and wondered if the pilot said that to the illegals he stopped. And he wondered if they understood.

Without warning the helicopter peeled away, its searchlight winking out. Over the radio he heard the call. Someone had a group of fourteen or fifteen illegals in the river, trying to reach the bank. Those were the people who were now righteously and truly fucked.

Rider started off again, cruising along a dirt cliff on the floor of a wide valley. He turned, climbed a gentle slope, and found himself within sight of the Rio Grande. As near as he could figure, he was no more than a mile or two from the point where Daniels and his raiders planned to ford the river and reenter the United States.

He rolled to a stop and shut off the engine, sitting for a moment and then cranking down the window to let the night air in. He'd hoped that the heat of the day had broken and that the humidity that had oppressed them for nearly a week would be gone. In seconds he was bathed in sweat and was tempted to use the air conditioner, but he didn't want to overheat the engine.

Outside, the night insects trilled. Something flapped past and climbed, losing itself in the blaze of night stars. This was the best of times for Rider, alone, in the deserted plains of south Texas, where he could imagine himself as a rancher or pioneer of a hundred years earlier.

The problem was the radio, which he had to leave on. It crackled and popped with messages from a dozen other places as the men and women worked to stop the illegals. And then came the message that he had been dreading.

"Attention, all units. We have a report of a group of vehicles rolling toward the border from Mexico that might have been involved in arson near Nueva Rosita. . . ."

There was other information, but Rider wasn't interested. All he cared about was that the border patrol was now alerted to the raiders. He was sure that they could bluff their way through, if they had to, but he didn't like the warning.

He reached across the seat and turned on the CB. He attached the antenna leads to the metal of his vehicle, turning it all into an antenna. He listened to Channel Fifteen but heard nothing from Daniels and the raiders. Of course, he hadn't thought he would.

For a moment he sat there, staring at the tiny, glowing lights on the radio, trying to decide if he should issue the warning, if they were close enough to hear it, or if he should just wait until he had a better feel for the situation. Patience, he decided, would be rewarded. He'd wait.

Sandi Paulding sat in the Humvee, the door open wide, watching the interior of the all-night drive-in. Sergeant Howard was sitting at the counter, drinking a huge chocolate shake and eating a massive hamburger. It was the compromise they'd worked out. He wouldn't complain anymore and she'd monitor the radio while he stuffed his face.

It seemed ridiculous to have the majority of an armored division on border patrol. It was true that there had been an increase in illegal immigrants sneaking across the border—not, as before, in San Diego, but in the uninhabited stretches of Arizona, New Mexico, or Texas. Moreover, bandits had been slipping across the border. They had stopped and attacked cars, and in one incident reminiscent of Pancho Villa, a gang of ten thugs had tried to rob a bank in a tiny border town.

Paulding didn't see how any of that would affect her. The Mexicans had been captured by the local police, and although it had happened a year ago, and formal protests had been lodged with the Mexican government, it wasn't seen as a trend. It was a gang that could have as easily been American.

For a moment she closed her eyes and wondered how things were going at the university. She'd been assured, by both the army and the university, that her job would be waiting when she returned, but she couldn't see that happening now. She'd been on active duty too long and a university was a dynamic place. She wouldn't fit in when she returned and she was sure that the administration knew that.

Sighing, she opened her eyes. Howard was turned slightly in his seat, talking to the waitress. She seemed fascinated by the NCO and his uniform. He pointed toward the Humvee and the waitress nodded. Then she turned and headed toward the rear of the restaurant.

The radio popped to life. "Caldron Two, this is Caldron Control."

The signal was a little weak, filled with pops and buzzes and static. It had to be the result of the metal roof over a part of the parking lot, and all the neon that was glowing brighter than Fremont Street in Las Vegas.

"This is Two. Go."

"Roger. We've gotten a report from the Mexican government about a raid into the Nueva Rosita area about an hour ago. They believe the raiders were Americans and are assuming that they'll be heading toward the border."

"Roger."

"Be advised that the men are armed and dangerous. If you spot them, call in. We'll apprehend them."

"Say again? Apprehend?"

"Roger. We're coordinating this with the border patrol and the FBI. We are to locate but not to take action. Do you copy?"

"Roger. Locate but do not take action."

"Check with Sit-rep every fifteen minutes starting at the bottom of the hour."

"Roger."

Paulding sat staring at the radio for a moment. This was every soldier's nightmare. Suddenly, instead of being a soldier, he or she was magically transformed into a police officer. No one seemed to understand that the police operated under a different set of rules. They arrested people for trial. The military's role was to kill people, destroy their equipment, and ruin their resupply capability.

She got out of the vehicle and walked to the door of the restaurant. Howard was finishing his milkshake. The waitress was standing near a coffeemaker watching him surreptitiously.

"Sergeant, we've got to roll."

Howard turned and looked at Paulding. Sucking his drink through the straw, he looked more like a high-school senior than an army sergeant.

Turning back, he put the glass on the counter, dug in his pocket and dropped a couple of bills beside it. "Got to roll. This should cover it," he called out.

The waitress's eyes got big as she watched the scene. It was something from television. She started forward, as if to kiss her war hero good-bye, but stopped short as Howard donned his boony hat and moved toward the door.

As he pushed it open he said, "You couldn't have timed that better, Major. Impressed the hell out of her."

"Well, I didn't do it for your love life. We've got to get back into the field." Paulding had reached her side of the Humvee and stopped. She stared at the NCO. "Got a bunch of Americans who might have done some damage in Mexico."

"Serve the beaners right. Teach them to stay on their side of the border."

A dozen retorts swam in Paulding's mind, but all

seemed inappropriate. Besides, it wasn't the time to talk
about race relations and discrimination. She'd file the information and make sure that Howard got another four-
hour block of instruction on interpersonal relations.

She got in and glanced into the rear of the vehicle.
Their weapons were there, along with the ammo, flares,
and even a couple cans of CS gas. The problem was that
no one expected trouble, so between them they had only
sixty rounds. Of course, Paulding had a pistol with three
magazines. That increased their firepower slightly but not
significantly.

Starting the engine, Howard asked, "Where to?"

"Back to our patrol zone. But we forget the northern
edge of it and concentrate on the area along the river."

"Looking at the map this afternoon," said Howard, "I
noticed a couple of fords marked on it. Figure that our
boys won't be using the highways. I would think that we'd
better watch them."

Smiling, Paulding pulled out her map and turned on
the light. "They're about five miles apart with high ground
between them. Seems if we set up on the high ground, we
should be able to spot their lights if they attempt to use either of the fords."

They left the outskirts of the town, turned down a dirt
road, and continued into the country. They topped a hill
where there was an open gate in the fence.

"Through there," said Paulding.

They turned in, drove slowly across the open ground,
the thick, dry grasses doing nothing to stop the dust cloud
they created behind them. They drove across the crest,
down to the bottom, where they found another fence. They
drove along it until they came to a cattle guard and entered
the next field.

From there it was easy to reach the high ground. Using the binoculars, Paulding could make out the ribbon of
the Rio Grande in the distance. The moonlight made it
easy to see, and on the open prairie it was nearly as bright

as early twilight. By staring at the dark shapes, she could discover which were bushes, or cattle or boulders.

"Think they'll cross here?" asked Howard.

Paulding lowered the binoculars. "I'm beginning to hope that they don't."

Daniels and his team were the first to reach the rally point. It wasn't much more than a wide spot on the road away from Nueva Rosita. As soon as the Blazer stopped, Daniels was out, standing by the side of the road, looking back. There was a rosy glow in the south that he was sure marked the location of the factory.

Amos leaned over, opened the glove box, and took out the mike. "All units. Report."

They went through the ritual, each of them checking in, each of them telling Amos that they were clear of the factory. One of them reported trouble but wouldn't explain. They were on their way to the rally point.

"Hyatt," said Daniels, "climb up on top and make sure that there is no pursuit. You see any flashing lights and we'll head for the secondary rally."

Hyatt stepped up on the rear bumper and raised himself cautiously to the top of the Blazer. Placing his feet carefully, he stood up and then lifted his binoculars to his eyes.

"Got one car coming. No flashers."

"You see the factory?"

"Nope. I can make out some flames. Looks like they're a hundred, two hundred feet in the air."

The oncoming vehicle slowed and pulled in behind them. Rogers leaped from it and ran toward Daniels. He couldn't contain his excitement. "We did it. Just like you said. We did it."

"We're still in Mexico," said Daniels. "It's not a success until we're in Texas."

"Another truck coming up," said Hyatt.

Amos came around the front of the Blazer. "Somebody ran into some trouble—Buchanan. I don't know what."

"We'll be out of here in three minutes," said Daniels.

Amos nodded. "Then I'm going to take a break." He disappeared around the front again unbuttoning his fly.

The Bronco stopped and the people piled out. Buchanan hurried forward. "We got trouble. Knight got hit. Killed. We had to leave him behind."

"Shit," said Daniels. "What the fuck happened?"

"Wise-ass guard with a pistol. Never saw the asshole. Opened up on Knight and killed him. Then wouldn't let us near the body. Kept us back."

"Shit. You had grenades."

"Figured that once the factory went up, the body'd burn, so who gave a fuck. Nothing to identify him anyway."

"His wife is going to create trouble," said Daniels.

Now Buchanan grinned. "I don't think so. She hated him. Been fucking around for months. Somebody give her some dough and she'll say he ran off. Everyone's happy."

Daniels checked the time. The pickup still hadn't reappeared. "You see anything?"

Hyatt said, "Nope ... wait. Maybe they're coming now."

"Let's get ready to roll. We get to the ford, everyone scatter. We'll debrief tomorrow afternoon at the headquarters. Until then everyone head home."

Daniels watched them climb into their trucks. Lights from the oncoming vehicle appeared and then turned toward them. It was the last of their raiders.

"We're going," yelled Daniels. He turned and jumped up into the Blazer.

Amos dropped it into gear and they rocketed onto the highway, passing the speed limit as they fled for the border. There didn't seem to be any other traffic on the road.

Using the radio, Daniels said, "Rear, drop back about a mile and keep watch. Let us know if any sign of a pursuit."

"Roger that."

Daniels laughed suddenly. He looked over the backseat at Gannon. "What you thinking now?"

"We didn't have to kill that guard."

"Sure we did," said Hyatt. "He was going to draw. Had to shoot him."

"Should have wounded him," said Gannon.

Daniels shook his head. "That's a load of shit and you know it. You shoot to kill or you don't shoot at all."

"Yeah."

"Doesn't matter now," said Amos. "It's done and we did what we wanted to do. That's all that counts."

"That and getting clear," said Daniels. "That and getting clear."

NICARAGUA

The camp was small, concealed in the jungle where they wouldn't have to worry about anybody stumbling on them accidentally. It was designed so that the defenders would have an opportunity to respond to an enemy threat, and laid out so that if the enemy force was overwhelmingly large, they could disappear into the jungle.

Martinez, having been awakened by Jones, who had the midnight-to-four guard tour, was lying just inside the defensive perimeter, listening to the quiet sounds as someone crept closer.

There had been more noise earlier, as some men worked their way through the jungle, but that had ended, replaced by the sounds as one or two men, good in the jungle, worked their way closer. Martinez had yet to spot them, or even see the movement because of the darkness, but he knew they were out there.

Leaning close to Jones, he said, "How many?"

"Point of one or two men, leading a force at company strength or less. Maybe no more than one hundred. Certainly no more."

"Yeah," said Martinez. He'd wondered if anyone would follow after the raid. The prisoners hadn't been very good, leaving a trail that was easy to follow. Now, three days later, it seemed the rebels had managed to track them.

Chavez appeared and crouched. He had moved through the night like a fog, making no noise. Chavez understood the jungle, and the night, and used both to his advantage. "Three men, on the right. Crawling toward us," he said.

Martinez jerked around and looked. Then to Chavez he said, "And two of them coming at us."

"I think they've got us surrounded," said Chavez. "They're going to want to destroy us."

"Alert the rest of the team and have Espinoza get on the radio to net. Let them know we could be in trouble."

"Rest of the team is alert."

"Good."

Chavez crawled off into the dark. As he did so Martinez realized that the night, which had been his friend, was rapidly becoming an enemy. They wouldn't be able to see the attackers if there wasn't any light. Any movement could be the enemy, or it could be a friend. It wasn't going to be one of the old World War II storm-the-enemy-bastions-and-kill-everyone fights. It was going to be a series of short sharp encounters.

Martinez was tempted to throw a grenade at the sound the enemy was making, but that might cause a sudden attack by all of them. At the moment they didn't know they had been detected. If he was patient, they might draw several enemy soldiers into a trap where they could be killed quickly and quietly.

He slipped to the rear, turned, and got to his feet. He didn't stand up, but bent at the waist so that his head was low, and worked his way to the center of the camp. Espinoza was hunched over the radio, a headset clamped over his ears, using the keypad so that he didn't have to make any noise.

"Anything?"

"Net is coming up," whispered Espinoza.

Martinez nodded, knowing that Espinoza would never see it in the dark. He focused his attention on the jungle. There were noises from the insects and the rattling of leaves as animals worked their way around in the dark. Small sounds that were always there, a part of the environment the way that cars and trucks were a part of the city. But there was also something else, and that was the noise made by the enemy. It was almost the same as that of the animals and insects. It was the small difference that had warned them.

One of the trip flares went off, a bursting of bright light on the perimeter. One man stood up, surprised, part of his uniform on fire. A single shot was followed by a wet slap, and the man fell. The flare burned on for another few seconds, but no one moved. Sound died away and the jungle was silent. Everything—even nature—was frozen in time. Nothing moved; everyone waited.

Martinez whirled and ripped a grenade from his harness. He jerked the pin free and let it drop, trying to pinpoint the place he'd heard the enemy last. He threw the grenade into the jungle like a center fielder trying to nail a runner going home.

Three seconds later the silence was ripped to shreds. There was a bright flash and white-hot shrapnel spun out, tearing at the vegetation and the enemy soldiers.

Firing erupted. The muzzle flashes of the enemy weapons sparkled in the jungle, looking like fireflies. Tracers slashed through the night, whining over the top of the tiny camp. The hammering of the weapons filled the night.

"Grenades," yelled Martinez. He dropped flat, pulled out another grenade, and then looked up; he hesitated and then threw his grenade at the center of a muzzle flash.

The grenades detonated one after another. There were fountains of sparks. Now there were screams of pain and surprise. Firing from the enemy increased, on full auto. Rounds slammed into the trees; bits of bark and leaf rained down.

The rush came from the right. A dozen soldiers, screaming as they fired from the hip. Tracers hit the ground in front of them and bounced up, tumbling.

Martinez turned to meet the threat. He threw a grenade, but it detonated behind the oncoming enemy. They were unaffected, screaming their rage. One of them hit a trip flare, illuminating the attack. Rifles from the interior opened up, chopping at the attackers. One fell. Then a second and third. The flare burned out.

Now there was screaming from all around the camp. The firing was increasing in intensity until it was a single long-drawn-out detonation.

"Here they come again," yelled Jones.

Espinoza approached. "Captain, net says there's nothing they can do. No one close enough to provide us support."

"Shit."

A round snapped by his ear and Martinez felt chills up and down his back. He dropped to one knee and glanced to the right. The jungle was alive with the enemy. Muzzle flashes strobed, giving all motion the unreal look of a silent movie.

"Maybe at sunup," said Espinoza.

"Thanks," said Martinez. He wiped a hand over his face and found it wet with sweat. That didn't surprise him.

There was motion on the left and Martinez spun to meet it. He didn't fire because he didn't know who it was. Maybe one of his men or maybe one of the enemy.

The man lifted a knife and swung at Martinez. He dodged, his arm up to push the flat of the blade away from him. The man stumbled and then turned. Martinez kicked, hitting the man in the knee. He howled in pain and tried to slash at Martinez, who danced back and raised the barrel of his rifle. He fired, heard the round hit and heard the grunt of surprise and pain, and then heard the body fall.

Whirling around, he saw another two men rushing at him. Martinez fired four times. The muzzle flash reached out and seemed to touch the men. They both went down without a sound. Neither moved.

Martinez dropped to his knees, his weapon in his hands. He watched the jungle in front of him. The enemy was still shooting, but it had tapered off. Single shots and then nothing.

Pulling back, he called out, "We take any casualties?"

Chavez appeared and said, "Munyo got hit. Jones is working on him. Nothing serious."

"Check the bodies."

"Yes, sir."

"Espinoza?"

"Yes, sir?"

"Get on the radio again. Let them know what's going on."

Espinoza worked his way back toward the radio while Martinez remained motionless for a moment, scanning the jungle. It was pitch black again and no one but the wounded was making any noise. One man was screaming. It sounded as if he was burning to death.

"Here they come again."

Martinez turned. He saw motion among the trees, but this time he knew that it wasn't his people. None of them was that far away. He came up on his knees, aimed over the top of the weapon, and fired, single shot, pulling the trigger as fast as he could. When the weapon was empty, he dropped to his stomach, ripped the magazine from it, and reloaded.

There was more screaming this time. Men howling at the tops of their voices. The weapons were pounding, the firing increasing in intensity.

Martinez popped up again. The enemy was closer. They were shooting as they ran. Martinez saw the jungle around them in between flashes.

Now more of his men were shooting, most on full auto. The strobing of the muzzle flashes combined into a single, bright light, giving the firefight an unreal look, a sickly, yellowish glow.

Grenades detonated. First one, then two, and finally half a dozen. There were screams of pain as the enemy was cut down. Men fell, missing limbs or hands or suddenly blinded. They shouted and yelled and prayed for help.

Martinez burned through the magazine, jerked it out, and tossed it aside. He reloaded, flipped the selector to full auto, and hosed down the jungle.

As quickly as it started, the attack broke. Martinez couldn't tell if they'd knocked down all the infiltrators or if some of them had fled into the jungle.

Martinez dropped to the ground for a moment, hugging it. He was aware of everything around him: the screams of the injured, the smell of the soil near his nose, and the odor of gunpower, sweat, and bowel mixed with the hot copper of freshly spilled blood.

He rolled to his back, looking up into the blackness of the thick jungle canopy over him. He took a moment, letting it wash over him, and then forced himself to move. He hoped that it was over now, that the enemy had been beaten badly enough that he would fall back and get out. That's what he hoped, but he wasn't sure.

Boyce sat in the rear of the C-130 cargo plane, insulated from the other members of his team by the roar of the four turboprops. The low red lights made it difficult to see the others. It was a good time because he didn't have to worry about answering questions, making decisions, or taking charge. For the moment all that was in the hands of the aircraft commander in the cockpit. Boyce was a passenger.

He closed his eyes, trying to relax. He didn't like jumping out of airplanes and he especially didn't like it at night. He would do it, but he didn't like it. And sitting there thinking about it wasn't helping. It was like the anticipation of a trip to the dentist when you knew he was going to be drilling.

A light touch on his shoulder caused him to sit up and open his eyes. The loadmaster was standing over him, leaning close. "AC would like to see you, sir."

Boyce nodded and reached to unbuckle his seat belt. He stood and followed the loadmaster to the front of the aircraft, then climbed up into the cockpit and sat down on the seat against the rear bulkhead. One of the crewmen handed him a headset.

"Can you hear me?" asked the AC.

"Yes."

"Got some radio traffic for you from your net control. Wanted me to advise you that one of your teams is in heavy contact."

"Where?"

"Code name of Cheyenne."

Boyce nodded, knowing that it was Martinez's team. They were in the hills and jungle to the northeast of Managua. The actual site of the camp was not known to him, just the general area. The other two teams, to the north and to the east of Managua, were not going to be able to support Martinez.

Boyce leaned forward, his elbows on his knees, one hand up to massage his temple. There was nothing he could do, either. If they dropped in now, there was no guarantee that they would be able to assist, even if they could spot the camp from the air.

"Status?" he asked.

"I don't know. We could put you in touch with your net and let them tell you."

"Please do it." He knew that there wasn't much more that could be said over the radio. COMSEC sometimes got in the way of trading information.

"Press that little black button when you want to talk. Release it when you're through."

Boyce pushed the button and said, "Montana Control, this is Six."

"Control here. You have been relayed the information about Cheyenne Six."

"Roger. Can you provide current status?"

"Cheyenne Six reports that they have repelled two assaults and are waiting the third. They have taken very light casualties. May have to E-and-E."

"Roger." Boyce sat for a moment, trying to think of something to help Martinez, but the captain was on his own. Too often that was the way the Special Forces operated. A small group of highly trained professionals out on their own, far from assistance.

"Cheyenne Six has requested assistance," said Control.

"Roger." Boyce thought of an air strike, but no one was on call who could get there. They had been promised close air from Texas, or from a carrier group in the Caribbean. But everyone was two or more hours away, and there was no guarantee that the pilots would be able to find the camp hidden deep in the triple canopy jungle.

Reluctantly Boyce pressed the button. "Advise Cheyenne that they are to escape and evade if they are unable to hold their camp."

"Roger."

Boyce looked up and saw the copilot staring at him. The man said, "Kind of hard-core, wasn't it?"

"Nothing I could do. They knew the score when they got into the game." He stripped the headset off and handed it to the flight engineer. "Thanks."

"Sure."

Boyce climbed down from the cockpit, feeling that he'd just thrown twelve men to the wolves. That was the trouble with covert operations. If something went wrong, the men involved were in deep shit.

·   ·   ·

Espinoza, lying on the ground near the radio, listened to the response. He used the keypad to acknowledge and then tore the headset off and threw it down. He crawled to the right and found Martinez.

"We're not going to get help. Montana said to E-and-E if we couldn't hold."

"That was helpful."

"Yes, sir."

"Prepare to destroy the main radio."

"Yes, sir."

Martinez crawled off and located Chavez. "Can everyone E-and-E?"

"Got two wounded, but neither serious. I think we can abandon the camp."

"Let's get ready to do that. Set the booby traps. We take as much as we can carry. Rally at the clearing four miles from here."

"We might be better off trying to stay here."

"No. They know where we are. They can get help and it doesn't look like we'll be able to. The best course is for us to get the hell out of here while we still can."

"I'll alert the others."

"CS to the north, grenades to the north, and we go out to the west. Down the hill. Wait for my mark. I'll throw a fragmentation grenade."

Chavez whispered, "I'll make the rounds."

Martinez moved toward the north and used his night binoculars. There were a couple of small fires burning, but they provided almost no light. Shapes were moving among the trees, looking as if they were preparing for the next assault.

Glancing at his watch, he decided that enough time had passed. He put the binoculars away and took out the last fragmentation grenade he had. He pulled the pin, dropped it, and then cocked his arm. With as much force as he could muster, he threw the grenade into the jungle. He could hear it as it snapped through the vegetation.

Three seconds later it exploded, the flash lost in the

veil of bushes, vines, and ferns. As it went off, the others began throwing their grenades. These fired with dull pops and then small flames as the CS poured from them.

The light gray cloud spread, blowing slightly toward the enemy line. Martinez was up then, crossing toward the southern side of the perimeter. He reached it and held, turning to watch as the rest of the team moved to join him.

The enemy began to fire, but it was sporadic, directed through the cloud of gas. Martinez dropped to one knee, his weapon held in his right hand as he stared at the southern side of the camp.

Chavez appeared, slapped him on the shoulder, and kept right on moving to the west. Martinez, ducking low, followed the master sergeant. Around him he was aware of the shapes of the rest of his team as they tried to exfiltrate.

Firing behind them increased now. A heavy machine gun opened fire, the huge round cutting through the jungle overhead. More AKs joined the fight. The enemy was repelling a phantom attack.

Chavez slowed and Martinez stopped. They listened for anyone in front of them, searched for them, but heard and saw nothing. They then started forward slowly, hoping to avoid any further contact.

To the right there was a wild burst of firing, AK against M-16. Tracers flashed in all directions, quick bursts of brightness and then nothing.

"Hope our guys made it through," whispered Chavez.

Martinez nodded but didn't speak. He hoped they themselves would make it through, too.

SAN ANTONIO, TEXAS

Major John Frankowski had spent an uncomfortable day in the ready room, hoping that something would happen so that he'd have the chance to get a little flight time. Anything to break up the monotony of sitting around waiting for the opportunity to take off. It was a carryover of the old days, when the air force had been afraid of a sneak attack. Now it was a routine that irritated the troops but allowed for intensive training during those few days when the pilots were required to be on alert.

Frankowski was a short skinny man with dark hair and bright blue eyes. It seemed that when he or his wife, Marie, another air-force pilot, had downtime, the other was scheduled to fly. Since Marie was a pilot on a transport, her flights sometimes lasted several days. John, as a fighter pilot, was rarely gone more than one.

Now he was surprised when the squadron commander, Lieutenant Colonel James Hahn, awakened him and told him to be ready for takeoff as quickly as possible. Not a full-fledged scramble with the pilots running out, but a let's-get-off-the-ground-without-delay.

"What's the problem?"

"Got some trouble down near the border. Mexican government is up in arms and we're going to throw up an air patrol to help them."

"Christ. A sophisticated fighter to be used for a job that would be better accomplished by a single-engine prop plane."

"Probably. But what we're doing is sending a message. Let the Mexican government know they can count on us. "Briefing in about ten minutes. You'll get everything that you need there. You'll be flight lead. Two aircraft. Along the border but do not cross into Mexican airspace. I believe, and we'll get the coordination before take off, that fighters from two other bases will also be responding."

"Great. The air full of jets."

"Ten minutes," said Hahn.

"Yes, sir." Frankowski forced himself to stand up. His mouth tasted like old shoes. And his head hurt from a lack of good, deep sleep.

He wandered into the latrine, splashed water on his face, and then brushed his teeth quickly. Finished with that, he staggered back into the room, put his toothbrush away, and headed out into the hallway.

The air-conditioning was working overtime. It seemed to be arctic cold. The light green walls, painted that color because some psychologist had decided that it was restful, bothered him. He figured that the walls should be bright red so that the men and women would be angry. Warriors, whether on the ground or in the air, should be angry.

He walked down to the briefing room, which looked

like a small movie theater. At one end was a raised stage, a screen, and the American flag. Sitting up toward the front of the ten rows of seats were a couple of other pilots. The theater was brightly lighted, so bright that it made Frankowski blink as he walked in.

On the stage was Captain Jeremy DuBose, the intelligence officer. Behind him, on the screen, was a section of map showing the Texas–Mexico border. DuBose held a mug in his hand. He was sipping from it when he spotted Frankowski.

"Now that we're all here we can get started. Gentlemen"—he glanced down at the one female pilot and added quickly—"and lady, our mission tonight is simple and quick. Recon along the border for about fifty minutes and then a return to base. Naturally some of the material we'll be discussing is classified as secret and will not be discussed outside this room."

Turning, DuBose pointed at the screen and began his briefing. Frankowski listened for a moment and then tuned it out. He knew what would be said, he knew it all because it was the same each and every time. Only when the slides showing the exact mission route came up, and when the weather briefing was made, did he pay attention. Both those were important aspects of the mission package. The rest was preprogrammed information handed out in the beginning of every mission.

Finally it was over and they were cleared to the aircraft for a quick preflight and then the run-up and commo check procedures. A standard mission, designed to fill squares on the training schedule and to promote goodwill with the neighbors to the south.

In the corridor one of the other pilots said, "Woke me up for this piece of crap."

"Could be worse," said Frankowski. "You could be flying a tanker. Around and around until it was time to give out gas and have the opportunity to turn into a glowing ball of debris."

"Sure. And I could be a civilian, too."

Daniels had wanted to get off the highway as quickly as possible. If the authorities decided to search for the men who had raided the factory, they would, quite naturally, patrol there. It was why the four-wheel drive vehicles had been used.

At the first opportunity they crashed through another fence and began driving cross-country. Daniels was nervous until they had climbed the first hill and disappeared behind it. The instant the highway faded from sight, he felt better.

On the radio he said, "Trail, be advised that we have left the main route."

The driver of the truck said, "Roger. We saw you go and are behind you."

"Close it up if you can."

"Will do."

They were bouncing over the rough fields now. Amos was pushing it as fast as he dared, leaning forward as if that would give him a better view through the windshield. The front wheels dropped away suddenly as they hit a huge hole. He stood on the brake, but the front collided with the other side and everyone was thrown back.

"Jesus," said Daniels.

"Didn't see it."

"Well, slow it down."

They drove out of the hole and continued to the top of the next ridge. Looking back toward Nueva Rosita, he could still see a glowing cherry cloud. The factory was fully engulfed and the local firefighters were having no luck. Even at twenty miles he could see the flames.

"They won't be putting that sucker out," said Hyatt.

"Not easily," said Daniels.

The radio crackled to life. "Ah, Front, this is Trail. I think we've got someone behind us."

Daniels twisted around but could see only the bobbing lights of the other two four-wheel-drive vehicles. The pickup truck hadn't been able to catch them yet.

"We slow?" asked Amos.

Daniels hesitated and then shook his head. "No. We go to the border."

"The Federales are rough," said Amos. "No constitution or lawyers to get in the way."

"I'm aware of Mexican justice," said Daniels. "You want to risk falling into their hands?"

"No . . ."

"Then get us the hell out of here."

Amos stepped on the accelerator and they rocketed to the top of a hill.

"Stop!" screamed Daniels.

As they halted, Daniels threw open his door and leaped out. He snatched his binoculars from the seat and focused on the ridge opposite them. The other two four-wheel drives appeared and slid to a stop behind him. Both the occupants leaped out, taking up firing positions near the front fenders.

"Christ," said Daniels as he saw the first of the muzzle flashes. "Jesus Christ."

The lights had appeared in the rearview mirror as rapidly growing dots in the distance. Whitney Garnett, the driver of the pickup truck, which was the rear guard, kept glancing up to monitor the progress of the oncoming car.

Lloyd Ladd, the passenger, was scanning the side of the road, searching for the point where the rest of the team had turned off the road a couple of minutes earlier. "There," he snapped, his right hand pointing. "Right there."

Garnett stepped on the brake and spun the wheel. The truck rocked up on two wheels, fell back, and shot forward. They dropped into the ditch and bounced up and out, slamming down to the dried prairie. The rear wheels bit at the ground, kicking out a plume of dust as they leaped forward.

"Still coming," said Ladd.

Again Garnett glanced at the rearview mirror. Bright blue lights began to flash on the top of the car. There was a cold chill in his belly and shivers up and down his spine.

They roared up a gentle hill. As they reached the crest Garnett slowed and risked a look to the rear. The police car had turned and was following them across the broken prairie.

"We can outrun them now," said Ladd. "They're going to break an axle or puncture the oil pan."

"Maybe," said Garnett. He hit the brights so that he could survey the ground in front of him. He pushed the accelerator to the floor, felt the wheels spin and bite deep.

They reached the bottom of the hill and began the rapid climb up another. For a moment the police car was gone, but it reached the crest and started down without hesitating.

"Still coming."

Garnett didn't respond. He wondered if he could put enough distance between them and the police car, turn off the lights, and then pull away to the east or west rather than the north.

"They're gaining," said Ladd.

Garnett could see that himself. "Get on the radio and warn Daniels. Then we'll stop and see if we can't slow them. At the top of the next hill."

"What the hell are you going to do?"

"Throw a couple of rounds at them. Get them stopped, and then get the hell out while they're thinking it over."

Ladd took the microphone and told Daniels that the police were catching them. As he finished Garnett stood on the brake. The wheels locked and the truck slid to a stop. Garnett grabbed his rifle from the rack in the back and jumped forward, crouching near the front fender.

Ladd did the same and then looked across the front of the truck. "We going to shoot?"

"No choice. Wait until they get a little closer. Aim just above the headlights."

Ladd didn't respond.

Garnett watched as the police car, the blue lights still flashing, came up the slope and slowed. He risked a glance at the top of the last ridge, but no support vehicles were visible.

"Now!" yelled Garnett. He pulled the trigger and felt the rifle buck. The muzzle flash stabbed out.

The police car spun suddenly, so that the driver's side was facing up the hill. The headlights went out as the passenger's door opened.

Garnett aimed and fired again, riddling the closest door with his rifle. He sprayed the top of the car and smashed the flashing blue lights. He then fired at the tires and the engine, trying to disable the police car.

The two police officers shot back with their pistols. One round smashed the rear window in the pickup and then punched through the windshield, leaving a starred hole.

Then, in the distance, came the wail of more police sirens. Ladd glanced over at Garnett and shouted, "We'd better get the hell out of here."

Garnett touched the selector switch, flipped it to full auto, and emptied the magazine, raking the side of the police car. He stood then, and ducking, almost like a man in a driving rain, he ran to the driver's side and got in. He propped his rifle up against the seat.

Ladd joined him, ducked below the back of the seat. "Go! Go."

Garnett stepped on the gas and the truck jumped from the crest of the hill. They bounced down it, thrown about the cab of the truck.

"No one coming," said Ladd.

"Tell Daniels."

"Right."

Daniels hadn't waited to see the outcome of the firefight. No matter what happened, it was providing them with the chance to get away. For a moment he wanted to remain, feeling like the old Indian chief who stood on the hill watching the younger braves attack. But that old chief had not needed to get away. Daniels and the rest of the raiders couldn't be caught in Mexico.

"Let's go," he said.

Amos glanced at him, as if wanting another instruction, and then started down the hill.

"Speed up," said Daniels.

"We need to give Garnett and Ladd a chance to catch up," said Hyatt from the backseat.

"Garnett and Ladd have their job to do. Ours is to get the hell out of Mexico."

"But we can't leave them."

"They can take care of themselves." Daniels turned away, ending the discussion.

"How much farther to the border?" asked Gannon.

Amos said, "I think it's maybe twenty miles. Maybe a little less."

"About an hour?" asked Daniels.

"I've got to hold the speed down," said Amos. "I don't want to drive us off a cliff."

Daniels turned around again, but could no longer see anything behind them. He was worried about Garnett and Ladd, but he didn't want the others to know that.

"We're clear," said Ladd over the radio.

Daniels picked up the microphone and acknowledged the call. "Hang back to make sure that no one else is behind us."

"Roger."

With that he felt the tension drain out of him. They were about to get clear and the one police car that had been following was stopped. They'd be back in Texas in under an hour and out of the reach of the Mexican authorities. There would be no way to connect any of them to the raid at the factory. The one man killed was left in the factory where the fire would burn the body so badly that no one would ever recognize it. With luck the fire would be hot enough that only a few bone fragments would be left. Maybe the authorities would believe it was a Mexican worker who had died.

They continued on with the other two four-wheel-drive vehicles. Amos slowed slightly as the ground got rougher. He concentrated on the terrain displayed in the headlights. Daniels just waited for the first sight of the Rio Grande.

"Coming up on the river," said Amos. "Another ten minutes."

"All right," said Hyatt.

Daniels grinned and then said, "Let's slow it down and make sure that we've got everybody with us."

They climbed the last hill, and as they crested it Daniels could see the river and beyond it Texas. Somehow the ground on the other side of the river looked better, brighter, more inviting. It was the base, the free zone, the area where they would finally be safe.

Gannon leaned forward, her face over the rear of the front seat. "Almost home."

"Right," said Daniels.

Amos stopped and then rolled forward so that they weren't silhouetted against the night sky. They stopped again and Amos switched off the lights.

Daniels picked up his binoculars and scanned the banks of the river as a precaution. He was about to announce that the way was clear when he spotted the black shape of a car below them, sitting near the ford. "Could be trouble," he said.

"What?" asked Gannon.

"Mexican police in front of us. One car. Not much of a problem."

"I thought there wouldn't be any killing," said Gannon.

Daniels shrugged. "When you make an omelet, you break the eggs."

"That's stupid," said Gannon.

"We going to break some more eggs?" asked Hyatt.

Daniels chuckled. "I hope not."

JUST NORTH OF THE TEXAS BORDER

It was Howard who spotted the lights first. He saw something on the hills on the other side of the river, bobbing across the landscape. They were points of light, barely visible. First a single vehicle, and then a second and a third.

"What we got there?" he asked.

Paulding turned her binoculars on the lights and studied them. "Two, three trucks, moving slowly. Not on a road. Or a really bad one."

"Coming at us?" asked Howard.

"More or less." Paulding lowered the binoculars and climbed into the passenger's seat of the Humvee. "Let's drive down closer to the river. No lights."

"Yes, ma'am."

They rolled down the slope, moving slowly. Paulding kept her eyes on the lights as they got closer. She tried to use the binoculars again, but the bouncing of the vehicle made it impossible for her to focus.

They stopped at the bottom of the slope about a hundred yards from the Rio Grande. Paulding climbed out and used her night glass. Now she could see the bulk behind the lights. Large boxy vehicles.

"Still coming at us," said Howard. "They have us outnumbered, too."

Without a word to Howard Paulding sat down. "Caldron Control, Caldron Two."

"Go, Two."

"I have three vehicles on the Mexican side coming at me. They're still about a mile from us."

"Roger. Do you require assistance?"

Paulding thought about that. To ask for assistance when all she knew was that there were three cars or trucks in Mexico seemed to be ridiculous. They might turn suddenly and then there would be no problem. Still, there had been that warning broadcast earlier. "Negative," she said finally.

"Roger."

She dropped the microphone to the seat and then turned her attention back to the oncoming vehicles. They had not varied their course.

Below those lights, parked on the bank on the opposite side of the river, Paulding made out a couple of dark shapes. She thought that she could see movement around them. Pointing it out to Howard, she asked, "What do you make of that?"

"Mexican roadblock?"

"That's what I thought," she said. "Looks like we're not going to have to worry about them getting over here."

"Unless they blow through," said Howard.

"Yeah. Unless."

The four-wheel-drive Blazer crept forward and Amos touched the brake. Below they could now see a couple of other vehicles that hadn't been there when they had crossed over from Texas.

"Slow it down," said Daniels. "Let's not rush into this thing."

The two other four-wheel-drive vehicles reached the hilltop and stopped. Daniels turned and saw them back there. None of them used the radio.

"What do you think?" asked Amos.

"I don't know." He glanced into the backseat. "Get your weapons out, loaded, but on safe."

"Yes, sir," said Hyatt.

Gannon didn't move right away. She stared at him and then ducked down, picking up the M-16 that she'd put on the floor. There was a magazine in the well.

"Advance on them slowly."

Amos took his foot off the brake and let them begin to roll forward. "Should I use the headlights?"

"Leave them off."

They had reached the midpoint of the hill when the lights of the cars below came on. The flashers on the top began to rotate. A searchlight stabbed out, flashed across the ground, and focused on the truck.

A man walked around to the front of one of the cars, stood in the headlights, and held up a hand. "You want stop," he said in accented English.

Amos asked, "What'll I do?"

"Stop."

"Yes, sir."

Daniels turned so that he was looking into the back of the Blazer. "If there is shooting, we'll want to spread out. Make it tougher on them."

"They're police officers," said Gannon.

"You want to go to a Mexican jail? They'll love you there. No lawyers, constitutional rights, or appeals." Daniels didn't wait for an answer. To everyone he said, "We have to shoot to kill and we have to get clear of here as quickly as possible."

The radio crackled. "What are we supposed to do?"

The police officer had a bullhorn that he raised to his lips. "You must come out with hands up. You must surrender now."

Daniels used his microphone. "We're going through. Follow the lead. Get ready." To Amos he said, "Start forward slowly. First sign of trouble, stop again."

From the backseat Hyatt asked, "How many are there?"

"I make it five," said Amos. "Maybe six."

"You will halt," ordered the police officer. "You will get out of the vehicle."

"Stop," said Daniels.

Again Amos stepped on the brake, but this time he used the stick to shift into neutral. He reached to the right and touched his rifle.

"Get out of your vehicle."

Daniels took a deep breath and let it out. He could feel the sweat on his face and body as it dripped. The pit of his stomach was ice cold, and for a moment he believed he was going to pass out. But then everything focused perfectly and sharply.

"On my command get out. Amos and Hyatt, you take those on the left. We'll take the rest on the right. I'll drop that son of a bitch in the headlights. On my command." He waited to let the instructions sink in and to give everyone a chance to check their weapons. *"Go!"*

Daniels threw open his door, forgetting that the dome light would illuminate them. The sudden flash surprised him. As he tumbled from the truck he glanced at it. Then, propping his weapon in the gap between the door and the side of the vehicle, he aimed at the stunned policeman, who stood still in the bright lights of his police car. Daniels aimed and fired and watched as he fell back, tossing his bullhorn in the air.

Another searchlight flashed, the beam on Daniels. The police officers opened fire, their rounds smashing the window near Daniels's head. The door shook under the impact of the slugs.

"Aim at the muzzle flashes," ordered Amos. He was lying prone, using the front tire as protection. He pulled the trigger slowly, rhythmically, as he tried to cut down the police officers.

On the other side of the truck Gannon opened up on full auto. She didn't aim. She just sprayed the area, hoping for the best.

The rest of them, spreading out on either side of the Blazer, began to shoot, their weapons joining the cacophony. There was a shattering of glass as the windshields and windows of the police cars were broken. One of the headlights was hit, flared, and went out. The searchlight went off suddenly and the side of the hill was dark again.

The other Blazers spread out and the passengers leaped out, firing at the police officers. The night was filled with gunfire, the hammering of the weapons, including a grenade launcher. A shotgun, used by the police, boomed and created a huge flash of brightness.

There was a scream and Hyatt yelled, "I'm hit. Hit bad."

Daniels ignored it. He tried to spot one of the men below him. He knelt, one knee on the ground, his rifle still propped on the side of the door. He fired quickly, remembering that someone had once told him the tendency was to aim high at night.

A police officer dashed to one side, as if he wanted to get to the wounded man. As he broke from cover Daniels fired, as did everyone else. The officer was hit, spun, and fell.

More firing came from the police cars. The shotgun fired again and again. Daniels shot back, finally flipping to full auto and holding down the trigger. The shotgun fell silent.

Firing from the police cars ended abruptly. Daniels and his people slowly stopped shooting until it was quiet. Daniels rubbed his eyes with the heel of his hand, staring down at the police cars. "We get them all?" he asked.

"I don't know."

"Someone look at Hyatt."

"Hyatt's dead," said Amos.

"Shit."

The radio came to life again. "What are our instructions?"

Daniels, his eyes still on the police cars, reached into the truck for the microphone. "Hold your positions for the moment. Garnett?"

"Garnett here."

"Cover the rear. I don't want anyone coming up behind us."

"Roger that."

"Amos, let's you and me walk on down there."

Amos stood up and walked around the front of the truck. He dropped the magazine from his weapon and slammed a new one home. He worked the bolt to make sure that a round was chambered. "Ready."

Daniels looked back at Gannon. She was sitting on the ground, her back to the truck. She clutched her rifle in both hands.

Daniels joined Amos and they began to walk down the hill slowly. They reached the first body and Amos knelt and tried to find a pulse. "Dead."

They walked around the car and saw two men sprawled on the ground. Amos kicked the pistol away from the hand of one of them. He checked the man and then stepped to the other. Both of them were dead.

Daniels covered Amos as he moved from man to man. "Let's take the weapons."

"I don't know," said Amos. "They could be traced if anyone gets them away from us. I don't think we want anything that will lead back to here."

"Good point."

Amos crouched near another man. "Hey, this guy's alive."

Daniels walked up and looked down at the wounded police officer. He raised his rifle, aimed at the head, and fired. The body jerked and the head exploded, splattering blood and brains over the side of the car.

Amos stood for a moment, staring down at the body. He didn't say anything.

"Let's get out of here," said Daniels. He turned and walked quickly back to his Blazer.

Standing on the hill on the Texas side of the border, Paulding could do nothing. She watched the firefight, able to see the lines of each side by the muzzle flashes of the weapons. The sound of firing drifted to them. First just a couple of shots, and then the dull, drawn-out detonation of two or three dozen weapons.

"Jesus," said Howard. "It's World War Three over there."

Paulding ducked down, picked up the microphone, and said, "Caldron Control, this is Caldron Two."

"Go."

"We've got some kind of firefight going on just south of the border."

"Say location."

Paulding turned on her flashlight and studied the map. She gave the coordinates.

"Wait one."

The firing tapered and then ended. Paulding stood up holding onto the microphone. The slope across the river was dark and quiet.

"War's over," said Howard.

"Caldron Two, do you want assistance?"

Howard spoke up. "They're going to cross now. You'd better get us some help." He opened the door on his side of the vehicle and leaned over to check his weapon.

"Roger," said Paulding.

"On its way. Break. Break. Caldron Two-six, this is Caldron Control. . . ."

Paulding tossed the microphone into the Humvee. "Let's head down to the river."

"I'm not sure that's such a great idea," said Howard. "We're badly outnumbered."

"We're just going to keep an eye on things until the backup gets here."

"Sure. And there weren't any Indians on the Little Bighorn."

"There's no reason to be paranoid," said Paulding. But she reached down and touched the butt of her pistol and then looked into the rear where the rifles were.

Howard let the Humvee roll down the slope but didn't bother to start the engine. He kept the lights off, too. He wanted to do nothing that would call attention to them.

"Looks like they're beginning to move," said Paulding.

"Maybe we should stop here."

"Nope. Let's get down closer to the river's edge. We'll stop there."

Howard, both his hands on the wheel, stared out toward the other vehicles. They, too, were moving without their lights. They had rolled around the police vehicles and had reached the edge of the Rio Grande. "They're coming across," he said.

"Stop right here."

Howard put on the brakes and then twisted around, getting his rifle from the rear of the vehicle. He made sure that the safety was on.

Paulding used the radio again. "Caldron Control, this is Two. They are on the move, nearly to the river. Say ETA of our support."

"Wait one. . . . No more than one-zero mikes."

"Roger."

Howard got out of the Humvee and moved toward the front. "They're entering the river."

Paulding was out now, standing at the side, her hand on her holstered pistol. They had no flashing red lights, no siren, nothing to identify them as an official vehicle. Turning, she leaned across the front and snapped on the lights.

"What the hell are you doing?"

"Letting them know we're here."

"Jesus, Major, they just shot the hell out of those Mexicans and you're going to let them know we're here."

Paulding pulled her pistol. It felt heavy in her hand. She glanced down at it and flipped off the safety. The vehicles were in the center of the river, splashing toward them. The fact that Paulding had turned on the lights hadn't slowed them or caused them to change their path.

"Get ready," said Paulding. "Here they come."

The first of the vehicles climbed out of the river, roared up the bank, and then stopped. The others fanned out behind the leader.

Paulding lifted a hand like a traffic cop and raised her voice, "Please step out of your vehicle and identify yourself."

"Major," said Howard. "This is crazy."

Paulding ignored him. "This is Major Paulding, United States Army. You are requested to vacate your vehicle and identify yourself."

The door on the passenger's side opened and someone got out. Paulding shifted around so that she was facing him, watching him closely. She felt the weight of the pistol in her hand, but didn't raise it. "Who are you?"

The figure stood staring at her. A moment later someone got out of the other side.

"Major," said Howard, raising his rifle.

Paulding said, "Take it easy. We don't want to have any trouble."

The first shot got Howard high, in the shoulder, pushing him back. There was a burst of firing, the rounds driving Howard away from the Humvee. He fell and rolled and didn't move.

Paulding snapped her pistol up and fired a single shot. She didn't see where it went. The windshield near her shattered. Rounds hit the vehicle. Something smashed into her leg and she felt it buckle. She fell back against the side of the Humvee. Another round hit her on the tip of the shoulder, numbing her arm and weakening her fingers. She heard her pistol drop to the ground. She tried to roll and fell beside the vehicle.

"Come on," shouted a male voice. "Let's get the fuck out of here."

Paulding heard the vehicles start to drive off. She tried to open her eyes, but couldn't see anything. In a moment everything was black and she saw nothing more.

NICARAGUA

The deep charcoals of the jungle had brightened so that the shapes were becoming more distinct. The animal life was starting to move, the monkeys swinging through the trees, calling to one another. The birds were squawking, dropping into the air, and then landing on lower branches.

Martinez was leaning against a tree trunk. His uniform was soaked, and his hands were clammy. His mouth was filled with cotton, but he refused to drink any of the water in his canteen. Not with the enemy close by. He might need it later.

Chavez leaned close, his lips only inches from Martinez's ear. "Gibson and Davis have made it."

"Espinoza and the radio?"

"Not yet," said Chavez. He glanced up. It was bright

enough to see some of the colors. Now the monkeys were visible as they sat chattering.

"I haven't seen or heard a sign that the enemy is following," said Martinez. "I think we got away from them cleanly."

"Yeah. I think so."

"We've got what, eight or ten of the team in now?"

"Ten. Still missing Espinoza and Jones. I wish Jones would get here. Brown isn't all that good as a medic."

Martinez took a deep breath and exhaled slowly. He wiped a hand over his face. He didn't like running. He didn't like abandoning his camp, but then, there hadn't been anything he could do. It wasn't the first time that a Special Forces team had been forced to escape and evade.

There was a low whistle and someone whispered, "Got somebody coming in."

Martinez came up, one knee on the soggy ground. He touched the side of his weapon, making sure that the safety was off. He checked the positions of the other members of the team. The sunlight was beginning to penetrate the triple canopy.

Jones appeared, moving slowly, weapon held at port arms. He stopped and waited, his head moving slowly from side to side as he searched for the others.

"Come ahead," said Chavez.

Jones grinned broadly as he moved in.

"Where's Espinoza?" asked Martinez.

Jones hitched a thumb over his shoulder. Martinez looked past him and saw the last member of the team. Espinoza staggered once but then spotted the others. "Made it," he said.

"Chavez," said Martinez, "five minutes and then we get out of here."

"We should let Jones and Espinoza rest."

"Later, farther from the camp. Maybe we can get some airlift and get the hell out of here."

"Yes, sir."

Martinez pulled out his map, opened it up, and then

refolded it so that his position was in the center. They were on the side of a range of hills that sloped gently into a valley several miles wide. A river was at the foot of the hills. Even though it was fresh water, they had to be careful. A species of freshwater shark lived in the rivers, and they could be as deadly as their saltwater counterparts.

Espinoza dropped to the ground near Martinez. The captain asked, "Have you reestablished contact with net?"

"No. Haven't had the chance and I didn't want to use voice. Pinpoints us too easily."

"The main radio destroyed?"

"Everything went up as we abandoned the camp. The enemy tripped a number of the booby traps as we got out. I didn't hear them following us. They were too busy trying to keep from getting killed."

"Yeah," said Martinez. He turned his attention to the jungle around him. It had been thicker higher up. Here there were stretches where the ground looked like it did in a well-manicured park. Thick grass growing on a dense bed of rotting vegetation. Short, stunted trees, some bushes and ferns, all damp with the morning dew. Wisps of white fog drifted along the ground or in the trees of the canopy, looking as if part of the jungle had caught fire during the night.

Chavez returned, dark smudges on his face where he'd hastily applied camo paint. "We're ready to move. Gibson has the point."

"Okay," said Martinez. He lifted his left hand, holding the under part of his wrist in front of his face. "We go in two minutes."

"Yes, sir."

Boyce and the rest of the B detachment were lined up in the door, waiting for the red light to go to green, but that didn't happen. Instead the loadmaster reached up and yanked the troop door down, closing it. The roar of the engines and the wind diminished radically.

Boyce tapped the loadmaster on the shoulder, leaned close, and shouted. "What in the hell is going on?"

"Sir, if you'd accompany me to the cockpit again?"

Boyce turned, unhooked the metal buckle of the static line, and stored it. He looked into the face of the sergeant major and said, "Have the men take their seats."

"What in the hell is going on, sir?"

"Damned if I know." He moved around the sergeant major and walked forward, then climbed up into the cockpit.

As he sat down the aircraft commander turned and yelled, "Colonel, I got a recall message. I was ordered away from the drop zone and not to let you or your team jump. You are to contact your net for instructions."

"What the hell?" yelled Boyce.

The pilot shrugged. "I have no clue as to what is happening. All I know is that we were recalled, that I authenticated and received the proper codes."

The flight engineer handed Boyce the headset again and then yelled, "You're on the proper frequency."

"Thanks." He pressed the button. "Montana Control, this is Montana Six."

"This is Montana Control. Be advised that your mission has been scrubbed and you are to return to base."

Boyce scowled but didn't ask for authentication. He recognized the voice of the operator. "What in the hell is going on?"

"Montana Six, be advised that we have lost contact with Cheyenne, Sioux, and Apache."

"Roger." Boyce fell back against the bulkhead. There were a hundred questions that he wanted to ask, but he would never get the answers over the radio. He sat there for a moment, his mind racing.

"Montana Six, you are to return to base."

"Roger," snapped Boyce. "We have turned around. Say status of Cheyenne, Sioux, and Apache."

"We have negative information."

There was nothing more to be gained on the radio. Boyce said, "Roger. Out."

As he stripped the headphone the AC turned and said, "We estimate arrival at Howard in just over an hour. That's pushing it."

"Shit," said Boyce. "Any of you have a clue as to what is going on?"

"No, sir. Just that we're to get the hell out of Nicaraguan airspace as quickly as possible and then return to Panama. That's it."

Boyce stood up and then climbed down out of the cockpit. He found Lombard and the sergeant major, and knelt in front of them. "I have no clue about what's happening. Contact has been lost with all three of our teams, and the air force has ordered the plane back to base."

"Shit," said Lombard.

"My word exactly," said Boyce.

John Frankowski, tucked into the cockpit of his F-16, orbited just north of the Mexican border. He was boring holes in the sky thirty thousand feet in the air. Glancing down, he could see almost nothing except the sunbaked ground.

This was the time that Frankowski liked the best. A mission, though it consisted of a huge oval patrol along the border, that was so simple he could complete it with half his mind. The aircraft was trimmed to hold his altitude. He scanned the instruments and then the sky around him. This was what flying was all about. Alone. The only problem was the damned radios. The FAA and the air base and his wingmen and operations. They kept intruding on his peace.

He slowly turned, glanced down at the Rio Grande. There was nothing that he could see. The river was a string, the highways pencillike ribbons, and the cities tiny checkerboards. Single vehicles and individuals were invisible.

He called the flight control center and requested a lower altitude. He was cleared to fifteen thousand feet and advised that there was no other traffic near him. He answered, "Roger. Beginning letdown."

As he reached fifteen thousand feet things came into focus. Now the cars were visible and he could make out a rancher, standing near a pickup. There was a herd of cattle walking slowly toward him, as if they expected to be fed.

To the right, on the other side of the border, he spotted a group of cars. A half dozen of them had lights flashing on top of them. There were men sprawled on the ground and others standing around looking at them. One of the men looked up, pointed, and the others scattered.

Frankowski kept his eyes on them because it was something different. Then, almost like a flashback to the missions he'd flown above Kuwait and Iraq, he realized that he was taking fire. The muzzle flashes of the pistols and rifles were nearly lost in the brightening of the morning.

"Strides Control, this is Strides Four-four. You're not going to believe this, but I'm taking fire."

"Say again."

"I am taking fire from a group of police officers in Mexico."

"Roger. Are you in danger?"

Frankowski wanted to laugh. They were shooting at him with pistols and rifles with effective ranges of far less than a mile. He knew the rounds would never reach him. "Negative. Say instructions."

"Wait one."

Frankowski was now beyond them, streaking away. If he cut in the afterburners and pushed it to the fire wall, he could easily outrun the bullets fired at him. The danger, if there was any, was of some kind of a fluke.

"Strides Six requests that you document the fire. Are you equipped with gun-camera tape?"

"Roger. Fully equipped."

"You are authorized to penetrate the southern ADIZ

for a single pass at the Mexican authorities. You are not to engage them, and you are to egress as rapidly as possible. You will then return to base."

"Roger. One pass and then I get out."

"Roger."

Frankowski twisted around to see his wingman back behind him. Using the radio, he said, "Did you copy?"

"Roger."

"You stay right back here. I'll make the pass and then we'll join for the flight to the base."

"Roger that."

"Beginning the turn now."

"Roger."

Frankowski came around, first to the north so that he could line up. Then, losing altitude, he dived at the group on the ground. As he approached he turned on the gun cameras and watched as the enemy grew rapidly. It was just like the Iraqis during Desert Storm. Standing behind their trucks or cars, firing up with rifles and pistols. It was possible to knock a jet down that way, but not likely. Jets moved too fast and the bullets were too slow, their effective range too limited. They would need machine guns, radar, surface-to-air missiles to get him, and even with that the odds were that he'd get through.

He stayed on the course, crossing the river, his nose pointed right at them. And then suddenly he was beyond them, climbing nearly straight up and turning to head back to the other side of the border.

"They're still firing."

"Roger." Frankowski glanced at the instruments, but everything was in the green. He'd heard nothing, felt nothing. He doubted that any of the bullets had even come close, let alone hit his airframe.

He rolled over and headed north, crossing the border. He looked down at the enemy ten or eleven thousand feet below. They were still shooting at him. He wished he could come around again, firing his rockets, let them see what a fully loaded aircraft could do. Put the fear of God into them like he had those Iraqi soldiers.

He crossed over into the United States, his mind holding on the turkey shoot that had started with the ground war.

"Lead, I've joined on your right wing."

Frankowski touched the radio button and said, "Roger that. Heading to the barn." He switched frequencies and said, "Stride Control, Stride Four-four. We're coming on in."

"Roger that."

Frankowski settled into the cockpit seat and wished that he could think of a reason to stay airborne for another couple hours. Of course he'd need to refuel and that meant talking to others. For the moment he had the peace of the sky to himself, but in minutes it would be gone and then he'd be landing. The flight was nearly over.

He saw the airfield in front of him and called the tower to let them know he was inbound with a flight of two. He turned on final a few minutes later, his wingman behind him. They crossed the threshold, let down slowly, and touched the black-smudged runway. He hit the thrust reverse and popped the drag chute, slowing rapidly.

He turned off on a taxiway and rolled to a stop on the tarmac in front of the operations building, in the parking spot for his aircraft. He waited, the canopy up and the hot air of the Texas morning swirling around him. The crew chief appeared, set the ladder against the fuselage, and waited.

Frankowski unbuckled his seat belt and shoulder harness, put his hands up on the side of the aircraft, and lifted himself up until he could stand on the seat. He turned and climbed down.

The crew chief appeared at his side and asked, "Just what in the hell were you doing? Sir?"

Frankowski was surprised by the greeting. He grinned and said, "Nice to see you, too, Sergeant."

"No, sir. I want to know what you've been doing to my airplane."

"Flying in circles, boring holes in the sky, and collecting a great deal of flight pay in the process."

"Follow me, sir," said the crew chief, turning and walking back along the fuselage. He stopped near the horizonal elevator and pointed.

Frankowski moved forward and saw the small round hole on the underside, and the larger hole on the top where the metal had peeled back like the petals of a silver flower. "What the hell," he asked.

"Bullet hole," said the crew chief. "Small arms. Rifle of some kind."

Frankowski laughed. "Taking fire in the United States. Un-fucking-real."

"Yes, sir. I've got to report this. Aircraft's grounded until we can get it repaired."

"Of course." Frankowski turned and headed toward the operations building suddenly exhilarated. He thought of Winston Churchill's line. There was nothing quite like being shot at without results. He'd forgotten what it was like to take battle damage until that moment. And he realized it was the excitement he craved. No way to find it again, unless the United States managed to find a war. He didn't expect that to happen.

SAN ANTONIO, TEXAS

Morris Reisman got off the aircraft and into the mugginess of the jetway. After the air-conditioned plane, and after the mountains of Nepal, the heat and the humidity were oppressive. But as he approached the terminal proper he could feel the cool dry air from the inside. The sweat that had beaded evaporated as he entered and worked his way through the crowd of stupid people who thought that the best way to hurry their relatives off a plane was to stand in front of the door so that no one could move.

He turned and walked down the concourse, past the bars and phones and bookstores. He found the baggage claim area and then surveyed the carousels looking for the one where his suitcase would appear. He had expected to be met as he got off the plane, and then at the baggage claim area, but there was no one looking for him.

"Typical," he said. "Just typical."

It was the flying that made him irritable. Confined to the interior of an airplane with a hundred and fifty other people he didn't know and probably wouldn't like. No way to escape them and their annoying habits, like the fat woman who thought the sound of her snapping gum was somehow pleasing to those around her. Reisman's answer had been to turn up the volume of his headset to drown her out.

He sat in one of the few chairs and waited until the buzzer sounded and the light began to flash, signaling the arrival of the luggage. Then, like Pavlov's dogs, the people crowded the moving belts. No one thought to stand back until his or her suitcase appeared. No, all crowd around blocking the view so that it was difficult for everyone.

Finally his suitcase appeared and he moved through the maze of people, snagged it, let the armed guard inspect the claim check, and then pushed his way out into the thick air of the humid morning.

"Christ," he said as his shirt became sweat-soaked.

A man in black came up to him and asked, "You Reisman?"

"Yeah," he said with relief.

"Come with me." He turned and walked back to a cream-colored station wagon. "Toss your shit in the back."

Reisman did as told and then climbed into the passenger's side. He realized that the engine was running and that the air-conditioning was on. He turned the vent toward his face and leaned into it.

"How do you like our Texas weather?"

"Sucks."

"Wait till it gets hot," said the driver. "By the way, name's Webster."

"This isn't hot?"

"Not yet."

"Great. I can't wait."

Webster looked over his shoulder and then pulled out into traffic. There was a blare of a horn and Webster held up the middle finger of his hand. "Assholes," he said. "Think they own the fucking street."

"Right," said Reisman.

They drove along the edge of the airfield, crossed a highway, and turned down one of the access roads until they were up on the freeway. Webster got them onto the main road without anyone else coming close to them.

"Okay," said Webster, "here's the scam. I've got to take you to Brooks Army Hospital first."

"What the hell for? I got all my shots before I started to travel and was cleared in New York."

Webster laughed, a hand pounding on the steering wheel. "Nah. That's where the story is."

"What in the hell are you talking about? I was sent here to cover the patrols along the border and the deployment of our forces. I haven't had a chance to check in with either the news desk or the military or even a hotel."

Webster swerved to the right suddenly and yelled, "Asshole," at the windshield. "Fucking guy got his driver's license out of a Cracker Jacks box. Old guys in hats. Watch out for them. Smash you in a minute."

Reisman took a deep breath and thought about closing his eyes so that he couldn't see what was happening. As much as he hated flying, he now wished he was in the airplane with the gum-cracking fat lady. Anything but the ride on the freeway with an idiot named Webster. And to make it worse, now it was beginning to rain.

"Anyway," said Webster, "story's at the hospital. Some assholes shot up one of our patrols. Killed one and wounded one. You're going to interview the wounded one."

Reisman glanced to the side. "For a moment I thought you were going to tell me that I had to interview the dead one."

Webster barked, a sound that might have been a laugh. "Dead one. That's good. Wounded one. Then I'm taking you over to talk to some colonel or general or some damn thing."

"I'd like to find a place to stay. Last time I was here the hotels filled up fast."

"Room's been reserved," said Webster. "Right on the freeway. Easy access to everywhere in San Antonio. Unless you want to stay at the Crockett Hotel right across from the Alamo."

"I prefer to get my own room," said Reisman.

"I'm following my orders. I drive you around because I know the city."

He turned onto another street and then stopped at the front gate of a military base. The guard came out, looked through the windshield, and waited until Webster rolled down the window. "What's your business?" asked the guard.

Webster flashed a card and said, "Press."

"Yes, sir, I can see that. What is your business here?"

"Got an interview with that soldier wounded this morning. Cleared through the base public-affairs office. Major Finchford."

"Please wait right here." The MP disappeared into a brick guardhouse.

"Haven't gotten over the restrictions imposed during Desert Storm."

"Christ."

"Right, but it gave them an excuse and they decided to stick with it."

The guard came out and handed them a paper pass. "Tape this to the inside of the windshield. It's good for three hours only. You must be off the base before it expires."

"Okay."

Stepping down off the curb, the MP pointed. "You follow this street to the first light, turn to the left, and you'll see signs that'll direct you to the hospital. Go immediately there and don't vary your route."

Webster nodded.

"Three hours," warned the MP.

"Right."

They drove to the hospital, and just like those in the civilian world, there was an expanse of parking lot filled with bright cars. The hospital loomed in front of them, looking foreboding, an architectural nightmare, designed when buildings on military bases were functional, with no requirement for beauty. It was a concept that explained the Pentagon.

Webster parked the car, turned off the engine, and then turned on the radio. "I'll wait here. Remember, you've got about two hours and forty-five minutes. Less when you figure we've got to be off the base."

"Right," said Reisman. "Now, who am I supposed to see?"

"Yeah, I suppose it would help to have a name, though I think if you ask for the soldier wounded this morning, they'll be able to direct you." He handed Reisman several sheets of paper. "Everything you need."

"Thanks." Reisman got out of the car and hurried across the parking lot. Rain soaked his hair and dripped from his nose and chin before he was halfway to the doors. At the reception desk inside, he told a nurse what he wanted. She checked the lists, found that his name was on it, and gave him directions to the right room.

He took the elevator up, got off, and looked at the long corridor in front of him. The nurses' station, where two men and three women stood, was to the right. Unlike a civilian hospital, one of the men wore fatigues and was probably an orderly of some kind.

He walked past them and found the room, the wide door partially closed. Quiet music was coming from the inside. Reisman pushed open the door, entered, and stopped, looking at the figure in bed. Bandages and tubes hid the shape of the body.

A man stood at the end of the bed, looking down, watching the breathing. "Can I help you?"

"Morris Reisman. Press."

"You're not needed here."

"No," said Reisman. "But there is a story here. The public-affairs officer, with the permission of the commanding general, authorized this visit. I won't be any trouble."

"Then sit down and be quiet for a moment."

"Certainly."

Commander Dees stood on the bridge of his destroyer as they crashed through the sea, watching as the water sometimes washed over the bow. It was a rough sea that jolted him sometimes and made it impossible to drink coffee. Not a quiet, pleasant sea, but a rough, nasty one.

"Lots of movement around Guantanamo," said Randolph.

Dees kept his eyes on the sea, trying not to see the Cuban mainland off to the left like a dark smudge at the bottom of a picture window. "Anyone concerned about it?"

Randolph fumbled a cigarette out of his pocket, buttoned the flap, and stuck the butt in his mouth. He turned his back to the bow and shielded himself against the bridge. He used his lighter, puffed, and then turned back. Taking the cigarette from his mouth, he said, "Not yet. I talked to Drummond again. I wanted to see if there were any rumblings that he hadn't stuck into the briefing. Something in one of those CIA reports of his."

"And?"

"The rumblings are, of course, that we, meaning the United States, are responsible for the assassination of Castro. That's from Cuba, of course." Randolph laughed. "We give Drummond a hard time, but the kid's sharp."

"Meaning?" asked Dees, not sure that he cared. He kept his eyes focused on the sea but his attention on what he was hearing from the exec.

"Pointed out something strange. The Soviet Union had supported Castro, helped to keep him in power for what, thirty, forty years? Gave him aid to the detriment of their own society and their own economy. Then Castro gets smoked and there isn't a word of protest out of Moscow."

"The Soviets were happy to see him go. They have already cut the aid to Cuba. Castro's death was beneficial to them."

Randolph took a long drag on the cigarette, blew out the smoke, and said, "Exactly. Drummond made the same argument to me. Moscow benefits from the death of Castro. So who's to say that they didn't pull the trigger. No one would suspect it. The blame, naturally, is put on the U.S."

Dees turned and studied his exec. "I can't believe that the Soviets would be that clever. Besides, their society has been collapsing for years. I talked to a friend who visited there. Knew a family or some damned thing. Lived with them in their apartment. In a building that was nearly half a mile long and seven stories high. The elevator, when it worked, was slow and jerky. They had two rooms and five people. One family, but only two rooms."

"Yes, sir?"

"The Soviets are having enough trouble as it is. Ten years ago I was convinced that we'd eventually have to fight them. Someday the Soviets would believe that the West was so weak, so immoral, that it would be time to strike. But not now. The Warsaw Pact is long gone. The Soviets didn't protest the death of Castro because it let them off the hook without them losing any face."

"So they take him out themselves rather than waiting for him to die."

"I suppose." Dees turned back and watched the sea in front of him. "There a point here?"

"Rumblings," said Randolph. "Cubans are blaming us and there are riots in the streets. . . ."

"Good for the morale of the people. Sacrifice isn't so painful if there is an enemy to hate and to blame."

"And there have been incidents at the base in the last

few days. Cubans firing at the compound and one group in an old car that tried to penetrate the perimeter."

"I know," said Dees. "I've been keeping up with the message traffic."

"Well, after talking to Drummond and hearing what was happening on Cuba, I was thinking that there might be a massed attack on the base."

"Cubans would never be that stupid. Not after what happened to Saddam Hussein." Dees grinned broadly. "We kind of beat him into the ground. A hundred-hour war. Think what would have happened if we'd been real mad."

"Another point, Captain," said Randolph. "Situation in Nicaragua is getting worse. The government there has asked for our aid. There has been a quiet alert announced. Troops are standing by."

Dees didn't say anything for a moment. Instead he thought about what he'd heard. Cubans who might be massing to attack Guantanamo. Government and rebel forces tangling in Nicaragua with the possibility that American forces would be involved in the fighting. And he'd seen a report this morning about some kind of raid into Mexico and a counterattack of some kind across the border. No one was sure if the Mexicans were responsible or if the raiders had shot up the American patrol.

"We're spreading ourselves a little thin here," said Dees.

"Reduced force in Europe and a closing of overseas bases," Randolph reminded him.

"And a reduced military force. We don't have the numbers that we did five or six years ago."

Randolph finished his cigarette and flipped it over the rail. The wind caught it and dragged it toward the stern. Changing the subject, he said, "I'll be glad when we get orders to return home."

"What?" asked Dees, surprised. "There are people who pay thousands for a Caribbean cruise and here you get one for free. Not only that, you get paid handsomely for doing it."

"But on those others I wouldn't have to work and there would be lots of women."

"We have women on board."

"Yes, sir, and with all the rules and regulations I prefer to think of them as sailors, not women."

"A most prudent course," said Dees.

"The only course."

Castro had been unable to sleep. The excitement of getting close to the American stronghold had not evaporated as they had retreated. Sitting under a tree, he had watched the sun come up and watched the faces of the men and women around him. Not the ragged men and women of a revolutionary army who had to make do with what they could find, steal, or capture, but part of the Cuban army with a specific mission. Take the American base once and for all.

Sitting there, with another day to think, Castro began to get scared. Up to that point, with the training and the march, there had been too much to think about, and when he had the time, he was too tired. But now, with nothing to do but wait for the sun to go down, he was scared.

Even though the officers and NCOs had told them, repeatedly, that the Americans were soft and weak, he knew the truth. Jamming had never stopped all the signals from Florida, and the new, powerful transmitters that the Americans used blasted a signal through a solid wall of interference. The government was powerless to stop it and that was what scared Castro. If the Americans had the money and the power and the knowledge to beam entertainment to the Cubans, shows from their networks dubbed into Spanish, then what secrets could they be hiding at the base. Weapons and secrets that would destroy them quickly, before they had a chance.

Another man slipped closer and dropped to the ground near him. "Getting hot," he said.

"Good growing weather. Hot and humid. Makes the crops shoot into the air," said Castro.

"Cigarette?"

Castro shook his head. "Better not. No one said we could smoke."

"Right. Always the way in the army. Tell you when to wake up, go to sleep, what to eat and when to eat it, and when you can enjoy a smoke."

"My name's Cesar Castro."

"Pablo Ramirez."

"You regular?"

"No, drafted for this. Not sure that I'm happy about it, but what can I do?"

"Yeah, what?"

They were quiet for a moment. A bird leaped into the air, squawked, and then disappeared. The treetops rattled, as if something were running through them.

"I'm a little nervous about this," said Ramirez.

Castro knew the feeling but didn't want to admit it. Instead he asked, "Nervous about what?"

"The Americans. I think they've got a few tricks hidden up their sleeves."

"Of course they do. If they didn't, they wouldn't be Americans."

"Still, there are a lot of them on the base."

"But the rewards," said Castro, realizing that he was beginning to sound like one of the sergeants in the lectures before the march.

Ramirez nodded but didn't respond. Finally he said, "I hope to get one of the Jeeps. I could use one of the Jeeps."

"A TV," said Castro, smiling. "I promised my family that I would get them a TV."

"A modest request. You'll have a better shot at it than I will. Probably more TVs around than Jeeps."

A shadow fell across them and both looked up. Castro held a hand above his eyes to shade them. He didn't recognize the man standing there.

"You men are supposed to be resting, not sitting here dreaming of riches."

Ramirez scrambled to his feet. "Just talking, Sarge. Nothing more."

"Get back to your squad."

"Sure, Sarge." Ramirez hurried into the camp, disappearing quickly.

Castro climbed to his feet slowly. He looked at the sergeant, unafraid of the man or the power he momentarily held. "Is this a wise thing we do?"

"Of course. The American base has been a thorn in our side for too long. What do you do to a thorn? You remove it."

"Our soldiers will be killed."

"For the glory of our land." Then, realizing that he was being drawn into a discussion with a private, his voice hardened. "You are to rest now."

"Yes, Sergeant." Castro hesitated, and then hurried toward the middle of the camp where the rest of his squad waited. The hours were slipping by too quickly.

NICARAGUA

Chavez slipped closer and lowered his voice so that it was an almost inaudible whisper. "I think there is someone following us now."

"How many?"

"No more than a squad in the lead element. There's a second group about half a klick behind, and I have no idea how many are in it."

"Damn," said Martinez. "I had hoped that we'd gotten away clean."

"There's a hell of a lot of people in this jungle today," said Chavez. "It's got to be some kind of a coordinated effort. Somebody in Managua has a big mouth."

Martinez's first instinct was to speed up. To run from the enemy. Once the fight had been broken and the E and

E had started, it was difficult to change the mind-set. He glanced at his watch and then looked up into the canopy.

"We'll never get airlift in and this is a crappy place for a fight." He pulled the map out and studied it quickly. The terrain for several miles around was the same. No good place for a fight. The words of an old cavalry officer, written at the time of the Indian Wars, came back to him. The Indians wanted to get them into a running fight so that they could pick off the soldiers one by one. The advantages went to the pursuers in that sort of a battle. "There's a stream half a klick from here," he said.

"We set up on one side of it and ambush when they try to cross?"

Martinez rubbed a hand over his chin. "Best place. Let them think they're driving us and then turn suddenly. Might hold up the others long enough so that we can get away."

"Okay, Captain."

The team began to move again, quickly and quietly, though not as quietly as before. Now that they knew the enemy had spotted them, it didn't matter. Getting to the stream was what mattered.

They rushed downhill. The oppressive heat of the jungle began to sap their strength, soaking them in sweat, dehydrating their bodies, but Martinez wouldn't allow them to slow down. They'd have their chance to rest later.

They stopped suddenly and Martinez could hear the quiet gurgling of a stream. He pushed his way to the front of the patrol and found Gibson crouched on the bank. The stream wasn't very wide or very deep.

"What's the holdup?"

"Didn't want to stir up the sand on the bottom," Gibson said. "Tell the enemy where we crossed."

Martinez was about to agree and then realized that it didn't matter. The enemy was behind them, they'd made no real effort to conceal the noise they made. If the enemy reached the stream and didn't see the silt floating, they might be suspicious.

"Cross it now," said Martinez. "It doesn't matter. Hold up on the other side."

"Yes, sir."

Chavez, his uniform black with sweat, moved up to them. He held his rifle in one hand and leaned the butt against his hip. "They're still back there."

"Go," Martinez said. But Chavez stood where he was, looking back into the jungle. There was nothing to see. The enemy was still too far away.

Martinez turned and moved to the muddy bank of the stream. There was a scrape mark where one of the team slipped. On a normal patrol they'd erase the sign. But this time not doing so might be good because it marked the place they'd crossed the stream.

Martinez stepped onto one of the large stones and then into the center of the stream. The cold water swarmed around his boot and over the top, pouring in, cooling his foot. He splashed out, felt his foot slip, and then caught his balance.

Chavez was right there. "We set up about ten meters back. Good fields of fire all along the stream. They'll never get across it."

"Good."

Martinez worked his way into the jungle and found a place where a tree had fallen to the side until it was caught by those around it, the branches intertwined. He knelt near the vertical trunk, looking under the slanted one. It gave him good protection on both sides but allowed him a wide field of fire to the front.

"Fire on my command," he said to the men on either side of them. They spread the word to the right or left, though it wasn't necessary. Everyone knew they would wait for him to spring the ambush.

For several minutes it was quiet in the jungle. The insects, birds, and animals that had been chased away by their movement to the stream began to return. There was a chattering above them. A mosquito dived at Martinez's ear, sending chills up his spine. But he made no move to swat it. Not with the enemy approaching.

There was a flash of movement that was gone instantly. Then khaki showed through the deep greens of the jungle. Martinez fixed his eyes on it and saw part of an arm holding a weapon. Suddenly the sounds that had been filtering back were gone again.

One figure appeared, looking more like a farmer than a soldier. He wore no shirt, and sandals rather than boots. He carried no weapon and Martinez knew he was a sacrificial goat, someone sent out to draw fire. The man looked at the scrape on the bank and then at the water where the silt still floated. He crouched, reached a hand down, and splashed his face. Satisfied, he stood and turned, walking back the way he had come.

There was more movement in the jungle and the soldiers appeared, fanning out slightly. They walked toward the stream, but hesitantly, as if they expected something to happen. The first of them stepped into the water and halted. He aimed his weapon at the jungle but didn't fire.

More of the enemy soldiers began to cross. One slipped into the water. Those with him laughed, but the sergeant silenced them with a single, quiet word. A man reached out to haul his friend to his feet.

The first of the troops reached the opposite bank, and as he grabbed at a thick vine to pull himself up, Martinez aimed at the center of his chest. He squeezed the trigger, felt the weapon recoil, and saw the sudden explosion of red around the man as he flipped back into the water.

"Fire! Fire! Fire!" he screamed as he swung his rifle, searching for another target. He pulled the trigger and hit another of the enemy, who dropped into the stream, blood spreading in the flowing water.

There was a loud crash, sounding as if everyone had fired at once. The bullets snapped through the air. The enemy soldiers turned to run and were cut down. Half a dozen fell into the water. One managed to climb out of the stream before he was hit, falling back. Another threw himself to the bank and tried to shoot but was hit in the head. The top of his skull exploded in a crimson cloud. He slipped down into the stream. Another tossed his rifle away but was hit before he could surrender. He fell facedown and didn't move.

Martinez emptied his weapon, ducked back, and yanked the magazine from it. He dropped it to the ground, pulled a fresh one from his pouch, and jammed it home. He charged the weapon and then leaped up, but all the enemy soldiers were down.

"Cease fire!" yelled Martinez. He stood there but didn't move forward. He was scanning the jungle beyond the stream, searching for anyone who might have escaped in that direction.

The last of the echoes died away and it was unnaturally quiet, no sounds at all. The light-colored smoke from the weapons hung heavy in the air. The water was pink.

"We check the bodies?" asked Chavez.

"No. Let's just get the hell out of here," said Martinez. "That large unit had to have heard the shooting. They'll be coming on quickly."

"Booby traps?"

Martinez hesitated and then said, "No. Too many civilians in the area, and if the enemy doesn't trip them, then we'll get some innocents."

"I don't think there'll be any innocents out here."

"Doesn't matter; let's get going. Who's on the point?"

"I'll take it."

"Then go."

"Yes, sir."

Daniels sat in his headquarters, a beer in his hand and a telephone at his side. The others were outside his office, also drinking beer and eating the lunch that two of the men who hadn't gone on the raid prepared. That was the good thing about the Defenders of the Texas Revolution. They had a place to go to relax. They didn't have to reappear in society without a few hours to decompress. Made it easier to go home and not seem out of place.

There were phone calls that had to be made. People had died on the raid: one left behind in the factory to be burned, another killed in the shoot-out at the Rio Grande and left behind. They had been so busy trying to get the hell out that they hadn't gotten Hyatt's body. Hadn't even thought about it.

Daniels reached out, touched the phone, and then remembered stories from the Vietnam War. Men and women seeing a military car turning on their street and dreading it because they knew what it meant. Someone was either seriously wounded or had been killed.

The point, however, was that the notification was made in person. Not an impersonal telegram or telephone call. Officers, a chaplain, maybe a doctor, calling on the relatives to let them know that their son, husband, brother, had fallen in battle.

"It's the least we can do," said Daniels, jerking his hand back from the phone, glad for the excuse. "Make the announcement in person."

He drained the beer, crushed the can, and tossed it at the wastebasket. He missed but didn't care. Picking up the beer cans was not his job.

He walked into the outer room. Those who had been on the raid were sitting soberly, drinking and eating. The empty beer cans made quite a stack.

Gannon spotted him and stood, forgetting about the plate of food on her knee. It fell on the floor. She raised an accusing finger. "You said that no one would get hurt."

"I said that we'd do our best to make sure that no one got hurt."

She polished off the beer and threw the can at the wall. It bounced and fell to the floor. "So how many do you think we killed?"

Amos, who had been sitting to the side, looked up. "No more than twenty, twenty-five. But when you raid into foreign territory, people are going to get killed."

"Shit," said Gannon. She turned and walked toward the door.

"Hold it!" yelled Daniels. "Where do you think you're going?"

"I'm getting out of here."

"Not until we get one thing straight. We're in this together. All of us. The weak link breaks the whole chain. No one can say a word about it. Those who died, we'll see that the families are taken care of, but we go running off at the mouth and all our good work is gone."

Rogers had been sitting quietly, eating a chicken leg. He was acting as if nothing had happened the night before. It was business as usual. "You all have to remember the reason for the raid. Keep that firmly in mind."

"Shit. People died."

"People die all the time. Nothin' we can do about it. But we talk out of turn and our good work is gone." Rogers put the leg bone on his plate and set it carefully on the table near him. He stood, looking directly into Gannon's eyes. "You all with us or against us?"

Gannon turned from the door to look at the others in the room, finally nodding. "I'm with you. I just didn't expect the results. Hell, Ralph gunned that guard down right in front of us. I didn't think it was necessary. We could have held him prisoner."

"Okay," said Daniels, "I think it's time that we talked about some things. You take a man hostage or prisoner, and he can fuck up your mission. If he's alive, he can do you harm. If he's dead, there is nothing he can do to you. That is the bottom line, it's the name of the game, the code of the west, the law of the jungle, and the way the cookie crumbles."

"Don't trivialize it," said Gannon.

"And don't make it more than it was. He was a greaser, a beaner who was taking food out of the mouths of good Americans. That is what is important here."

The warning bell sounded suddenly and a red light began to flash. Amos leaped to the switch and cut it off.

He moved to the window, looked out, and said, "Police on the compound."

There was a sudden buzz but Daniels shouted it down. "What is everyone's problem here? We have done nothing and we are in possession of no illegal weapons. Everything is locked away, so everyone fucking relax."

"Two cops," said Amos. "And an army officer. Pistols but no riot guns or backup. Looks routine."

"Everyone sit down and relax. Have a beer. Have some more chicken."

There was a knock at the door and Daniels nodded. "Let them in, Sergeant."

Amos did as he was told and then stepped to the rear, his back against the wall so that he would be behind the cops and soldier when they entered the room.

As they did so Daniels moved forward, grinning, a hand out to be shaken. "Good afternoon, gentlemen. How may we be of service to you?"

The lead cop, a burly man in a tailored uniform, a Smokey the Bear hat, and a pistol in creaking leather, didn't bother to shake hands. He stopped three feet from Daniels and said, "A group of Americans raided a factory in Mexico last night, killed a number of workers, then murdered a number of Mexican police officials before crossing into the United States, killing an American soldier and wounding another."

"I'm afraid that we know nothing about that," said Daniels reasonably.

"Where were all of you last night?"

Daniels stared at the cop for a moment. "We're under no obligation to answer any of your questions." He saw the cop was about to protest and held up a hand. "But we're reasonable people. We were engaged in a night exercise, here on the compound."

"Can you prove that?"

Daniels waved a hand at the others around him. "They all saw me here."

"Uh-huh. And is there anyone who can vouch for them?"

"Do you have any proof that we weren't here?" asked Daniels.

The cop didn't answer. The soldier, a major in dress greens, stood silently, watching the people with a look of disgust on his face.

"We were all here," said Daniels. "You're welcome to ask each of us individually."

"You have weapons," said the cop. "I'd like to examine them."

Daniels took a deep breath and then shook his head. "I don't want to seem uncooperative, but without a warrant I don't think I'll allow that. We've complied with all local, state, and federal regulations. We pay our taxes, obey the laws, and you harass us because you think we might have been involved in something. No proof, just speculation."

The soldier finally spoke. "We have a dead soldier, and if we learn that you are responsible, the entire weight of the United States Army will fall on you."

Daniels turned his attention to the soldier. "Major, we're on your side. We want a strong defense. We believe all military personnel should be well paid. We wouldn't do anything to hurt the army."

The cop looked around for a moment, at the people, at the food and the open cans of beer. He pointed at a rifle on a table. "Booze and weapons don't mix."

"That's right. You'll notice that there is no magazine in it. If we had training to accomplish this afternoon, the beer would be in the refrigerator. Now, if there is nothing else that we can do . . ."

"We'll be keeping an eye on you," said the cop.

"That could be construed as harassment. Our attorneys will be looking into it."

To the others the cop said, "Let's get out of here."

They headed for the door, but before they left, the major said, "If I learn that it was you, I'll be back."

"Sure, Major."

They left and Amos closed the door behind them and watched them through the window. "They're in the car."

"Okay," said Daniels, "that'll give you an idea of what we're up against. Try to help our fellow countrymen and the police harass us."

Gannon said, "But they're right."

"And no one will know that if we keep quiet. Anyone have a problem with that?"

There was no reply. Just silence. Daniels finally said, "Good. We've got that straight."

PANAMA

The meeting was conducted in a small, air-conditioned conference room. There was a table holding a variety of cold beverages, another with a coffeepot, and a third that held a slide projector with a carousel on the top. The four officers sat around a small conference table, an empty chair at its head. There were notepads in front of each chair. A sergeant in a clean, well-pressed uniform stood at parade rest near the door.

Boyce, who had gotten no sleep the night before and who had expected to be in the jungle, was getting irritated. He'd rushed from the airplane to his own comm center to see if anything new had developed on the net, but they had no information. All nets were down and there had been no contact with any of them. One going down wasn't unusual, especially given that all the equipment had been built by the lowest bidder, but all three wouldn't go down at the same time.

Finished there, he'd gone to the office, but no one had any additional information. Orders had been waiting for him to report to the conference room. He, along with Lombard, drove over and the two were now sitting, waiting for someone to appear. Boyce played with the flash on the beret sitting on the table in front of him. Lombard sat quietly, looking as if he was about to fall asleep.

"Gentlemen," said the sergeant suddenly, "General Keaton."

Boyce and Lombard got to their feet and watched Keaton and his aide enter. Keaton took the seat at the head of the table and then waved at them. "Be seated, gentlemen."

Boyce didn't wait for the general to start the briefing or ask for questions. "Just what in the hell is going on here?"

"Colonel Boyce," said Keaton, "I'm sorry for the sudden change in plans but the situation has changed radically in the last twenty-four hours."

"I know. I've lost contact with my three teams in Nicaragua."

Keaton took a deep breath and then glanced at the coffeepot. The sergeant caught the look and jumped toward it, filling a cup quickly and placing it in front of the general. When Keaton had his coffee, he said, "We've gotten some top-secret assessments from both the CIA station in Managua and our own intelligence people at the embassy. Situation is going to hell in a hand basket and the Nicaraguan government is asking for American military aid in the form of weapons, ammunition, and most importantly troops."

"Christ," said Boyce. "What in the hell is going on up there?"

"The insurgents are beginning to make their push. I think they believe that the time is right for them and that we won't intercede."

"What gives them that idea?" asked Boyce. "We rolled through Iraq."

Keaton nodded and his aide spoke. "That was the Middle East and this is Central America. The feeling among the various factions is that the United States, to avoid being called a bully, will not interfere in the internal workings of the various countries."

"Though we've been doing it for years," said Boyce.

"Not openly. Economic aid, military aid, advisers, but not armed soldiers."

"And none of the countries have asked for our military assistance in the last thirty years. Now they have. Now they're afraid of losing their power, they know that we can keep them in power. They saw what happened in Kuwait. We asked for free elections. We asked for reforms, but we demanded nothing. I think, based on that, they're going to use our help and expect little in the way of interference."

Keaton took over. "Rationale doesn't matter. The point is that the government has already approached us for assistance, military assistance. The Eighteenth Airborne Corps is ready to board the airplanes and drop into the capital."

"Then we should have gone in yesterday," said Boyce. "We should have been on the ground now."

"No!"

"Excuse me, General," said Boyce, "but we could have been acting as pathfinders. DZs set up and ready—"

"No," said Keaton again. "They'll probably be landing at the airport." He grinned. "Not the way the Eighteenth likes to make its entrance."

Boyce had to laugh. "No. They like to fill the skies with chutes."

"The point," said Keaton, "is that we've been asked to assist and we need you here to help coordinate. The old mission is canceled in light of the new."

"Then I need to get my people out," said Boyce.

"As quickly as possible," said Keaton. "They may be

going right back in as pathfinders because they've seen the country and are familiar with it."

"Right now we're having some trouble. . . ."

"I'm not interested in excuses," said Keaton. "You are authorized to do whatever you have to so that the teams are recovered, but they will be out within the next twenty-four hours and ready to deploy with the forward elements of the Eighteenth."

"Yes, General."

"You will have your people here, ready, within twelve hours. Airlift is available and waiting. Coordination with Colonel Glen Canon for air-strike capability if you need it. That's how important this is becoming."

"Understood, General."

Keaton got to his feet, glanced at the two Special Forces officers sitting at the table. "Gentlemen, as our British friends used to say, the balloon is about to go up. Let's be ready."

Boyce said, "Yes, sir," and watched Keaton disappear through the door. When the general was gone, he turned to Lombard. "We're in some deep shit here."

There was nothing that Lombard could say.

Reisman sat quietly, watching the breathing shape in the bed. He leaned toward the man and asked, "You know what happened?"

"Yeah. I know."

Reisman's eyes stung from lack of sleep. Crossing a dozen time zones, airplane rides, and airport food exhausted him. Then there had been a rush to get him to Texas, so that he had gotten no real rest. His sleep schedule out of phase, he was wide-awake at two or three in the morning and dragging about noon. He was hungry at the wrong times.

And now he had to play games with a man who would answer one question at a time. And just the question asked. Reisman knew that if he asked if the man knew what time it was, he'd say, "Yes."

"You want to share it with me?" asked Reisman.

"No."

The body on the bed stirred, groaned, and the eyes fluttered open. The man got up and walked to the door. He leaned out and shouted, "Nurse."

Reisman was on his feet and moved to the bed. The woman there reached up, fingered the tube in her nose, and then looked at the IV hung next to the bed. She lifted a hand weakly and let it fall back. Her color was bad and her eyes were bloodshot.

"Who you?"

"Reisman. Press. You up to a couple of questions?"

She closed her eyes in answer.

Reisman stood there, looking down at her, wondering if she had gone back to sleep. A nurse burst into the room and moved rapidly to the bed. She looked down at the patient, checked her pulse, and lifted an eyelid to examine the pupil.

"She say anything?" asked the nurse.

"Just asked who I was and then closed her eyes."

"Should she have known you?"

Reisman shook his head. "No."

"Fine. If you'll wait outside with the other gentleman, I'll do my job."

Reisman turned and walked out of the room. He found the other man standing in the hallway, leaning against the wall. "I guess she'll be fine," he said.

"Nurse tell you that?"

"She was awake and spoke to me," said Reisman.

"Fuckers gunned her down," said the man.

Reisman held out a hand and said, "Morris Reisman."

The man hesitated, took the hand, and shook it. "Roger Nagy. Sorry, but the reporters have been around her like vultures."

"Doing their jobs," said Reisman.

"Just as the Nazis were doing theirs. Wonder why

that excuse didn't work for them, but all you reporters seem to think it excuses your intrusions?"

Reisman shrugged. "Public-affairs officer cleared me in here. I guess he thought that I could be of help."

"Doing what?"

"Sometimes," said Reisman, "if the information gets out, those who know something come forward because they know others are looking for it. They provide pieces to the puzzle and we end up learning the truth."

Nagy took a deep breath and breathed out audibly. He reached into a pocket, took out a cigarette, and then remembered that he wouldn't be able to smoke it. Holding it in his hand, he said, "We don't know who it was. Shot it out with Mexican authorities, crossed into Texas, and then shot Sandi and her sergeant."

"Sandi?"

"Paulding."

"And you are?"

"From the headquarters company. We didn't want her to awaken without a familiar face around."

"Uh-huh."

"We don't know exactly what happened. She made a call on the radio, but before the backup platoon could arrive, the enemy, whoever they are, shot Sandi and got out. Our people found them. Got a medivac in." He shook his head. "Shouldn't have happened."

"Why was the backup so slow?"

"Because we didn't think that we really needed it. Our job was recon. Give the information to the border patrol or the local police. The army is not a police agency, though the Congress keeps trying to force us into that role."

The nurse came out and closed the door. She looked at the two men and said, "She'll be fine. She'll probably sleep the rest of the day."

"How badly hurt is she?"

"Wounds are painful and she might have stiffness in her shoulder, but she should recover fully."

Nagy asked, "Is it all right if I wait in the room?"

"She's going to be sleeping, but you can stay if you want."

"Thanks."

Nagy and Reisman entered the room again. Reisman walked to the bed and looked down at Paulding. She was pale, looking sick, but even with that he could see that she was a good-looking woman. He watched her sleep for a moment.

"There is no reason for you to be here," said Nagy. There was an edge to his voice, telling the reporter he wasn't welcome.

Taking a card from his pocket, Reisman gave it to Nagy. "I'll be in touch. I'd like to talk to her, when she's up to it."

"Check in with the public-affairs office first."

"Sure."

Frankowski, along with a dozen other pilots, a few ground-pounding officers, and the intelligence sections, sat in the briefing room while Colonel Hahn paced on the stage. He glanced at his watch and then the clock on the wall above the door and at the empty place. A moment later a pilot opened the doors, hurried to his seat, and sat down, trying to look as if he'd been there all along but failing miserably.

"Okay," said Hahn. "Sterne, tell the guard that no one enters now. The briefing is beginning."

"Yes, sir."

Returning to the podium, Hahn said, "There has been an official protest from the Mexican government. They have mentioned, specifically, our flyby this morning."

"Under orders," said Frankowski.

"Under orders," agreed Hahn. "But they have also protested the destruction of their car factory and they're blaming the United States for that. Diplomatic relations are strained and I understand that they are considering a move to throw our ambassador out of their country. Or we're going to recall him."

"What does this have to do with us?" asked Sterne.

"We have a huge common border with Mexico," said Hahn. "It makes the possibility of covert crossings simple. . . ." He leaned on the lectern and clasped his hands. "You know, I know, and the Mexicans have to know that they can do nothing against us. Declaring war would be ridiculous. Our technology, training, and ability would sweep them from the skies and lay waste to any military force."

"Then there is nothing for any of us to worry about," said Sterne.

"But the lessons of the past aren't all that clear. Pancho Villa raided. Hit and got out. No problem. That is the lesson they'll remember. They'll dip deeply into the past, forgetting that what was possible a hundred years ago is no longer possible. We'll have combat air patrols along the border to stop it."

"How long?" asked Frankowski.

Hahn shrugged. "As long as it takes. If the FBI can find the raiders and turn them over to the Mexican authorities, then tensions will ease. That's if the raiders were American citizens and not someone trying to topple the current Mexican government. If the raiders can't be identified, tensions will rise, and if the Mexicans try something in retaliation but we stop it, that'll turn the heat up another notch."

"This is ridiculous," said Sterne. "Fucking stupid."

"In a world where macho counts, where a country's strength is seen as something to be attacked, where governments think in terms of getting even, I can see where this can escalate quickly into a full-scale conflict. Can't let this go unpunished."

"Stupid," said Sterne.

Frankowski grinned. "I'd like a chance to get even with the dumb son of a bitch who put the hole in my airplane."

"See," said Hahn, pointing. "That's what I'm talking about. Two seven-year-old kids standing in the school yard making faces at one another. Someone threw a snowball and now we have to prove they can't get away with that."

"I was kidding," said Frankowski.

"Yeah, but the governments aren't," said Hahn. "And that's the real problem."

NICARAGUA

They fled the ambush as quickly as they could disengage. They left the dead and wounded where they fell and didn't attempt to exploit the advantage. They got the hell out as fast as they could, heading downhill to a point where the jungle thinned.

After two hours of solid hiking they stopped. This time Martinez told the men to take a break, drink some water, and eat some of the MREs. Half the men on alert while half relaxed. Jones checked their wounded and found that they were ready to run if it came to that.

Espinoza set up a small UHF radio, strung up an antenna in the low branches of a tree, and then crouched at the base of it. When he was ready, he asked, "You want me to make contact with net?"

"Go ahead," said Martinez. "Let them know that we

were attacked, have wounded, but we're clear for the moment."

"Yes, sir."

Martinez moved to the north, along the path they had followed to get where they were. He scanned the jungle, the trees, bushes, ferns, grass, and undergrowth. By studying it carefully, he could spot their path. Little things like a bent branch of a bush or a twisted leaf that was not aligned with the others.

There was movement in the jungle, but it was the animal life and not the enemy.

Chavez came up behind him and crouched. "We're to get the hell out."

"What?"

"Recall. Get to the closest LZ as quickly as possible and get the hell out. Choppers are airborne and ready to come in just as soon as we give them the word."

"What in the hell is going on?"

"I don't know," said Chavez. He sat down, his back to a tree trunk, and pulled off his boony hat. His face was wet with sweat, his hair soaked. "Somebody has a bug up his ass."

"We haven't done very well here," said Martinez, his voice low.

"Got those people away from the bad guys and sent them home."

"Yeah, but that's it." Martinez checked the time. "You look at the map?"

"Not yet. Brought you the word."

Martinez twisted around, propped his rifle up, and pulled out his map. "Jungle," he said. "Jungle and hills."

"Looks like there might be something here, about what, two klicks?" Chavez pointed at the map.

"Or here," said Martinez. "That'd be about half a klick beyond your LZ."

"On a line," said Chavez. "If the jungle is as thin as it is here and we don't have any trouble with the bad guys, we could be at the closest in an hour."

"On a chopper heading home in about an hour. I think we should move now."

"Yes, sir. Should I take the point?"

"We'll get there faster if you do. Give the men on alert a chance to get a cold drink and then let's get going."

Chavez nodded, got to his feet, and moved off to spread the word to the others. Martinez kept his attention focused on the back trail. Still no sign that the enemy was coming. They had held up at the ambush. No one wanted it to happen again.

Five minutes later, Martinez got to his feet. He moved back to Chavez and said, "Let's get going, Sergeant."

Chavez moved to the south, waited until the rest of the team was up and ready, and then stepped off. In seconds he had disappeared into the vegetation. The team followed him in single file, the men carefully checking the jungle around them, heads swiveling as they moved. They spread out as far as the jungle would let them, each man keeping the man in front of him in sight but losing sight of the point.

Martinez scanned the jungle where they had rested but saw that the men had left no easily seen signs. They picked up their trash, had used the vegetation to conceal themselves, but now that they were moving, the plants were springing back into position. In an hour it would be nearly impossible to tell where they had been.

Martinez joined the end of the line, but he kept checking the rear. He listened for unnatural sounds, sudden flights of birds or scrambling of the monkeys. He listened for the snapping of a twig or the misstep of an impatient soldier, but he heard nothing.

They marched through the steambath heat of the jungle; the canopy over them trapped the moisture, holding it close to the ground. Sweat couldn't evaporate in the humidity, so that it was as if each man was wrapped in a wet towel. It dripped down the face and soaked into the already saturated collar. They had to be careful that they didn't dehydrate.

They were moving down off a mountain, the slope becoming more gentle and finally leveling. They worked their way across the horizontal valley floor, the jungle thinning as they altered their direction, heading toward the northwest. It became more like a manicured forest than a thick jungle. The animal trails were wider and more easily identified.

Martinez was thinking of calling a halt for ten minutes, but Chavez stopped them. The men drew together and then fanned out in a rough circle, each man facing out, searching for the enemy that seemed to have lost them.

Chavez worked his way to the rear, found Martinez, and said, "We're getting close to the first LZ."

Martinez slipped to one knee and tried to wipe the sweat from his face, but the sleeve of his uniform was already soaked. "Looks like we've given them the slip."

"Maybe," said Chavez, "but if they figured we'd want airlift out, maybe they leaped ahead of us. There aren't that many good LZs around here."

"You could have gone all day and not said that. But then, I was thinking the same thing. Let's keep moving."

Chavez nodded and in a few moments they were again hiking through the jungle, but more slowly as Chavez searched harder for the enemy in case they had somehow figured out the team's destination.

As they climbed a gentle slope the jungle thinned. Sunlight streamed down in large shafts. There were huge, bright spots that seemed to glow green. Chavez held up a hand, and the team scattered.

When Martinez approached, Chavez pointed. "LZ is right through there."

Martinez moved a little closer. Through a gap in the vegetation he could see the LZ. There was a single tree growing at the far end that was out of the way. Plenty of space to get one or two helicopters in. Grass that was knee-high covered the ground.

"Looks peaceful," said Chavez.

"Take a couple of men and swing around to the right. Carefully. See if there's any sign of an ambush."

"Take thirty minutes to do it right."

"Take the time," said Martinez. "We're close to getting out of here."

"Yes, sir."

"I'll head in the other direction. Leave Espinoza and the wounded here to guard our trail. In an hour or so we'll be on our way in."

Chavez pointed at a couple of the men and led them off into the jungle. Martinez ordered two of the others to follow him. He told Epinoza to make radio contact.

On the circuit of the LZ Martinez and his men found nothing. There was no sign that anyone had been in the area for months. He halted at the far end and watched Chavez and his men come out of the jungle.

"Looks clear," said Chavez, his voice louder.

"Let's get ready to get the hell out of here," said Martinez.

This time they walked through the center of the clearing. Martinez wanted to make sure that nothing was hidden in the grass, that there was no great hole that could suck in a helicopter or kill a man who fell in. He needed to make sure that there were no stumps to impale a chopper and that the ground was level and smooth.

As he reentered the jungle and walked over to Espinoza, the radioman was crouched, facing to the south. He turned, looked up at the captain, and said, "There's something coming."

Martinez dropped and stared into the jungle but heard and saw nothing. "You sure?"

"Sounds like a squad, maybe more."

"You make contact?"

"Yes, sir. Helicopters are inbound. We'll need to pop smoke in about twenty minutes."

Chavez appeared, crouched, and pointed to the south. Martinez nodded and then said, quietly, "Twenty minutes."

"There's someone out there," said Chavez.

"Yeah. I think we'd better prepare to stop them."

"I could do it with three men," said Chavez.

"You, me, and two others," said Martinez. "Cline, I think. And Jones, in case one of us gets hit."

"Yes, sir."

Martinez stood and worked his way to the rear. He found Alvarez and knelt near the lieutenant. "You're going to have to get the men ready at the edge of the clearing. When the choppers are down, hold it until we can get back."

"You'll be . . . ?"

"Back about half a klick to block the trail. Espinoza should stay in contact with the choppers."

"Yes, sir."

"Get moving," said Martinez.

He turned and headed back to Chavez. The sergeant had found Cline and Jones, and all were ready. He waved at them, and they began to move through the jungle slowly.

Martinez found the perfect place to set up an ambush. The enemy would have to move through a light patch of jungle while they could hide in the dense growth.

Cline set up two claymore mines, angling them away from the center. It would force the enemy into the middle, where the killing ground was the clearest.

Chavez looked at his watch. "Fifteen minutes," he whispered.

Martinez hoped it wouldn't be that long. The sounds were getting louder now: the quiet rustling of cloth and the occasional squeak of leather or the rattle of metal. The enemy was moving carefully.

Martinez strained to hear the distant sound of the choppers. The instant he heard them, he would order Cline to fire the claymores. The enemy, no matter where he was, would take cover. The few minutes bought by the maneuver would be enough to let them escape.

The quiet pop of a helicopter's rotors cut through the

undercurrent of sound. Martinez turned to look back toward the LZ but could see nothing through the thick canopy.

In front of him the sound was getting louder and he saw a flash of movement. He pointed at Cline and nodded. Cline understood the signal and triggered the claymores. There was a crash, followed by a second one. The explosion shook the jungle as the steel balls cut through the vegetation and the enemy soldiers. There were shouts of surprise, pain, and then orders. Firing erupted. Bullets snapped overhead, slashing at the trees, branches, and leaves.

Martinez pointed a thumb over his shoulder. Chavez, seeing the signal, stood and began backing away, his weapon pointed at the enemy. Cline followed.

Two men appeared suddenly, running toward Martinez. He flipped the selector to full auto and pulled the trigger, firing in short bursts. One man was hit and went down immediately. The second dived for cover.

Firing from the enemy increased. Martinez, hugging the ground, began to retreat. A grenade exploded to his right, the dirt, shrapnel, and debris raining into the jungle with a sound like frying bacon.

That didn't slow Martinez. He kept crawling, thought that he was clear, and got to his feet. Then, hunched over and keeping his head down, he ran through the jungle, hurdling a fallen tree. He caught up with Cline.

"Go. Hurry."

The helicopters were closer now; the sound of the turbine engines and the popping rotors dominated the jungle. The firing behind was tapering off, and Martinez knew that the enemy was beginning to maneuver.

Chavez had stopped and was facing to the rear. Both Martinez and Cline ran past him, and as they did so Chavez whirled and joined them.

They reached the edge of the LZ and saw a cloud of green smoke billowing from the center. At the far end, above the trees, the sunlight was winking from the windshields of the choppers.

Martinez saw Alvarez and yelled, "Get moving."

Alvarez didn't speak. He spun and waved a hand. The team filtered out of the trees, running toward the center as the first of the choppers flared. The rotor wash flattened the grass, sucked the green smoke up, swirling it around.

The helicopter touched down, and as it did so Alvarez and five of the men leaped into the rear. Door guns were leveled but remained silent.

The second helicopter touched down behind the first. Martinez and the rest of the team ran for it. The deep grass made it difficult. It seemed to claw at him, trying to drag him down, slow him. He was running in slow motion, and it seemed that the helicopter was getting no closer.

There was noise behind him, but Martinez kept his attention focused on the chopper and didn't turn. He saw a man moving, twisting his weapon around, but he didn't begin to fire. There was a popping behind him. Someone shooting at him.

He ducked once, instinctively, and nearly fell, but then was up and running well, dodging to the right, out of the line of fire. As soon as he was clear, the door gun opened fire, the muzzle flash easily visible even in the brightness of the afternoon.

Martinez reached the door, stepped up, and felt a half-dozen hands grab him. He was lifted from the ground as the chopper leaped into the sky. Twisting around, he could see the enemy firing up at them. Red tracers, looking pink in the sunlight, flashed downward, disappearing into the jungle.

And then they were hugging the trees as they raced from the landing zone. Martinez sat up and looked out the cargo-compartment door, but the LZ and the enemy soldiers were gone.

"Everyone clear?" he asked.

Chavez, shouting over the roar of the turbine and the

pop of the rotors, said, "We're all clear. Everyone out and no new wounded."

"That was close," he said.

"Closer than it should be," said Chavez.

Martinez nodded, but smiled broadly. They had cheated death again.

SAN ANTONIO, TEXAS

Reisman walked out of the air-conditioning of the hospital into the blazing heat and oppressive humidity of the late afternoon. He walked across the parking lot and found his car with the driver sitting on the hood, staring up at the thick clouds. The radio was turned up and it seemed the Cubs were losing another.

"You ready?" asked Webster, without moving.

"Who's in command around here?"

"Of what? The base?"

"The commander of the unit where that officer was assigned."

Webster hopped down off the car, walked around to the driver's side, and opened the door. Pulling a notebook off the front seat, he flipped through it and said, "General Nickson."

"I want to see him."

"Our pass is about to expire, and once we're on the base, we're not supposed to be driving around the facility. We go to our destination and then we get the hell off."

"Where do we find this Nickson?"

Webster tossed the notebook back into the car. "I'd have to look it up, but we really should head to the gate."

"Couple of minutes one way or the other won't matter."

"You spent much time on military bases?"

"I was in the army back in the late sixties. Spent some time in Vietnam."

"Then you should know that they hold you to the very letter of the law. Speed limit says fifteen, they mean fifteen, not sixteen or seventeen, but fifteen. They say our pass expires in three hours, it expires. I fuck this up and we won't be granted the privilege of returning to the base."

"I still want to see the general."

"We'll have to drive to the gate and get our pass renewed. I thought you were all fired up to get your room and get to work on the important story."

Reisman rubbed his chin and then grinned. "I think I might have found the real story."

The helicopters took them out to a carrier in the Pacific. They landed on the flight deck, amid the parked fighters, transports, and reconnaissance craft. As they hit the deck they were surrounded by sailors, swarming around them as if they were the newest exhibits in a zoo.

Men with stretchers and a couple of women in crisp white were moving toward the lead helicopter. Jones leaped off and trotted toward them, his words lost in the sound of the turbines and the wind across the flight deck. The two wounded men got themselves out of the choppers but then were forced onto the stretchers. Jones looked over at Martinez, and then followed the medical people and the stretchers off the flight deck.

An officer in sweat-stained khakis pushed through the crowd, stopped in front of Martinez, and saluted. "Welcome aboard. I'm afraid that your stay is going to be a short one."

"Time enough for clean clothes and a shower?"

"No, sir. Time enough for a cold drink, to hit the head, and that's about it."

Martinez looked at the crowd around him, sailors in clean uniforms, though a few were slightly grease-stained. He felt the cooling breeze blowing over the flight deck. And he thought about the five or six thousand sailors on the ship complete with closed-circuit television, movies, and air-conditioning. A floating city in the middle of the ocean.

Turning, Martinez called, "Sergeant Chavez?"

"Yes, sir."

"The men will have a few minutes. Make sure that no one strays too far."

The navy officer said, "Rubens, take these guys below and see that they get something cold to drink."

"Aye-aye, sir."

The officer pointed to a gray-painted plane sitting on the deck a hundred feet away. "The crew is aboard and waiting for you."

"Thanks, Lieutenant," said Martinez.

He followed his men as they entered the island set on the side of the flight deck. They climbed down a ladder and were shown a latrine. Martinez stopped in front of a sink, looked at the mirror over it, and grinned at himself. Sweat-damp hair hung down and his face was a nightmare mask of camo paint now smeared into an ill-defined mess. He turned on the water, surprised that it was hot, and then adjusted it. He bent, scooped water up in his hands, and scrubbed at his face.

Chavez came in, his face mostly clean, though there were remnants of the camo paint at his hairline. "Navy knows how to live. Ever think that we joined the wrong service?"

"Constantly." Martinez straightened and looked at himself. He rubbed a hand through his hair and then reached for a paper towel.

Finally the rest of the team finished, and were escorted back to the flight deck. Now they realized how bright it could be on the ocean. The sunlight reflected from the water, making it much brighter than it got on land, or in the jungle, where the sunlight was filtered through the canopy.

The transport was smaller than the C-130 that had carried them into Nicaragua, and was set up like a commercial aircraft with individual seats rather than the red webbing that was used in some military aircraft. The loadmaster walked down the center aisle making sure that all were belted in.

Before the engines were started, he said, "Takeoff won't be quite as smooth as you've become used to. Because we've got a fairly short runway, we need to hit full power and speed as quickly as possible. There will be some discomfort."

"Great," said Alvarez.

Martinez fastened his seat belt, looked at the gray-painted bulkhead, and shook his head. An hour earlier—he looked at his watch—two hours earlier he had been running through the jungle, an enemy force chasing him. He'd been involved in a firefight and then had gotten out, using helicopters brought in for the extraction. Now he was sitting in the safety of a transport on the deck of an aircraft carrier. No time for transition. One minute under fire and the next peace and calm.

In that moment he understood some of the pressure that was on by police officers. He'd always laughed at the stories of cops under fire because they were never involved in firefights with a thousand armed men. The police were usually the ones with the reinforcements, and in their line of work the shooting lasted a minute or less. In the army the fights could last for hours or days and the enemy could number in the thousands.

The problem wasn't the numbers, the types of weapons, or the length of the fight. The problem was the calm of one moment being replaced, with no chance to think, with the danger of the next. One minute trying to fire as many rounds as possible, to knock down the enemy, and the next sitting in the car, or driving to the station where there was no more danger.

Martinez now understood that. He felt his belly churn and felt the chills up and down his spine. He thought of things that he should be doing and then rejected them because he was on a transport, on a carrier, in the middle of the ocean. None of it was important because of his current situation. He'd lived on the edge for several days and now the edge was dulled. All he had to do was sit with his seat belt fastened and relax. It was difficult, but that was all he had to do.

The first of the engines roared to life. The plane was closed up and the air-conditioning came on. The second engine was started, and after a few moments the aircraft began to move.

"Here we go," said Alvarez.

Martinez closed his eyes and tried to relax, but the nervous energy of the last few days had failed to burn out. He kept opening his eyes to search for the lurking enemy, though no enemy was near.

He was shoved violently back in the aircraft as they took off. They climbed steeply into the nearly cloudless Pacific sky, wheeled around, and headed toward the southeast and the coast of Panama.

As they leveled off and the drone of the engines was reduced, Chavez leaned over. "I don't like this sort of thing. Jerked out of the jungle at the last minute."

"Actually," said Martinez, "I kind of liked it, given the circumstances."

"No, sir," said Chavez. "I meant that we were basically recalled. I don't mind getting out. I don't like getting out on such a priority basis. Whatever they have in mind is going to be worse than what we faced."

"We'll have time to prepare for it," said Martinez. "Besides, it was getting hairy in the jungle."

"Only because the air support didn't arrive."

"We didn't give it time. And the choppers did arrive. At the right time."

Chavez shrugged. "Coordination was a little sloppy."

"Which could be our fault. We lost radio contact because of the attack."

"Sure."

They lapsed into silence. Martinez tilted his seat back as far as it could go, surprised that the navy would spend money on such a luxury but grateful for it. He closed his eyes and relaxed, letting his mind drain. He tried to think of nothing at all. Not the recent days in the jungle, not the firefight, and not the reason for the sudden recall.

A moment later he jerked wide-awake, aware of everything around him. He sat back, took a deep breath, and wished that it hadn't happened. He knew the cause. Tension, pure and simple. The mind had relaxed, but the body hadn't gotten the word.

He relaxed again, his eyes closed, and he thought it would be impossible to sleep. But the next thing he knew he was being shaken awake. Chavez was grinning at him.

"We're about to land, Captain."

"Good," said Martinez.

The plane touched down, taxied, and then rolled to a stop. Martinez and the team waited until the loadmaster had opened the hatch. Then they lined up and exited slowly, stooping and climbing down into the late-afternoon humidity of Panama. Thunderheads were building in the west, dark ominous clouds that threatened rain.

A Jeep roared across the tarmac and stopped close to them. A sergeant leaped out, ran forward, and asked, "Captain Martinez?"

"Here."

"General Keaton and Colonel Boyce would like to meet with you."

"Right this minute?"

"Yes, sir."

Martinez handed his weapon to Chavez but then said, "Last time this happened the general was less than pleased with me for showing up in a dirty uniform. I think I'll take time for a shower and a shave."

The sergeant looked as if he was going to protest but merely said, "Yes, sir."

"You have transport for the men?"

"No, sir. Just you."

Martinez climbed into the Jeep, held out his hand for his weapon, and said, "Sergeant Chavez, please join me. We'll get some transport arranged."

"Yes, sir."

They rode off the field to a small one-story building. The driver said, "You can find a phone in there."

Chavez hopped out and disappeared inside.

"I'll take you to the transient quarters."

"Fine."

In a few minutes Martinez had checked in and had sent the driver toward the clothing store to get him a fresh set of fatigues. While he showered and shaved, the driver bought him the new clothes, and about the time that Martinez had finished with the shower, standing under the fine spray just because it felt so damned good, the driver was back. Martinez shaved quickly, donned the clean uniform, pulling the tags from them. He knew that he didn't look more like a recruit than a professional soldier, but his uniform was clean, so that the general wouldn't be insulted as he had been the last time Martinez reported directly from the jungle.

They then drove off for the headquarters where the general and Colonel Boyce were waiting. Martinez still carried his weapon, afraid to leave it unattended in the

VOQ room. Had the others been with him, he could have let Chavez or Alvarez guard it.

Inside, he walked down the hallway, was directed to a conference room by a small black woman in a perfect uniform. He opened the door, where both the general and Colonel Boyce were waiting.

Boyce jumped up. "Captain Martinez, what in the hell happened?"

"Colonel?"

"Radio contact went down and then—"

"Enemy hit us at the camp. Company-sized operation, maybe a light battalion."

"Gentlemen," said Keaton, "you can discuss that later. Right now we've got a new problem."

"Certainly, General," said Boyce.

"If you'll sit down." Keaton looked at Martinez. "Would you care for a Coke?"

"No, sir."

"Then let's get started."

Boyce waited for a moment and then asked, "Do you have any idea what happened to the other teams?"

"No, sir. All I know is that we were hit with a large force. Had they been better trained or had there been more of them, we'd have had trouble getting clear."

"Gentlemen, I might remind you that time is running out. I want to be able to field the teams within the next twenty-four hours," said Keaton.

"Jesus," said Martinez.

"Exactly, Captain," said Keaton. "The problem is that we need pathfinders on the ground for the deployment of the Eighteenth Airborne Corps if the Nicaraguan government asks for it."

"We just got back," said Martinez.

"Then you know the situation in Nicaragua," said Keaton. "You'll be debriefed by intelligence and then resupplied for the flight to Managua."

Martinez looked at Boyce, hoping that the colonel

would add something, but the man sat quietly. Martinez repeated, "We just got out of the field."

"This isn't a big deal," said Keaton. "A few markers for the Eighteenth and they'll take care of the fighting. Hell, you could probably take a commercial flight into Managua and then drive out. There is going to be no opposition."

"Yes, sir," said Martinez.

Keaton opened a leather folder, took out a single, eight-by-ten black-and-white photo, and pushed it toward Martinez. "That's Colonel Jesus Castillo."

Without looking at it, Martinez said, "I know."

"He's the real thorn in the side of the government. He's agitating the country, creating more trouble than he's worth. If you should happen to see him, I don't think anyone in Washington, or in Managua for that matter, would mourn his loss."

"Is he a target?" asked Martinez.

"If you see him and have the opportunity," said Keaton, shrugging.

"Noted," said Martinez.

"You may keep the photograph," said Keaton. "In case you need it."

"No thanks."

Boyce finally spoke. "Be twenty-four hours before the flight. Time for a little rest, a steak, and then a quick mission without too many problems."

"Yes, sir," said Martinez.

"We go in tomorrow night at zero-one-zero-zero, prepare the DZs, and wait for the airborne to hit about zero-five-zero-zero," said Keaton.

Martinez sat quietly, staring at the maps, unable to believe it. He said, "Yes, sir."

"We'll have the op order cut tomorrow morning and that'll give you the rest of the day for your planning."

Martinez realized that there was nothing he could say to stop this. The decision had been made. It violated everything he knew. No time for planning, no time to study the terrain, the latest intelligence. Just drop back into Nicaragua and be ready for the Eighteenth when it arrived.

He looked at the general and said the only thing that he could think of. "Yes, sir."

NUEVA ROSITA, MEXICO

The man was older than anyone else in the room. He was larger, with thick black hair slicked down, a big belly hanging over the leather of his black belt, and small, hate-filled eyes. He looked at the assembled men, all dressed in khakis, all wearing sidearms, and all waiting for him to say something.

He looked from face to face and then said, "I am Colonel Juan Guerrero. I have seen the destruction of the factory, I have spoken with the police officials, and I have examined the river crossing. I think I can say without fear of contradiction that it was the Americans. They invaded our country, killed our countrymen, and have gotten away without punishment. The American government is denying all knowledge of the activity and they are planning no retribution against those who raided us."

A murmur spread among the assembled men. One of them said, "The gringos care nothing for our people."

"Exactly," said Guerrero. "Because of that we have been authorized by the government in Mexico City to exact retribution for the outrage."

There was an explosion of noise as each of the men began to talk or shout questions. Guerrero grinned broadly, thinking that he had calculated correctly. The men felt their manhood had been challenged. Foreigners had invaded their country and it was time to get even with them.

"Our authorization is not official," said Guerrero. "Our government will disavow knowledge of our activities if any of us are captured. Our government, like that of the Americans, will say that it was a private group, criminals, who raided across the border."

Guerrero let the men talk then. Let them discuss the problem among themselves. Let them get used to the idea of raiding a city or town in Texas. He stood in front of the group, professionals who had been handpicked after Guerrero had been told of the raid early in the morning. He had been authorized to retaliate as quickly as he could arrange it.

Finally he stopped the discussion. He raised his voice and called, "Let me have your attention. Now. Let me have your attention."

As they fell silent he said, "I have a plan designed to exact the largest price from the Americans." He turned to a map on the easel standing near him. He picked up a pointer and snapped it against the map. "There are a number of targets. Here. Here. And here. Small towns on the Texas side of the border away from large cities where there would be a large police force that could respond quickly."

"Any specific target?" asked a man.

Guerrero nodded. "They destroyed a car-manufacturing plant that employed over three thousand of our countrymen. There are a couple of plants—one clothing maker, and three petroleum-processing plants—that we could destroy in retribution. My inclination is to hit the plant here. It's only fifteen miles from the border, would tend to burn well, and allow us to get in and out in less than an hour."

"How many men are you going to take?"

Guerrero moved away from the map, set the pointer down, and then walked around to sit on a desk. "Forty men, armed with automatic weapons including a half-dozen grenade launchers, two antitank weapons, and one rocket launcher. With those we don't even have to get close to the plant. High explosives launched from outside the fences will do it."

"Then why the extra men?"

"To make sure that we can get close and that we can get out. Nothing left to chance. If they try to stop us, we shoot our way out."

"Won't they be expecting this? Won't they be watching the border."

Guerrero grinned at them. These were not dummies, wanting only revenge. These were thinking men who wanted to inflict damage and then get out. The raid wouldn't be a success if they didn't get away with it. "They'll think that we, the 'greaseballs' to the south, will talk before we act. They think they can buy us off. They won't think that we'll be able to retaliate quickly."

"When do we act?"

"At the earliest tonight. At the latest tomorrow. It won't take long to put this together. The weapons and the transport have been provided and there will be a diversion near Nuevo Laredo so that the Americans will be kept busy."

"Good," said one of the men.

Guerrero nodded and decided that it would be a solid group. They had a better-than-even chance of pulling it off and making the Americans look bad. He stood and returned to the map to begin the detailed briefing.

•   •   •

Late in the afternoon one of the sergeants walked through the camp, getting everyone ready. He stopped near a small knot of men who were sitting on a couple of rotting logs and announced, "We go tonight."

Castro looked up, held a hand above his eyes to shade them, and felt his belly grow cold. To that point the coming fight had been like a scheduled visit to the doctor. It was something in the future. Now the future was gone and all Castro could do was nod dumbly.

"I want everyone to check his weapon, make sure that it is clean and well oiled. I want everyone to check the equipment he is responsible for and to make sure that it is all working properly. There will be an inspection of rifles and ammo in fifteen minutes."

"Yes, Sergeant," said one of the men.

As the sergeant walked off toward another group one of the soldiers said, "About time. We've waited too long for this."

Castro looked at the man, Salidar. He was younger than most of the soldiers. His uniform was newer, cleaner, and he took good care of it as well as of his boots and equipment. Castro knew that most of the others didn't like him.

Salidar stood up and said, "We've got work to do." He hurried off toward the camp where they'd left their gear.

"Too excited," said Espidito.

"Yeah," agreed Castro, crouching next to his weapon and rucksack. He touched his rifle. There was no dirt on it. He picked it up, pulled the magazine from it, worked the bolt, and looked down the barrel.

Satisfied that it was clean, he reloaded, but didn't chamber a round. He set it on safe and then turned his attention on the rest of his gear. He made sure that his knife was sharpened and free of rust. In the tropics things rusted quickly.

Finished, he sat back and waited for the sergeant to return. He tried to think of what life would be like after they had driven the American invaders into the sea. He wondered what sorts of booty would be found on the base. Maybe the TV that he wanted. Probably lots of radios. Clothes. Boots. Maybe he'd be lucky enough to get a car or a Jeep, though he believed the officers and top NCOs would make off with them.

A group of men appeared in the trees, and Castro stood up, holding his rifle at port arms. The men moved among the soldiers, inspecting the gear and the weapons, nodding or mumbling comments. When they came to him, a man snatched the rifle from his hand, turned it around, examined it for dirt or rust, and gave it back to him. A sergeant looked at the rest of his gear and then nodded. They moved on without a word to him.

When they were gone, the men broke up into small groups, none of them sure what they were supposed to do next. Espidito walked over, crouched, but didn't speak.

Castro looked down at him and asked, "What do you think?"

"About what?"

"Will it be tonight?"

"Of course. They can't keep us out here forever."

Castro nodded at that, but wasn't sure of the wisdom. They could keep the men out there forever if that was what they decided to do. With the NCOs ready to beat up or shoot anyone who protested, they could keep the men there until Cuba sank into the sea.

A few minutes later the sergeant returned. He stood for a moment, his hands on his hips, and then said, "You people will prepare to move out."

"We take all our gear?" asked Espidito.

"We're not coming back here," said the sergeant. "You take everything you want to keep."

"Yes, Sergeant."

Castro shouldered his pack and then set his weapon butt first on the ground while he held on to the barrel. He looked up into the canopy and saw that it was beginning to get dark.

"Anytime now," said Espidito.

"Yeah," said Castro. He was beginning to get nervous. He was beginning to get scared.

It was very late when Reisman finally got permission to see the commanding general. He was warned that he was extremely busy and couldn't waste much time but was willing to give the little he had to spare to representatives of the working press.

The office was small, poorly furnished, and hot. It wasn't the typical office of a general and Reisman was surprised. Even in Vietnam the generals had managed to find air-conditioned comfort. They lived in house trailers with all the comforts of a stateside post while lower-ranking officers and enlisted troops lived in rat infested bunkers within a few yards of the enemy.

The general, a phone cupped against an ear, signaled Reisman to enter. He pointed at a chair and mouthed, "Sit down."

Reisman collapsed onto the seat and wiped the sweat from his face. The general turned his back and lowered his voice. Reisman waited patiently and studied the room. Spartan was the word that came to mind. Nothing ornate, everything functional.

Finally the general turned, hung up the phone, and leaned his elbows on the desk. "I don't have much time. We're moving out in less than an hour."

"Then let's get started," said Reisman. "Why so fast?"

"Situation. Need to get into position."

Reisman took out his notebook, folded it open, and asked, "Just what is going on?"

"Ah," said the general. "That's a complicated question. . . ." He sat quietly, staring up at the cracked and stained ceiling.

"The raid into Mexico?" prompted Reisman.

"Yes. There have been rumblings that the Mexicans

are going to retaliate." The general laughed. "You'd think they'd know better by now; the idea's ridiculous. Yet intel says they still plan on coming. We're deploying with our full strength along the border to prevent a raid into the United States."

Reisman sat there, staring at the general. "You can't be serious."

"I'm afraid that I am. The Mexican government is making noise, of course. I don't blame them. We'd react the same way."

"You really expect a retaliation raid?"

"I wouldn't be surprised if someone down there doesn't make the attempt."

"You have anything definite?"

The general turned, touched a pile of papers. "No, nothing definite."

Reisman sat for a moment, trying to compose another question, and then realized that he'd taken that as far as he could. They were going to deploy in case the Mexicans tried to get even.

"What happened this morning?"

The general thought about that for a moment. "Some kind of raiders gunned down a couple of our people. One killed and one wounded."

"You don't seem too concerned."

"That'll be enough of that! There just isn't anything that we can do about it now. We don't know who did it. The FBI, Texas Rangers, and a couple of officers from our CID are investigating the incident."

"Any leads?"

"Nothing," said the general. "If you're finished with this, I have work to do."

Resiman didn't move. "I'm not getting what I want."

The general raised his eyebrows. "I'm not particularly interested in that."

"General," said Reisman, "you have two soldiers down and all you can say is that you have the CID on it?"

"Nothing more to do. I have over twelve thousand

men and women assigned to this division. I have had more people killed in training accidents. At the moment there is nothing that I can do. The running of this division takes top priority."

"Then you don't care."

Now the general laughed. "No, Mister . . . ?"

"Reisman."

"You're not going to bait me with that. It's too simple. I care about all the soldiers assigned to this division. But there are times when I have to ignore the individuals. Now, I'll be happy to put you in touch with the CID investigators and even have them answer your questions."

"What I'd like to do is go along tonight."

"No, I don't think so."

"Something you don't want me to see?"

The general leaned forward, elbows on his desk, and stared at the reporter. "Why do you all reach into the same bag of tricks?"

"General, I'm just trying to do my job here."

"Sure." He took a deep breath. "Not going to be easy. Up all night with lousy coffee."

"General, I served a tour in Vietnam."

"As a reporter or a soldier?"

"Soldier."

"Okay," said the general. "If you were a soldier, then you might still understand some of this. . . . I'll have someone from the public-affairs office get with you."

"I'd rather be with the troops in the field."

"Of course you would." He fell silent and then consulted a list that he took from a side drawer. "Got an MP unit where you might not get in the way."

"I want a line unit," said Reisman.

"Line unit might not want you. They've got more important things to do. The MP company is the best I can offer."

Reisman stood. "Okay, General, I'll go with them."

The general picked up the phone, touched the buttons, and spoke quickly. "Get Captain Liemback here." As he hung up he said, "Liemback is in command of the Seventh MP Company."

"Thank you, General."

"Just one thing. Captain Liemback is in command. He gives you an order, you obey it, just like you were in the army. He'll be charged with your safety."

"Of course."

"Now, I've got a great deal of work to do."

"Thank you, General." Reisman left the office, walking out into the growing dusk, and found Webster and the car. "I'm going with the division on the deployment."

"The hell you say."

"You can take off."

"What about your bags? And that hotel room you were so all-fired hot to get?"

"Keep the bags in the car. I'll check in when I have the chance."

"This is stupid," said Webster. "You've got other things to do."

"The story," said Reisman, "is at the border and that's where I'll be."

"You even know the office number?"

"I'll get it from Directory Assistance if I need it. I'll see you later," said Reisman.

Webster climbed into the car and looked out the window. "Suit yourself."

CUBA

They made their way through the jungle, moving slowly and carefully, trying to make no noise, trying to show no lights, trying to get into position without alerting the Americans.

Castro felt the sweat form and drip. He felt cotton form in his mouth from the exertion of fighting the jungle. Or maybe it was because he was scared. No longer was it something in the future. The attack was about to begin and there didn't seem to be anything or anyone to rescue him.

There was a crash to the right as someone fell. Castro turned, but in the blackness of the jungle he couldn't see who is was. Just the sound of someone scrambling to his feet and then a grunt as he apparently stumbled again.

They slowed and then stopped. Castro sat down on the damp ground, his rifle clutched in both hands, the butt on the ground between his feet. He leaned his forehead against his wrists and closed his eyes. His body was soaked with sweat. His palms were slippery, his clothing drenched. His mouth was the only thing that was dry.

The whispered word came to him. "Five minutes. We go in five minutes."

Castro turned his head and passed the word along, listening as the order moved down the line and then there was silence except for the quiet scratching of claws in the trees, the buzz of insects, and the occasional call of an animal or bird.

A sergeant suddenly appeared out of the quiet gloom of the nighttime jungle. "On your feet," he whispered and then moved on.

Castro stood, touched the safety on his rifle to make sure that it was still on. He wanted to check the magazine, but couldn't see it in the dark. He left it alone and waited.

Around him the jungle came alive. He could hear quiet voices, the rattling of equipment, and the metallic workings of bolts. The men were preparing to hit the American base.

They began to move again, but slower, as if they expected the Americans to appear at any moment. Castro stepped over a log, searched the ground under his feet, and then looked up. Through a gap in the trees he could see the lights of the base. And noise: car engines, generators, jet engines, and loud rock-and-roll music.

They worked their way forward another fifteen or twenty meters and then stopped again. Castro crouched at the very edge of the jungle, looking down on Guantanamo. It looked peaceful and unprotected. It looked as if it would be easy to overrun.

Castro saw movement as the sappers moved to the fence, crouched and then stood, moving from side to side. In a couple of minutes they disappeared.

"Let's go," said the sergeant. He ran down the gentle slope toward the holes created by the sappers.

Castro followed, his eyes on the ground near him

first, and then at the holes in the fence. He stopped for just an instant, a knee on the ground. There was more open ground in front of him, a paved street, and then a series of short white buildings.

Men raced passed him, their weapons held high. There was a burst of fire, a single weapon, and then silence. Shapes appeared all around him. Castro knew that it was time to move.

He reached the road, leaped a short white fence bordering it, and then ran toward a darkened building. All around him were the others, moving silently forward as they searched for the enemy.

Castro stopped at the corner of the building, then slipped along with his back to it. He peeked around a corner, saw nothing other than his fellows. He ran to join them as they filtered through the base. For the moment no one had been alerted about them.

Castro slowed down, breathing hard. It seemed that the attack was going to be easier than he had thought. No resistance by the Americans. He'd expected a tough fight just to penetrate the fence.

Shots rang out to the right. It sounded like AKs and there didn't seem to be any answering fire. Glancing in that direction, he spotted the muzzle flashes and then the tracers as they leaped across the open areas or tumbled into the night sky.

There was an explosion close by, the hot air washing over him. Something thudded into the wood of the building just above him. He ducked instinctively and then leaped to the side.

He heard a scream, either of pain or surprise, and then more shooting, now from in front. Castro stopped, unsure of what to do. Most of the men who had been around him had disappeared into or behind buildings. He felt alone with shooting all around.

He started forward again, now terrified. He reached out his hand, like a blind man in unfamiliar surroundings.

He saw someone moving in front of him, but didn't know if it was a friend or foe. "Hey!" he called.

The man turned and froze, staring into the darkness. He said, "Shit," and turned to flee. As he did so Castro fired, the muzzle flash reaching out a meter or two. The tracer seemed to fly high, over the man's head.

Castro was going to shoot again, but something caused him to hesitate, and the man disappeared around a corner. Castro ran forward, but his target was gone.

A siren began to wail. It started low and built until the sound pierced the air. Lights began to flare all over the base and it seemed suddenly that every jet was taking off at once.

Captain William A. "Wild Bill" Ramey had been told that something was brewing, that a lot of people, mainly men, had been moving toward the base and that something, some kind of demonstration or commando-type raid, might be coming. He, along with his company of marines, was to be alert, ready to respond, in much the fashion that a police force would respond to a riot. Be ready, be armed, but don't shoot first.

Ramey, who had picked the name Wild Bill himself, didn't like orders that limited his options. He preferred orders that opened them wide. He wanted to be able to deal with a threat with everything at his command, rather than worry about the opinions of paper pushers and politicians. Those who were not on the scene often had different views than those who were.

For the last week he had inspected his men daily, checking their weapons, the ammunition supplies, the grenades, squad automatic weapons, the antitank weapons, and everything else that he could get his hands on. He had been delighted by the heightened state of alert, at the evacuation of dependents, civilian employees, and nonessential military personnel, but knew that the odds of something happening were almost nonexistent. He knew that the Cubans might stage a riot at the wire, throw some firebombs over the fence, but that was all he expected.

The first burst of fire had been barely audible over the rock music on his tape player. Ramey had been lying on his bunk, listening to Stevie Nicks and Tom Petty, when he thought he heard firing. By the time he'd gotten up, beer in hand, and turned off the tape, the firing had ended.

Ramey walked to the window and looked out on what seemed to be a peaceful base. Nothing was apparently out of place and the firing could have been an aberration, a guard with an itchy trigger finger who would find himself in hot water in the morning.

Turning from the window, Ramey walked back to the tape player, but didn't turn it on. Instead he stood with his finger on the play button, his eyes closed, as he strained to hear. Still there was nothing.

And then another burst, followed quickly by another and then another.

His door burst open and Ramey dived over his cot, his hand reaching for his pistol. As he rolled against the wall, whirling to aim, he saw Sergeant Bruce Jenkins.

"Base is under attack."

"I know," said Ramey, climbing to his feet. "Let's get the men out there."

"Where?"

"Sound of the guns," said Ramey. "Always ride to the sound of the guns."

"Yes, sir!"

Ramey opened his locker and took out his body armor, pulling it on over his OD green T-shirt. He wore dress pants and low quarters, but didn't take time to change. He found his Kevlar helmet and buckled the chin strap. He secured his pistol belt and then grabbed his rifle.

Outside, he saw that the men were already forming into platoons, the platoon leaders getting them ready to move. Ramey ran to the front, saw Jenkins, and asked, "Any word?"

"No, sir."

The siren began to wail then and lights flared. Attackers would want it dark. Defenders would want all the light they could get. Flares burst overhead, either fired by artillery, ships, or dropped from aircraft.

"Sounds like the trouble is on the west," said Ramey.

"Yes, sir."

"Harris, take your platoon to the right and then west. Philips, you go left and then west. The rest are on me, right up the middle."

"Rules of engagement," shouted Harris.

"Sounds like they've been superseded," said Ramey. "Enemy is shooting. We are authorized to fire for our own protection, which means if you can't identify the son of a bitch, you kill him. That's the rule."

"Yes, sir."

"Go!" ordered Ramey. "Go!"

"Follow me!" shouted Harris as he ran between two buildings and then turned.

As Philips did the same Ramey waved an arm. "Let's go, boys. Cut them down."

Ramey ran into the darkness between the buildings. They were brick structures three stories high, the lights showing in a few windows. Behind some of the windows were faces of sailors, wondering if it was some kind of marine exercise or if it was something more ominous.

As they neared the firing Ramey slowed and then slipped to the side, into the shadow cast by a building. He held up a hand as the rest of the men scattered, taking what cover they could. There was sound in the darkness just beyond them, and Ramey wanted to let it come to him.

The enemy appeared suddenly, running toward the center of the base. There was no question that they were invaders from the outside.

Lowering his own weapon, Ramey shouted, "Stop them!" He fired on full auto, the weapon crashing.

All around him his men opened fire. Fifty weapons,

all on full auto. The firing blended into a single, drawn-out detonation. The muzzle flashes were one strobe light that illuminated the enemy. The first rank went down under a hail of bullets. Men screamed as their bodies were torn to shreds. The odors of battle and death filled the air.

Ramey emptied his weapon, ducked down, and yanked the magazine, tossing it away. He jammed a second one home, pulled the charging handle, and popped up. The darkness in front of him was alive with fireflies. Bullets snapped through the air. Ramey fired into the muzzle flashes of the Cubans, short bursts of two, three, or four rounds.

A shape materialized near the side of the building and Ramey turned toward it. The man fired, the round went wide. Ramey heard it slam into the building. He fired back and saw the man lifted from his feet. He fell to the ground and tried to get up, but Ramey shot again, driving him down, finishing him.

Firing around him was slowing. The marines had beaten back the enemy assault. Ramey was up on his feet, moving forward cautiously. He reached the body of the man he'd shot and stepped on the fingers, making sure that the man was dead. He kicked the rifle away from him.

Now there was firing to the right. Harris and his platoon had run into something and engaged them. Ramey glanced over his shoulder. There was a burst; one man firing down into the body of a fallen attacker.

"Let's move it," shouted Ramey. He turned, slipping along the side of a building. A moment later he could see the muzzle flashes of the firefight. "Harris, where are you?"

"Here."

There was a sudden burst of fire into the air, tracers rising.

"Support on the left," said Ramey.

"Got it."

"Jenkins, to the right of me. Up around them. Second squad."

"Yes, sir."

Now he could make out the shapes of the Cuban soldiers. They were engaging part of Harris's platoon. Maybe fifteen or twenty of them.

Suddenly Jenkins yelled, "Coming at us."

Ramey turned in time to see another twenty men loom out of the darkness. He fell back, thinking that the wall of the building was closer than it was. He dropped to the ground on his back and bumped his head. Pain flared, and for a moment he couldn't see, but then his eyes cleared. He rolled to his belly as the rest of his men opened fire.

"Here they come again," yelled Jenkins.

Ramey grinned and waited. It was turning into a turkey shoot.

The sudden appearance of American soldiers surprised Castro. He thought that they'd get away with it. Some shooting as base security people, the few that were stationed there, came forward. But now there seemed to be too many of them.

He ran across an open space between two buildings as firing erupted. He saw half a dozen of his fellows fall, dead. Others were hit, wounded, and screamed as they scrambled to get clear.

Castro dropped back into the cover of the building and fired into the mess. He pulled the trigger slowly. A round splintered the wood near him and he jumped back. He pushed the barrel of his weapon around the corner, holding the rifle out to his side and shooting without looking. He was just putting out rounds with no idea of where they were going.

He emptied his weapon and then moved back from the corner. He reloaded and looked up to see one of the sergeants standing over him.

"You come with me."

Castro got to his feet and nodded. Together they ran

along the building, hesitated at the side, and then sprinted across the open ground. They reached safety and the sergeant said, "You guard the door. You protect my back."

"Yes."

The sergeant disappeared inside and Castro turned, watching the ground around them, listening to the pounding of hundreds of weapons, the sounds loud and long, punctuated by the explosions of grenades. In the distance a flare burst into brilliance, and as it swung under its parachute the light bounced around, giving life to the shadows.

Castro swung his rifle at every movement, ready to blaze away. He turned once and did fire, the single round smashing a window with a crash of glass. He laughed at himself but noticed that his hands were still shaking.

The sergeant reappeared, carrying a large bundle. "Place is loaded with stuff. You'd better grab some of it before the officers find it."

As the sergeant ran off toward the west and the hole in the fence, Castro turned to look into the doorway. It was dark inside. He took a step up and then moved into the building. He turned, his back against the wall, and looked out. No one around. The firing was in the distance. Maybe the defense of the base was collapsing already. That had to be why the sergeant was grabbing the booty. Get the good stuff before everyone realized what was happening.

There was no sound in the building. Castro slipped into it deeper, touching the wall, feeling his way along with the toe of his boot. He found a door, reached for the knob, but didn't turn it. He hesitated outside the door, wondering what was on the inside, afraid.

Outside, there was a loud crash that shook the building. Dust cascaded from the ceiling and Castro sneezed twice. He leaped to the other side of the hall and then whirled, looking back at the rectangle of the door. No one appeared there.

Moving on, he found an open door and stepped into the room. Light from outside made it easier to see. There were a couple of chairs, one of them dumped over. Castro found a refrigerator and pulled the door open, horrified by the bright light on the interior. He slammed it and backed away.

He left the room and stopped in the hall. The firing had moved away from him. It was distant now, as if it was on the other side of the base. He grinned, figuring that the fighting was now beyond him, that they had pushed the Americans across the base. He had survived the assault and would be able to get away with his life.

He moved along the hall, found another door, and forced it open. The curtains were drawn, so that there was only a small gap in them. He moved to the window and pushed the curtains to the side. There was a bullet hole in the glass.

Turning, he saw what he wanted. There was a small TV sitting on a table. He walked over to it and picked it up. It was lightweight. Easy to carry. He'd take it outside, then see what happened to his friends.

He put his rifle to the side and got down on his hands and knees, feeling the wall, searching for the plug. He found it, pulled it free, and stood. He wrapped the cord around the TV and then reached for his rifle.

There was sound in the building. Footsteps running along the hall and then someone on the stairs. Above him were more running men. And then a shout, the words in English.

Castro now wished that he'd found someone to guard his back, to warn him in case the Americans returned. He tried to find his rifle, but didn't want to move and he didn't want to give up the TV. That was the reason he had come. Find a TV for his family and now he had it in his hand.

He turned and looked at the window. That was his escape. Out the window, along the building, and then to the fence and the jungle beyond it. His rifle was gone and he decided that he didn't care. He had his TV.

Quietly he worked his way across the room, pushed the chair to the side, and opened the window. He stuck his head out and saw that the way was clear. He was going to get away.

And then the world crashed down around him. The door burst open with a loud, frightening bang. Someone dived into the room and yelled, "Halt."

Castro didn't. He tried to get out the window. He didn't look back as the windows around him exploded under the hammering of an automatic weapon. There was a sudden burst of pain, a white-hot tearing in his shoulder, back, and hip. He lost his grip on the TV and heard it fall to the ground, breaking.

He tried to turn, to tell the man that he only wanted a TV for his family, but slipped out, falling. He didn't understand what was happening to him. And then he understood nothing.

OFF THE COAST OF CUBA

Dees was in the CIC, looking at the various electronic boards that displayed the locations of the ships in the American fleet, the Soviet trawlers that were always hovering around to gather electronic intelligence, the various aircraft that were in range of the defensive weapons, and anything else that could affect the mission of the ship.

One of the men turned in his chair, took off his headset, and said, "There's something going on ashore."

Dees moved closer and looked at the screen. "I don't see anything."

"Buildup of heat and carbon dioxide here," he said, pointing. "Could be nothing. Could be a herd of cattle that have moved in, though the gas concentration is wrong." He grinned. "Cow farts are methane."

On the screen was a map of Cuba, the bases used by

the Cuban military displayed, as were the primary and secondary roads, cities, and concentrations of industrial or commercial enterprises. Flights by Cuban aircraft were also displayed, but all the Cuban aircraft were well away from Guantanamo.

"Isn't that a little strange?" Dees asked.

"No . . . well, I suppose, Captain."

"They're congregating on the northwestern end of the island, as if they expect some kind of an attack from there. Looks like a combat air patrol."

"Maneuvers?"

Dees studied it for a moment and then noticed a second group standing over the Great Bahama Bank as if they were ready to intercept fighters launched from Homestead Air Force Base in Florida.

"I don't like that. Has Drummond seen this?"

"No, sir."

"Have him report to me down here."

"Aye aye, Captain."

Dees watched the board, then turned to take in the data from the other displays. Electronic intelligence, gathered by satellites and sensors, aircraft and ships, all relayed, refined, and displayed in the CIC of his ship so that he could make independent, split-second decisions if radio communication was lost with his next higher authority.

Drummond appeared and asked, "You wanted to see me, Captain?"

"What in the hell is going on?"

Drummond looked at the screen, at the moving blips, at the stationary targets and the displays of various information. "Buildup on the western side of Guantanamo with air cover inserted into the slots where logically they could expect to find our fighters for a response."

"You suggesting that there is something going on in Cuba that you didn't brief us on?"

"No, Captain. I told you that the Cubans would be making some kind of retaliatory raid because of the assassination of their leader. Even though we weren't involved, they're going to blame us."

"Captain, I've got a call through here. There is an attack on the base," said the radioman.

"Pipe it in."

"Aye, sir."

Dees listened for a moment and realized what was happening. He turned and said, "I want the exec on the bridge. Drummond, you come with me. If there is any change in any of the aircraft, if they head toward the base, I want to know."

"Aye, sir."

"Where the hell's the *Kennedy*?"

"Here, sir." A sailor stood and pointed at a dot off the eastern edge of Cuba. "About two hundred miles out."

"Has the CAG on *Kennedy* launched any aircraft?"

"No, sir."

"Keep me posted," said Dees.

He turned and hurried from the CIC, working his way up to the bridge. As he entered, one of the sailors announced, "Captain's on the bridge."

Randolph came to him. "What's happening?"

To the officer of the deck Dees said, "Come around to three-three-zero degrees at full speed."

"Aye, sir."

To Randolph he said, "There's some kind of activity around Guantanamo. We're moving to support."

"Aye, sir."

Dees turned and stepped out on the wing where he could catch the fresh sea air. He looked at the horizon, searching for some clue about the situation near Guantanamo. He thought he might be able to see something if it was happening at a high enough altitude.

Randolph joined him. "What in the hell is going on?"

"That's the question," said Dees. "Cubans are causing some trouble. We're moving to support."

There was a burst of light above the horizon that

dimmed rapidly as it descended under its parachute. It was a pinpoint in the distance.

"Flare," said Randolph.

A sailor appeared. "Captain, I have a report that the base at Guantanamo is under ground assault by a battalion-size force. Marines are moving to intercept and engage."

Dees felt the blood drain from his face and his stomach turn over. He had always privately believed that the beginning of the next great global conflict would be an attempt to remove the base at Guantanamo. With the Soviet Union in disarray, with the Warsaw Pact gone, and with communism failing around the world, he wasn't sure what the attack meant.

"Drummond!"

The young intelligence officer, his khakis now sweat-stained, appeared. "Aye, Captain."

"The situation at Guantanamo."

"Aye, sir. Current report is that the enemy is in the wire and maybe has penetrated the base proper."

"Jesus Christ," said Dees. "What in the hell is going on?"

Frankowski had thought that he was going to fly in support of the border patrol, but now that had been turned upside down. Hahn had searched out the pilots and told them there had been a change in plans and to report to the briefing room in ten minutes.

The intelligence officer, DuBose, was standing behind the podium, waiting as Frankowski entered. He slipped into a seat, saw that nearly everyone was at the briefing, including those who had been at home. The intelligence officer glanced at the filled auditorium and decided that it was time to begin.

"Ladies and gentlemen," said DuBose as the first of the slides appeared, "it looks as if the Cubans are making a push to take the Guantanamo base away from us. Although the ground force employed, at the moment, seems to be irregulars, they do have air assets available."

The slide changed, showing the location of the Cuban fighters. It was a handmade slide with poorly drawn figures. A smudge near the center could have been a thumbprint or an area of interest.

"Right here," said DuBose, pointing, "is the first line of defense, designed, apparently, to intercept anyone coming from Texas."

He went on to detail what was known about the fighters that were airborne, the weapons systems on the fighters, the Soviet doctrine of deploying fighters so that they could make use of the ground-based antiaircraft defenses if they got into trouble, and then detailed those, including the ranges of the various missiles.

He put up pictures of Soviet-built fighters, most of which would be considered second line. There was nothing newer than a MiG-27. He spoke quickly of their capabilities, their updated radars that included look-down, shoot-down capability, and of some of the newer air-to-air missiles.

He finished with the colored pictures of the fighters and then sequenced through silhouettes of them. He would hesitate and then name the fighter. It was a crash course in visual identification.

After fifty such slides he stopped and began to outline the details of the surface-to-air missiles. The old SA-2 Guideline, which had been deployed in Vietnam, was being phased out in Cuba, but some remained operational. He also addressed the capabilities of the newer missile systems.

He finished the briefing by talking about the antiaircraft artillery. These were weapons that fired 12.7mm rounds, 20mm shells, and 30mm exploding bullets. There was also the S-60 that threw huge shells into the air to explode, creating a cloud of shrapnel.

He also gave the launch characteristics of the missiles, the radar signatures of the surveillance and acquisition radars, and firing features of the artillery.

He finished, leaned on the lectern, and scanned the audience. There was sweat on his face and it looked as if he'd just preached the sermon of his life. "Now," he said, "are there any questions?"

Without waiting, a pilot yelled, "Have we identified the locations of the fixed sites and will they be plotted on our navigation charts?"

"Fixed sites have been located, but many of the newer SAMs are mobile and can be erected and launched in a matter of minutes. We don't believe that the Cubans have many of them, but then, the radar signatures will give them away."

"What's the Cuban order of battle?"

DuBose ran a finger down the list of slides and used the microphone. "Put up number two-oh-six, please." He waited, saw it, and then said, "There's your order of battle. You'll see the front-line fighters. If you run into any Cuban fighters, those, because of their all-weather capability, will be what you'll see."

He fell silent and let the men study the list of fighters and their bases. After a couple of minutes he changed to the next slide. "Those are the bases for those fighters. Route packages have been designed to avoid them."

"Rules of engagement?" asked another.

DuBose glanced to the right, where Hahn sat. The commander stood and faced the men and women. "If it's coming at you and it is not a friend, then the assumption is that it's hostile and you are authorized to engage it. If it is fleeing, then you let it go."

Frankowski was surprised. He asked, "Won't shooting down Cuban fighters, especially over Cuban airspace, start a war?"

"It could be that the war has already started," said Hahn. "If they come at us, we knock them down. They have two other choices. Flee or land."

"Yes, sir," said Frankowski.

Hahn stood there for a few seconds more, staring at his pilots, looking as if he wanted to give them a pep talk and then deciding against it. He moved from the stage and took his place in the front row.

The intelligence officer took over again. "I think that we can forget about starting a war with Cuba. The first move has been made by them. It is their forces who are attacking our base at Guantanamo. The positioning of their airborne alert aircraft indicates that they expect a retaliation strike. To engage them will not be an escalation of hostilities." He glanced at the CO to see if his words were correct.

Hahn nodded. "Our orders have been cleared by Washington. Takeoff is in thirty minutes. Flight leaders will be Frankowski, Levin, and Brannigan. Flight assignments are posted. There is no time for further questions. Let's get rolling."

The men and women came to their feet and Hahn crossed the stage to exit from the main door. As soon as he was gone, the room exploded into sound with everyone talking at once. It was almost like the night that Desert Shield had become Desert Storm. No moment of transition, though everyone had suspected that it was coming. Now, suddenly, they were going into a shooting war with weapons pods loaded and armed. They were cleared to fire.

Frankowski leaped at the door, stopped short, and looked at the black phone on the wall. It was a base phone, good only for communications with other phones on the base. He needed a Class-A line, but even if he had one, he couldn't call his wife. Because she was assigned to a different squadron, Marie didn't need to know what he was about to do. She'd have to hear about it on the news, as soon as the CNN reporters could get clearance to broadcast.

"Major," said a voice. "We've got to get moving."

Frankowski turned and looked into the face of one of his pilots. A young woman, no more than twenty-three, fresh from college, ROTC, and flight school, stationed here on her first assignment.

"I'll follow you, Spencer," said Frankowski.

Another voice, from near the main doors to the building announced, "Van's ready."

Frankowski hurried down the hall and turned into the locker room. He still needed to get into his flight gear, survival vest, and grab his helmet. He snagged them, slammed his locker, and then ran toward the doors. It wasn't that he had to run; he needed to. Suddenly the adrenaline was pumping and he was filled with nervous energy. During all this time Spencer stayed close to him.

At the door he stopped and saw the second van approaching. He pushed open the door and stepped out into the night.

"What's it like?" asked Spencer, her voice quiet.

"Just like the training flights except it's all live fire. Just think of it as an exercise, do the job you were trained to do, and it'll work out perfectly."

"Shit," she said.

"Yeah. Exactly."

Martinez and his team were on the tarmac, near a C-17, when the Jeep roared up and screeched to a stop near him. Boyce leaped out and hurried toward him. "Word just in. Eighteenth has been diverted."

"What?"

"Trouble in Cuba and the lead elements of the Eighteenth are going in there with the remainder of the corps being held in reserve for the next forty-eight hours."

Martinez grinned and asked, "That mean we've been scrubbed?"

"Hell no," yelled Boyce, grinning right back. "Means that we still have a job to do, but now we've got to do it with no outside assistance."

"Christ, Colonel, that's impossible, even for the Special Forces. We go from a force of nearly forty thousand to what, a hundred?"

"We've got to get in, get the DZs marked, and then move toward the capital. Guerrilla tactics. Disrupt the lines of communication, destroy their supplies, and make a general nuisance of yourselves."

Martinez shook his head. "Colonel, you know that's not the way things operate. We can't jump in there cold. We'll get our butts shot off."

"You were there just hours ago."

"The situation has changed radically. We were dealing with the locals, providing assistance to interdict the rebels, now they've got a full-blown revolution going on. We don't have the intelligence, the equipment—hell, the reserves—to do anything but get killed."

Boyce looked at Martinez and then at the team. They were short the two men who had been wounded. They were not well rested, having just gotten clear, didn't have the proper briefings, hadn't been given the time to formulate a plan. They just happened to be in Panama, ready to move. Several other army units were mobilizing, but the word had filtered down too late. The plan had called for the XVIII Airborne Corps to handle it. No one thought that anyone else would be needed.

"Crisis management," said Boyce.

"You know that crisis management is another term for fucking up and trying to recover. Wouldn't be a crisis if someone hadn't stepped on his dick."

Boyce stood there for a moment before saying, "Sometimes we have to throw men into the breach because there is nothing else we can do. You have to buy us some time."

"Just what in the hell is going on?"

"Cubans launched an assault on the base at Guantanamo. A serious assault, though it looks as if it's going to be repelled. For the moment they need the Eighteenth there."

Martinez understood. The attack against an American

base couldn't be allowed to succeed. The rebel assault on Managua wasn't as big a problem and once the Eighteenth began to drop in, the rebel attack would be beaten.

"Maybe we should delay for twenty-four hours," he said.

"We tried to push that through, but Keaton was insistent."

"We could try our own chain of command to Bragg."

"I think that this is something we have to do. If I thought it was going to result in a number of unnecessary deaths, I'd call it off."

"Yeah," said Martinez.

Boyce held out a hand. "Good luck and good hunting."

"Thanks. I think we're going to need it."

CUBA

"Counterattack!" yelled Harris.

Ramey ran toward the right, hit the side of the building, and glanced to the west. The shapes of running men appeared but the firing was sporadic. Men shooting from the hip, the shots not aimed at all.

"Skirmishers out," said Ramey.

Marines fanned out along the sides of the buildings, taking what cover they could find. Others kicked their way into the buildings, smashed the windows, and waited for targets to present themselves.

Firing erupted. Single shots as the men spotted the enemy and tried to kill him. Flares burst overhead, bright, greenish-yellow lights swinging under their parachutes, making the shadows and shapes jump.

Ramey, sweat-soaked and suddenly tired, fell back toward the RTO. He crouched near the man and asked, "You establish radio contact?"

"Got base defense. Some lieutenant colonel is coordinating it."

"Marine?"

"I sure as hell hope so," said the RTO.

There was a loud crash and Ramey ducked instinctively. As debris rained back he heard a rattle of dirt against the building.

"Close," said the RTO.

"They're hitting us pretty heavy here. There a chance for some support?" Ramey asked.

The RTO spoke into the radio, giving his call sign and then a quick synopsis of the situation. He was quiet for a moment and then said, "Roger. Out." Looking at Ramey, he shook his head. "Pressure everywhere."

The firing was increasing. Ramey, his weapon held in both hands, kept his eyes on the side of the buildings, searching for the first sign of a breakthrough.

Half a dozen men rounded one corner, firing into the shadows as they ran. The muzzle flashes reached out, touched the bodies of the marines. One man went down, his hands around his thigh. Another was pushed back, falling into a shadow and disappearing from sight. Two others dived for cover, scrambling for the protection of the building.

The Cubans burst into the open. Ramey twisted around and lowered his weapon. He pulled the trigger as a dozen other marines opened fire. The shots ran together. The enemy skidded, a couple were hit, and the others fired back. Tracers crisscrossed. A man screamed, the sound like tires on concrete.

Ramey, his weapon empty, fell back to his butt and jerked the magazine free. He slammed the fresh one home, charged the weapon, and opened up again. The muzzle flash made it hard to see beyond the end of his rifle. The flare overhead burned out, plunging them into darkness.

"On my right. Coming at me."

"Ammo. I'm out of ammo."

"Get that guy."

Ramey turned toward the last shout and saw someone running right at him. He aimed carefully, looking over the top of the barrel and ignoring the iron sights. He fired once, twice, three times, but the Cuban kept right on coming as if he hadn't been hit. He staggered once and then seemed to reach out like a kid falling into the arms of his parents. He fell facefirst on the ground in front of Ramey.

All the enemy were down now. A marine stood over one and fired down into the body. Two other marines moved from dead man to dead man, taking the weapons away from them in case they weren't as dead as they appeared.

For a moment it seemed quiet. The firing in that little square had ended, but then Ramey realized that the firefight continued all around him. He stood, kicked the body of the dead man, and then ran forward.

Jenkins appeared. "We're holding now. Was hairy for a minute there."

"You see where they're coming from?"

"West side. I don't know how big the force is."

"We have a perimeter set?"

"Yes, sir. We hold all of the buildings on this block. I've got men in them now. We're clearing them."

"Good. We've got radio contact with base defense. We just need to hold out until the situation stabilizes."

There was a wild burst of firing. Both men turned but could see nothing because of the buildings. Overhead, tracers danced and flew and burned out.

"We've got a real problem," said Jenkins. "The Cuban government could throw their whole army into this."

"Pull the perimeter in so that we can defend it. Once we've got that situation stabilized, we'll begin to worry about more immediate problems."

"Like ammo?"

"We use the enemy weapons and their ammo if we have to," said Ramey.

"Aye aye, sir."

•   •   •

At Homestead Air Force Base, Florida, the airplanes of the XVIII Airborne Corps were sitting on the runways and taxiways, the soldiers still belted into the webbing, waiting to take off. Major Ross Dempsey was pacing in the grass at the side of the aircraft. The air was filled with the smell of partially burned jet fuel and high humidity. It was like walking around a gas station wrapped in a warm, soggy blanket.

Dempsey wanted a cigarette. He needed to smoke but knew he couldn't. Not with airplanes so close, one or two with their engines running. Lift-off could be imminent, except that the word was that they were to hold.

A Humvee appeared near the operations building, its lights cutting through the darkness. Unconsciously Dempsey patted his pocket, checking for his cigarettes. Satisfied that he hadn't forgotten them, he dropped his hand.

"You think it'll be the word?" asked Master Sergeant David Channing. Channing was a career NCO, happy with his position. He got to do what he wanted and didn't have to play the political games of the officers.

"No," said Dempsey. "They'd have radioed and the pilot would have cranked the engines."

The Humvee followed the edge of a taxiway, diverted to the grass to pass an airplane, and then turned, so that it was aimed at Dempsey and Channing. It stopped short and a tall, thin man, Colonel Martin, exited.

Without preamble he said, "Once we get the word that the Cuban fighters have been engaged, we'll launch."

"Situation on the ground?"

"As good as can be expected. Our people rose to the occasion. A surprise attack like that should have overrun the base in an hour or less. It's not as if we were expecting them."

Dempsey reached into his pocket for a cigarette, realized for the hundredth time that he couldn't smoke on the flight line, and let his hand drop away. "When do we take off?"

"I don't know," said Martin.

Dempsey turned and looked at the aircraft. One of them was shutting down its engines. The noise level on the airfield dropped off slightly.

"Maybe we should let the men out of the planes," said Channing.

"No," said Martin. "We could get the word for take-off at any moment. It'd take thirty minutes just to get the troops loaded again."

"In squads," said Channing.

Dempsey spoke up then. "The men have been cooped up in there for a couple of hours."

"Won't hurt them," said Martin. "I spent ten hours once, waiting for the word to come down."

Dempsey nodded but knew that it was getting unbearably hot in the aircraft. The hatches were open, but the Florida air didn't circulate. It hung there like a load of dirty laundry.

Looking at his watch, he said, "Been about six hours since we've had a meal."

"Have them eat on the planes," said Martin. "Hell, we can't let them go dropping trash all over the flight line. Air force would have a fit, yelling about FOD."

"What?" asked Channing.

"Foreign Object Damage. Debris that gets sucked into a jet engine. Little bit of metal, hell, a stick, a bird, a tin can, sucked into an engine can destroy it."

Dempsey looked up at the high tail of the aircraft, nearly invisible, even with the lights of the airfield. It was painted a flat dark green with none of the bright insignia that had once marked all aircraft. Now they used flat paints and curved surfaces to reduce hot spots and radar signatures. Everything to keep the enemy from sighting them and then shooting them down.

Dempsey wiped the sweat from his face and rubbed

it on his jungle-camouflaged BDUs. "How long do you think it'll be?"

"As long as it takes," said Martin.

"Great. Just fucking great."

They were now cruising off the coast of Cuba, far enough away that the Cuban defenses couldn't reach them. Fighters, launched, could hit them, but there would be warning and Dees had the Sea Sparrow and the Phalanx antiaircraft gun that used depleted uranium in the slugs to fight back.

"Tomahawks are ready, Captain," said Randolph, stepping out onto the wings.

"Thank you." He stood looking toward the horizon. Cuba was hidden beyond it.

"They've asked for support and the firing has been cleared by Washington."

"You know," said Dees, "that it didn't used to be like this. Ships could see their targets. They were in danger as they engaged the enemy. But we're in no danger. The Cuban air force is posed to repel a threat from the United States. *Kennedy* is in position to protect us from air attack, and if *Kennedy* can't do it, we've got the defensive weapons."

"There a point here, Captain?"

"Just that it doesn't seem right that we can engage the enemy without being in danger ourselves. We shouldn't be able to shoot at an enemy we can't see."

"Yes, sir."

Dees turned to look at Randolph. "Let's fire the Tomahawks."

"Aye, sir." Randolph entered the bridge.

Dees moved to the left and stared out. A moment later there was a roar from the rear and the first of the missiles leaped from the tubes. It sank toward the water as it picked up speed, the yellow orange of the flame reflecting from the surface of the sea.

The glow from the rocket engine shrank as the missile leveled off only five meters above the wave tops. In an instant it was gone, and if the men had done their jobs correctly, it would land within meters of the target. The high-explosive warhead would destroy a portion of the enemy's ability to make war.

A second missile was fired and then a third. They seemed to be flying together in a loose formation. Dees watched them until they were gone.

Randolph reappeared and said, "First volley is away, Captain."

"I saw."

"CIC reports the situation has stabilized on the base. At least for the moment."

Dees laughed. "We're in combat."

"Yes, sir."

"We're fighting, defending Guantanamo. Sure doesn't feel like it."

"I understand that it was this way for a lot of soldiers in Vietnam. Spend the day fighting the war, walking through the jungle, in firefights, flying over the jungle in helicopters, and at night, back at a base camp watching TV and drinking beer."

"Air crews had the same situation in Korea and World War Two. Heavy combat, fighters all over them, ten-percent casualties, and then back to England to hang around pubs and chase the English girls."

"Aye, sir."

Another of the cruise missiles was ejected from the tube, the flames from the engine momentarily lighting the side of the ship. There was a sudden roar from it as it dropped away, seeming to fall before beginning its flight. In a moment the second and third were also launched. In moments all were gone, racing to their destinations.

From the bridge came the announcement. "Missiles away."

"Thank you," said Dees.

"Think we should go down to CIC?" asked Randolph.

"No reason to."

"Follow the progress of the missiles and make sure that they land where they're supposed to."

"That's the one thing that I never worry about," said Dees. "I have faith in our people."

But just the same Dees walked into the bridge and then out so that he could watch the missiles on the display boards below. As he reached it one of the sailors announced, "Captain's at CIC."

The men didn't move. They remained in place, watching everything that was happening around the ship. Military courtesy took a backseat to the necessity of watching the various equipment displays.

"First volley is two minutes from impact."

"Show me," said Dees.

A display on a screen faded and was quickly replaced by another at a smaller scale. The missiles appeared at the bottom, raced halfway up the board, and then vanished.

"Impact."

"Targets hit?" asked Dees.

"Wait one, Captain." The operator pressed a button, studied the display for a moment, and then turned, grinning. "Good hits."

They watched the second salvo disappear and knew that they had landed right where they were supposed to. Dees clapped the sailor on the shoulder. "Good shooting."

"Thank you, Captain."

"I'll see if they want us to launch anything else," said Randolph.

"Go ahead," said Dees. "I hope they don't."

"No, sir," said Randolph.

As the exec left, Dees returned his attention to the display screens. It was a hell of a way to fight a war. Just like a video game, but in this one men got killed. The light-colored blobs on the screen, looking like those in the video games, represented real people who died real deaths.

It all lost something in the translation from real life to a computer-generated display. Not the way it should be, but the direction war had taken.

"No activity directed toward us."

"I didn't think there would be," said Dees.

HEADING TOWARD CUBA

Frankowski and his flight of four was off as quickly as they could do it. Spencer was his wingman and Ronald Hobbs was the second element leader, with Richard Spelman flying in the slot. They had rolled down the runway and lifted into the night sky, aiming at the bright stars on the southern horizon.

Frankowski reached the flight level and the vector and then relaxed slightly. He remembered that when he had been a wingman, it had been easy to sit back and let the other guy worry about the navigation, the weather conditions, the tanker's position, and all the other little problems. It was easy to sit there and complain, but now the burden was squarely on his shoulders. It was the price of command and the major's leaf.

But he'd found the tanker easily thanks to the radar

operators in the aircraft who had vectored him in until he spotted the KC-10 orbiting over the Caribbean. They slipped up close, took on more fuel, and broke away with no trouble.

The weather was clear and at altitude it was possible to see a long way. The sea spread out below them like a carpet with an occasional lump of an island twinkling with light. Frankowski kept his eyes moving from the scene outside to the instruments and radars in the cockpit. He was looking for the MiGs that the intelligence officer had told him were patrolling the skies over Cuba.

As they neared the target, with nothing showing on the radars and with the AWACS yet to check in, Frankowski keyed his mike. "Strides check."

"Two," said Spencer, letting him know that she was still with him.

"Three," said Hobbs.

"Four," said Spelman.

Frankowski turned his attention to the GPS navigation system. According to it, he was no more than a hundred meters from where he was supposed to be. Navigation by the seat of the pants no longer existed.

The radio suddenly erupted. "Attention all aircraft. Attention all aircraft. This is Crystal Ball. We are up and on station. Be advised that the situation is still green. I say again: The situation is still green."

"Nice of them to blow our ears off," said Spencer.

"Nice of them to let us know what we already know," added Spelman.

"Knock off the chatter," said Frankowski, though he understood it. They were nervous. It was the first mission against an armed and hostile force. Kind of like the first missions over Iraq when Desert Shield evolved into Desert Storm. He hadn't known what was going to happen. No one knew if the Iraqi air force would come up and fight or if they'd flee at the first chance. No one had any clue about it and he'd wondered how good the Iraqi pilots would be. They had supposedly had experience, in live fire, against the Iranians. Frankowski and the majority of the people he flew with hadn't been in a real dogfight. They'd trained with pilots from Vietnam who told them that when the shooting starting, the training took over, and he'd been through Red Flag at Nellis Air Force Base in Las Vegas, but the first time was different. It was no longer theory.

They raced through the night sky, approaching the coast of Cuba at over five hundred miles an hour. Each pilot alone in his or her cockpit with only the instruments, radars, and radios for company. At altitude, with a flight leader taking charge for the navigation and the situation, there wasn't much to do but think about what might happen.

Frankowski keyed his mike. "Coming up on Cuba. Let's clean them up."

"Weak guns," said someone.

"ID," requested Frankowski.

"Strides Two has weak guns."

That meant that the surveillance radars of an antiaircraft battery had painted the flight. It was nothing to worry about at the moment. They were still too far away from the enemy to acquire and engage them.

"Roger guns," said Frankowski.

Far off, at one o'clock, a string of tracers climbed into the night sky. It was so far away that it was barely visible and could have been someone clearing a gun.

Now, with the AWACS up and running, they heard a half-dozen other flights, those that had come up off Homestead or from the carriers deployed in the Atlantic or the Caribbean report in. Frankowski announced his presence.

But the question remained. Would the Cubans engage the Americans? The radar sweeps and the launching of patrol aircraft were posturing that didn't lead to engagement. When the time came, they could turn to run.

And then the question was answered.

"SAMs coming up!"

Frankowski didn't recognize the voice and there was nothing on his own instruments to confirm the call.

AWACS, its radio louder and more powerful than those of the fighters, boomed, "Whose got the SAMs?"

"Texas flight. Take it down. *Down*."

"Iowa is breaking to the right."

"Texas got the SAMs at the two o'clock. Double ringer. Let's lose the tanks."

"Iowa. Light your burners."

There was a moment of silence and then, "Texas has MiGs at the ten o'clock. They're closing."

"Texas, go to afterburners, now."

Frankowski wasn't sure where the engagement was going on. He thought they were on the eastern route package, but didn't know. He could see nothing. The radio signals were strong.

On his radio he said, "Let's be alert now."

"Stinger, you have one right behind you. Break. *Now!* Go to burners."

"Stride Lead, can we go to burners?"

That was Spencer, wanting to get into the fight now that it had started. Frankowski understood. He wanted to get into it, too, but the mission required that they stick to the preprogrammed heading. They could not deviate unless attacked.

"Guns to the front," said Spelman.

"Roger guns." Now there was another string of tracers, but this one was closer, the glowing red balls streaking up from the blackness of the ground.

"Stinger, I got him. Look at the son of a bitch burn."

"Good shot. Good shot."

"There's one on your tail."

Frankowski twisted around, looking for the enemy MiG, but realized it could be a hundred miles away. Someone had made the call in the blind and now every American pilot over Cuba and the Caribbean Sea was looking for an enemy fighter that wasn't there.

"Texas, he's on your tail."

Frankowski relaxed for a moment, the sweat dripping along the side of his face.

"Strides, we have guns at one o'clock and three o'clock, all firing."

There was a bright flash from the flak, but it was far off to the right, too far to be dangerous. But they started coming closer and closer, and Frankowski began a slow letdown to throw them off.

"SAMs!"

But there was nothing around Frankowski. There had not been a telltale burst of fire on the ground and there had been no radar indications. He kept his eyes moving, from his instruments to the sky outside to the ground below him. The sky was clear around him.

"Coming up at the eleven o'clock." The voice was filled with awe and Frankowski recognized it as Spencer's.

Suddenly there was flak bursting all around them, and Frankowski knew that it wasn't going to be the turkey shoot he'd faced in Iraq. The Cubans were going to fight.

They were suddenly buffeted by the flak. Shrapnel rattled against the aircraft. Frankowski ignored that, watching the oncoming fighters. Then, unexpectedly, the jets rocked up on their sides, turning to flee.

"MiGs on the run."

Frankowski didn't care. He lit the burners, ordering his flight to do the same, as he tore after the enemy. They dodged and weaved, as if trying to evade him, but he followed them, trying to get a good lock. The instant he had it, the pipper flashing and then solid, he launched a missile. It dropped from the wing station, the engine igniting and shoving it forward, the brightness overwhelming Frankowski.

"SAM! SAM! SAM!"

Frankowski broke away from the pursuit. On the ground he saw the flash as the missile came off the launcher. The size of the fire shrank and turned toward him. Frankowski turned toward it, trying to break the lock of the guidance system. He pushed his stick forward and dived at the missile, the flight right behind him. Triple A opened up, the tracers flashing up past them. Bright bursts of flak exploded around them. Frankowski rolled right, then left, and finally hauled back on the stick, climbing out and then rolling over again, diving at the ground.

It hadn't been like this over Iraq. The ground fire had been minimal. Lots of antiaircraft, but not real flak or missiles. No enemy fighters.

Now the flight had spread out, each pilot moving out of position as they turned and twisted to lose the missile and to dodge the flak. The SAM followed Frankowski for a moment longer and then spiraled off, climbing upward until the rocket burned out.

Frankowski climbed again, away from the alley of flak and tracers. As he straightened he said, "Strides check."

"Two."

"Three."

"Four."

"Out of burners," he said.

All around them there were more calls of SAM missiles and antiaircraft fire. Others were engaging MiG fighters. But for the moment Frankowski and his flight were in the eye of the storm. No one was shooting at them and there were no MiGs up searching for them.

And then it all went to hell.

"SAM at one o'clock."

Frankowski spotted it, but before he could react, another was launched, and then another. He turned, diving at the SAM site, wishing that the Wild Weasels were there. He turned again, twisting away, and then began a rapid, nearly straight-up climb, trying to fool the Cuban radar and missile.

For a moment it looked as if they would evade all the missiles. And then the enemy commander salvoed all his weapons. The blast of the firing engines lighted the ground, making it look like daytime.

"Coming up! Coming up!"

"To the right!"

"Hit the burners!"

One of the missiles spiraled away and detonated half a klick behind them. Another turned with the flight and exploded behind them. Over the roar of the jet engines, Frankowski heard the detonation and felt the shock wave from it. His jet was shoved forward and downward as he fought the controls.

As they rolled right and left, trying to avoid the enemy missiles, with tracers slashing the air around them and calls of MiGs from everywhere, Frankowski realized that the tap points had been exaggerated. He hadn't expected the enemy until they were well over Cuban airspace.

Frankowski rolled, climbed nearly straight up, and then rolled over into a dive. He jinked right and left, trying to avoid the enemy missiles and to break the radar or IR locks of the tracking systems.

There was an explosion on the ground to his left as a missile slammed into the earth. Another flashed under them, climbed, and then detonated far from the flight. Suddenly he had flown out of the storm.

"Strides check."

"Two."

"Three."

"Four, but I'm way behind you now. How about slowing it down."

"Out of burners," said Frankowski.

"What in the hell are we doing here?" asked Spencer. "Providing targets for the enemy gunners?"

"Cut the chatter," said Frankowski. Even Spencer should have known the answer to that question. They were tying up the Cuban assets so the transports could get through to put the infantry on the ground at Guantanamo.

"SAM coming up!"

Before Frankowski could react, the missile slammed into Strides Two, exploding, the fiery cloud engulfing the whole aircraft. Frankowski expected it to emerge unhurt, but that didn't happen. There was a sudden rain of metal parts as the expanding cloud darkened and disappeared in the night sky. Flaming wreckage fell toward the ground.

"Jesus Christ," said Four.

"Two's gone," said Three.

"SAMs!"

Frankowski felt the blood drain from his face and he was suddenly dizzy. Too much happening too fast. Flak burst and the shrapnel hit the fuselage. There was a buffeting and warning lights began to flash. There were buzzers and fire warning lights on the panel. The controls were suddenly stiff, sluggish, as if the hydraulic lines were gone. The nose dipped and Frankowski fought to bring it up.

"SAMs!" warned Three.

Frankowski couldn't worry about that. His aircraft was beginning a slow roll to the right that he couldn't stop. He fought it, using the stick and rudders, and was aware of the tracers streaking past his cockpit. Great glowing orbs of red and white that now seemed to be larger than basketballs.

"Three's in trouble."

"SAMs!"

"Hit the burners," ordered Frankowski, but as he did so nothing happened. The remaining two planes flashed past him, suddenly flying much faster. That was what saved him.

SAMs lifted from the darkened ground, bright pinpoints of flame, leaping into the air. They turned slowly and then began to track the movements of the two lead jets.

One of the pilots, Frankowski didn't know if it was Hobbs or Spelman, tried to turn away from one missile and flew into another. There was a brilliant explosion that was so bright it hurt the eyes, but the plane reappeared, almost intact. The canopy flew off and it looked as if the pilot was going to get out. The jet shuddered once, like a big dog shaking itself. And then it exploded. There was no chute.

"Christ," said Frankowski, suddenly sick to his stomach.

The last plane turned twice and dived for the ground, a missile turning with him. He pulled around, climbed and dived, and the missile went spinning off on its own.

But a second came at him and exploded, the edge of the flame just touching the jet with enough force to flip the plane. The pilot, either Hobbs or Spelman, righted it and the canopy popped clear. The jet, trailing smoke and flame, climbed higher. More fire burst along the underside, covering the belly and trying to spread onto the wings.

"Get out!" yelled Frankowski.

Just as he spoke the pilot hit the ejector and was blown clear of the aircraft. The chute opened beautifully, and although there were Cuban gunners shooting at him, the tracers seemed to be wide. The beeper of the emergency radio attached to the parachute began to wail.

Now there was only Frankowski's aircraft and all the enemy gunners turned their attention to him. The flak became thicker and the tracers filled the night sky, some of them punching through the wings and fuselage of his aircraft. He could feel them as they tore the thin metal skin and destroyed the avionics, the wiring, the control cables.

Frankowski turned to try a run toward the Caribbean Sea. If he could get there, search-and-rescue helicopters from Texas or Louisiana would be over him before he could hit the water. In Cuba it would be impossible for them to get in. If he could reach the Caribbean.

Then the fire that had been concealed under the belly of his fighter began to creep up the sides. The flames were blown back along the fuselage. Twisting around in his seat, he could see a long looping trail of black smoke that was barely visible in the night sky.

The enemy fire grew thicker as if the enemy sensed that the plane was about to die. Frankowski dodged through the curtain of flak and tracers while the warnings kept wailing and the lights kept flashing. Heat and light began to fill the cockpit and he whispered to himself, "Just another minute. One more minute."

He could see the first thin line of the water that marked his sanctuary. And then the airplane rolled over as the last of the control cables were severed. Fire burned away part of the airfoils and the tail. The plane was no longer controllable.

Frankowski reached down and blasted the canopy free. As the fresh air swirled around him, blowing away the smoke, he could see the coastline clearly. A few seconds more and he'd be clear of Cuba. Just seconds. He didn't eject. He stayed with the plane as it lost altitude.

Then it was time to get out, before the aircraft was too low and there wouldn't be time for the chute to open. As he tried to eject the plane shuddered once, as if suddenly cold. Frankowski pulled the handle and then pulled the blast shield down, over his face. He was blown sharply clear, down and away from the cockpit.

Letting go of the blast shield, he twisted and watched as his plane suddenly nose-dived. There was a thud, a burst of fire from the engine, and then the aircraft exploded, disintegrating in the air. Frankowski turned away, but he was too far from the explosion to be hurt.

Looking up, he saw that he had a full chute. And then, looking down, he saw that he'd gotten over the coast of Cuba, and that the land was three or four miles away. If the Cuban patrol boats weren't out, then he had nothing to worry about, except for the sharks and barracuda and jellyfish.

He hit the water, his raft inflated, and the radio transmitter began to squawk. Frankowski scrambled up over the side and rolled into the bottom of the survival raft. He stared up into the night, thinking that it could have been worse. At least he had survived.

FLORIDA

They decided that they couldn't keep the men cooped up on the airplanes indefinitely. They had to be allowed out, if only for fifteen or twenty minutes, a few squads at a time. So now there was a steady stream of men moving from the aircraft and out onto the grass between the taxiways and runways. They milled around, a few smoking, though they had been told not to, the rest trying to stretch out the kinks in legs, arms, and backs.

Dempsey was standing with his back to the operations building, staring at the night sky and wishing that something would happen.

"Here comes Martin again," said Channing.

Dempsey turned and saw the Humvee that Martin had parked near the operations building had backed away. He looked at the lines of soldiers and wondered if he should order them back onto the planes.

The Humvee turned onto the taxiway, dodged around the aircraft, and then stopped near Dempsey. Martin climbed out and yelled, "Let's go."

Dempsey was going to say something, to ask questions, but then whirled. He waved a hand over his head and shouted, "Pack it up. Let's go. Take off."

A few of the NCOs stood and then took up the chant. All along the line men were shouting. A few cigarettes were tossed and stomped. The men rushed to the hatches and climbed back up into the aircraft.

Martin said, "Air routes are cleared. Shouldn't be any trouble from the Cuban air force."

"Our boys brush them aside?" asked Channing.

"I'm afraid that we lost a number of people knocking down the Cubans."

"Shit," said Channing.

"Just get onto Guantanamo and throw the bastards off. That'll make it all worthwhile."

"Yes, sir," said Channing.

Martin watched the soldiers as they rushed onto the aircraft for a moment and then said, "Good luck to you. I wish I was going along."

"Grab a weapon," said Dempsey. "We'll find room for you."

Martin hesitated. He glanced to the rear, at the operations building, and then at his driver in the Humvee. He looked as if he was going to accept the invitation, but finally shook his head. "I'm afraid that I'm needed here to coordinate this activity."

"Suit yourself," said Dempsey.

The lead aircraft started its engines. Another followed and the level of noise on the airfield began to rise rapidly. The stench of jet fuel filled the air.

"Good luck," said Martin.

Dempsey took his hand, shook it, and said, "Thanks. See you in a couple of days."

"I hope so."

Dempsey joined the line of men climbing into the rear of the closest C-17. As he boarded, the loadmaster closed the troop door, locking it. Dempsey reached a web seat, buckled himself in, and felt the aircraft lurch once.

"Here we go!" yelled a sergeant.

"This is it," said another.

Dempsey laughed and asked, "Why does someone always have to say that?"

"Captain, Ramey," called the RTO. "We've got to secure the airfield."

Ramey, crouched near the entrance to a barracks, turned and saw the RTO coming toward him. The last thing he wanted was to be identified as an officer by a private who'd never seen combat before. That was why there was no saluting in the field and why Ramey stayed away from the RTO as much as possible. The enemy knew that the men around the radio were important. Don't shoot the radio operator, but kill the men with him.

The RTO reached him and knelt next to him. "We've got to secure the airfield," he repeated.

Ramey glanced in the direction of the airfield but couldn't see it. The terrain and the buildings were in the way. High overhead the flares, now detonating in sequence, were providing continuous illumination. "Okay. Roger the call."

"Defense Six, Titan Six rogers."

"Sergeant Jenkins!" yelled Ramey. He waited and then called again.

"Yes, sir," said Jenkins, running up to them in a crouch.

"We're going to abandon the position here."

"Yes, sir. I might remind you that we have a defensible perimeter established."

"We're going to help secure the airfield."

Jenkins grinned, his face a strangely colored mask in

the swaying light of the illumination flares. "Means that somebody is coming in."

"Right. I want to peel off in platoon order. Harris in the lead."

"Yes, sir."

"In five minutes."

Jenkins nodded and stood up, bent at the waist, and hurried off.

Ramey fell back, leaning against the wall of the building. The firing had dropped off in the last few minutes; the majority of it was taking place along the northern edge of the base.

He climbed to his feet and ran across the open area between the buildings, watching as the marines in Harris's platoon slipped out of the line and formed at the rear of the perimeter, facing the airfield.

The captain moved along the line and passed the word to the other platoon leaders. Huxley would stay back, a rear guard to make sure the enemy didn't hit them from behind. When Ramey saw that the company was ready, he waved a hand.

Harris saw it, acknowledged it, and the platoon, by squads, filtered out from between the buildings, moving slowly, checking the bodies of the dead in their path.

Ramey and two more platoons followed along in support. They worked their way across the base until they were close to the airfield proper. The firing there had increased. Tracers flashed upward. The twinkling of the muzzles of half a hundred weapons lit the night.

Ramey halted, pointed right and left, and watched as his marines fanned out. They used the available cover, the wrecked trucks and Humvees, a burned-out building that was still smoldering, the fence poles and light poles and telephone poles, each with a glowing red light on top.

"Go!" he yelled.

A squad darted from protection, ran across the open ground, and threw themselves down. A second squad took off, but were only halfway across the open area when the firing erupted. Two men fell, hit. The first squad opened fire, the tracers smashing into the enemy line.

"Go!" Ramey leaped up, firing from the hip. He jumped over a rucksack, ran to the right, and hit the corner of the building. Around it, on the other side, the airfield was spread out.

Firing came from a hangar and the three trucks parked near it. A line of tracers flashed, struck the tarmac, and tumbled off.

"There," yelled Ramey.

"Got it," said a sergeant. He moved to the right, tapped men, and ordered, "Come with me."

Firing from the rest of the company poured into the hangar. There was a bright flash as a grenade detonated short of the trucks and the hangar.

The Cubans were shooting back with everything they had. A dozen, two dozen weapons on full auto. The marines returned fire quickly. A larger weapon began to hammer, the tracers from it floating toward the hangar. A truck exploded, the flames shooting a hundred feet into the air. One man, screaming, ran, the back of his uniform on fire. He was cut down and left to burn at the edge of the tarmac.

Ramey peeked around the corner and then burst from cover, running to the right. He dropped into a shallow drainage ditch, scrambled up the opposite side, and faced the enemy in the hangar. From there he would watch the marines work their way toward it.

They reached the edge of the tarmac and poured their fire into the two remaining trucks. A marine came up, threw a grenade, and dropped back to the ground. A moment later the truck exploded, throwing flaming debris across the tarmac. Cuban soldiers in the last truck abandoned it, running for the safety of the hangar. None of them made it.

The Americans spread out, running across the tarmac. Two of them stopped near a small door. One covered while the other ripped it open, tossed in a grenade, and threw himself to the side. When the grenade exploded, both men leaped up and dived through the door.

Other marines threw grenades in the broken windows or other doors. Firing from around the hangar grew in intensity. Ramey ran toward the hangar; taking cover behind a barrel lying on its side, he peeked over the top and then rushed forward.

Around him the rest of the platoon swarmed out of the darkness, running for the hangar. Ramey reached one of the doors as two sergeants approached. He nodded at them and then dived through.

He rolled away, surprised at the noise inside—it seemed as if a thousand men were firing, but it was the sound echoing from the metal walls. A round struck a girder near him and whined off. Ramey crawled to cover, and then studied the situation.

Bodies were scattered across the concrete floor. A single jet, sitting toward the rear of the hangar, had been hit by rifle fire and grenade shrapnel. Hydraulic fluid was leaking from it like blood.

The marines had taken positions near the doors, behind the cover there, or in a couple of offices that had windows facing into the structure. They were firing into a couple of offices on the other side of the hangar and at a couple of enemy soldiers crouched behind girders or barrels, or a bright yellow tug used to pull aircraft out onto the tarmac.

Ramey dropped the magazine from his weapon and slapped another one home. He whirled around aiming; the targets were easily visible in the lights of the hangar.

A figure behind the tug popped up and Ramey fired, taking off the top of the Cuban's head, blowing him back. Blood and brains sprayed the wall.

Then, suddenly, the firing from the enemy ceased. A single weapon flew out of the office to clatter on the floor. A white flag appeared, waving rapidly as someone shouted, "We quit."

Ramey yelled, "Cease fire."

One by one the marine weapons fell silent. Then someone called, "Come on out. Hands up."

A man appeared at the doorway, one hand in the air but the other clamped to his shoulder, which was stained bright red. A second man stood up and then a third. The last two tossed weapons out onto the concrete.

"Come on," said a marine.

Another marine stood, his weapon pointed at the surrendering Cubans. He advanced two steps and then thought better of it. He stood his ground, covering the enemy.

Marines began to appear, moving toward the cowering soldiers. Others checked the bodies, taking the weapons. Ramey stood and walked toward the body of a marine. He knelt and felt for a pulse, surprised by the steady though weak beat.

"Medic!"

A man with a kit with a bright red cross on it ran over. He crouched near the wounded man and began to work.

The RTO appeared and gave the handset to Ramey. "Defense Six, Titan Six actual. We have secured our section of the flight line."

"This is Defense Six. Fire a green flare from your position."

"Roger that."

With the RTO trailing, Ramey stepped from the hangar. His men were holding the tarmac, a supply building, the drainage ditch, and the hangar. To one of the sergeants he said, "Fire a green flare."

"Yes, sir." The shell climbed into the sky, burst like a fireworks bomb on the Fourth of July, and died out.

Around him Ramey saw others firing the green flares. It looked as if the whole airfield was in their hands.

Over the radio he heard, "Be advised that aircraft are inbound. Provide them with cover."

"Roger that."

Ramey looked up and spotted the landing lights of the

first of the aircraft coming in. Beyond them, in the east, was the first faint hint of dawn.

Dempsey stood, facing the other men in the aircraft. The noise of the engines wasn't as loud as it would have been in one of the old C-130s. He could talk to the man next to him in a normal tone of voice.

Now he addressed the entire plane. "Gentlemen, in a few minutes we'll be landing at Guantanamo. The instant we've rolled to a stop, the ramp will be down and all the doors open. Get out to the grass on the sides of the runway and prepare for an assault. The airfield is supposed to be in our hands, but let's not take any chances."

He looked into the faces of the men, now all painted in dark greens, grays, and blacks. They all wore helmets, the chin straps buckled, flak jackets that would stop most rifle bullets, and BDUs designed for the tropics. The one thing that struck him was the youth of the men with him. All so very young.

"Once the aircraft have cleared the runways, we'll fan out and link up with the marines. Remember, there are a lot of our people on the ground, so be sure of your targets before you fire. Any questions?"

"We're about a minute from touchdown," said the loadmaster.

Dempsey nodded at him. "Let's get this done as quickly as possible."

Someone said, "Yes, sir."

Dempsey sat down and strapped in. He closed his eyes momentarily and wished that it was going to be a parachute assault rather than a landing. Safer to go out at five hundred feet than to land on the airfield, unless the marines held it, and they wouldn't be landing if the marines didn't.

He glanced at the men, bathed in the red light that wouldn't destroy their night vision. They held their weapons in their hands and sat up very straight.

The sound of the engines changed and a moment later there was a bump and then a bounce as they touched the ground. The engines roared and the men were thrown around as the pilots stood on the brakes, trying to stop the aircraft. The instant they stopped, the rear ramp began to lower and the troop doors were thrown up.

Dempsey jumped to his feet and ran down the ramp, turned, and dropped to the ground. He glanced right and left and saw the soldiers were all around him. The engine sounds of the airplane changed and it rolled away, taking off a moment later.

With the sounds diminishing behind him Dempsey noticed how very little firing there was now. In the distance was a quiet boom and a flurry of tracers climbing upward.

The perimeter of the airfield itself looked peaceful enough. Dempsey spotted half a dozen men moving along it. They turned, ran across a taxiway, and then headed toward him.

"Hold your fire," said Dempsey. He got to his feet and began to move forward cautiously.

The men crossed the runway, walking toward him. As they got near, one of them called, "Glad that you could make it."

"Where's the war?"

The man shrugged. He pointed toward the north, where the last of the firing was dying out. "Over there, I think. But we've got the situation in hand."

"Good," said Dempsey.

"Welcome anyway," said the officer. "Now we can repel the counterattack, if they try."

"Nice," said Dempsey. He felt like laughing but not because anything was funny. It was the nervous energy of waiting to go into battle and then being denied the opportunity.

"If you'll follow me," said the officer, "we'll get you integrated into the perimeter defense."

"There'll be a number of additional flights," said Dempsey.

"Yes, sir. We're ready for them."

There was a sudden boom, much closer. The men all ducked, Dempsey slipping to one knee. The officer laughed now. "Maybe it's not quite as cut and dried as I made it out to be."

"Maybe," said Dempsey, but he knew the battle was over.

NICARAGUA

They'd landed in the thick jungle clearing, no more than two klicks from the capital city, using the cover of darkness to parachute in without letting the rebels know they were coming. Martinez and Chavez had gotten the team put together, got the maps checked, and figured the compass heading. The air force had put them right where they wanted to be.

Intelligence told them that the main rebel headquarters, with Jesus Castillo, was moving into the city at dawn. The attack on the presidential palace, coordinated with parts of the army, would begin at seven. If the rebels could snare the radio and TV station as well as the presidential palace, then announce the coup to the world, they might pull it off.

Chavez pointed to the south and said, "That way. Two klicks."

"Take the point," said Martinez.

Chavez got up and moved to the front of the line. He waited as the rest of the team fell in behind him and then started off for the capital. They moved as rapidly as they could, the men checking the jungle all around them as they moved through it. The chances of an ambush being in place were small, but they were taking no chances.

They worked their way up a slope and then stopped a dozen meters from the top of it, fanning out and resting for a moment. Each man was responsible for the jungle right in front of him, and for the men on either side of him. They stared into the darkness that was slowly fading into the brightness of morning.

Ten minutes later they were moving again, now making better time because they could see the jungle around them. The dark shapes developed into ferns and bushes and the trees that climbed two hundred feet into the air. Birds leaped into the sky, wheeled and lighted, squawking. Monkeys ran through the canopy, chattering at one another, covering any sound that Martinez and the team might be making.

They worked their way down the slope into a broad valley. Chavez turned slightly, following the valley floor as it led out onto the plain where Managua sat. In the growing light, through gaps in the vegetation, they could catch glimpses of the city.

Chavez stopped them again. Martinez slipped into the center of the group and studied the map carefully. He'd marked nothing on it, but he remembered what the intelligence maps he'd seen in Panama had shown. They were close to one of the rally points that Castillo would be using.

Moving toward the forward edge, Martinez knelt next to Chavez. "Over there. Quietly."

"On the way."

They started again, moving slowly now, placing their

feet carefully to avoid making noise. They'd taped down their loose equipment, folded the flaps of cloth over and taped them, and had gotten rid of anything that would rattle. Now they were moving like the early-morning mist.

Chavez halted them twenty minutes later. Martinez moved toward the point and slipped to his belly next to him. The master sergeant put his lips near Martinez's ear. "They're about fifty to a hundred meters ahead of us. Two hundred of them."

Martinez glanced at Chavez and raised his eyebrows. "Two hundred?"

"More or less."

Boyce landed in the back of a large helicopter that touched down on the grass outside the embassy building. The marine guards, dressed in jungle-camo BDUs, rushed out to them, and one reached up to open the cargo-compartment door.

Boyce leaped out, looked at the closest marine, and asked, "Is the ambassador on the compound?"

"Yes, sir. If you'll follow me."

Boyce turned and shouted, "Lombard, get the men integrated into the marine units and meet with their CO."

"Yes, sir."

"Let's go, Sergeant."

The marine turned and trotted toward the front door of the embassy building. They ran up the stairs and entered. There were sandbags piled just inside the doors, creating a small bunker. The barrel of a squad automatic weapon was pointed at the door and set to cover the approach.

They ran to the center stairs and climbed to the second floor. Armed guards in BDUs and body armor stood there; near one was a tripod-mounted machine gun. If someone broke into the building and got past the bunker, the machine gun, which commanded the whole lobby, would cut them down.

The ambassador was in his office, sitting at his massive desk, dressed in a charcoal-gray suit, brilliantly white shirt, and a blood-red tie. He looked up as the marine opened the door.

"Colonel Boyce to see you, sir."

The ambassador rose and held out a hand. "Colonel Boyce. I'm Ambassador Danford."

"Mr. Ambassador."

He waved at one of the chairs. "I don't suppose you want to waste time on civilian preliminaries."

"I'm sure that you're aware of the situation here, Mr. Ambassador."

Touching a file in front of him, Danford said, "I have the CIA report right here. The station chief has confirmed it."

"I have men in the field now, trying stop the coup."

"Do you think they'll be successful?"

"Mr. Ambassador, I was promised the assistance of the Eighteenth Airborne Corps, but they have been diverted into Cuba."

"Will the coup succeed?"

"I think you're in a better position to answer that than I am, sir."

"The government here is shaky and it won't take much to topple it," said Danford. "I think they have the support of most of the top officers, but again, if the wind changes, they'll all switch sides. They're going to protect themselves as best they can."

Boyce took a deep breath. "If the Cubans had decided to make their move a week from now, we'd be in better shape."

"Makes you wonder if this was all coordinated."

"If the situation deteriorates too much," said Boyce, "I can get air support out of Howard in Panama. There is a marine strike force on the ground there, and another available in Florida. Transport is now the problem. Eighteenth diverted most of the newest transports."

Danford laughed. "We've got the soldiers and marines, just no way to get them here."

"Taxpayers don't want to spring for a bunch of modern transports that we probably don't need anyway. Hell, if the Cubans hadn't jumped, we'd have all we need."

"Certainly," said Danford. He opened the file, glanced at the top page, and then asked, "You think you have enough to take care of the problem?"

"We can make a dent in it," said Boyce.

Danford closed his eyes and pinched the bridge of his nose. "I don't want to be remembered as the man who let the communists back into Nicaragua."

"At the moment we've got it covered. There are troops and aircraft on standby if we need them."

"Okay," said Danford. "If you need anything, let me know."

Boyce got to his feet. "Thank you, Mr. Ambassador."

Martinez pointed to the right and left and the men slipped through the jungle. Ortega pulled a claymore from his pack and aimed it forward. He handed one to Davis and a third to Munyo.

The captain waved a hand, and the team began to move forward, almost on line. They halted at the edge of the tree line and spread out. Martinez took a grenade and held it up so the rest of the men could see it. He pulled the pin and held his hand up, the fingers out. Counting down to zero, he threw the grenade as far as he could, over the closest rank of enemy soldiers.

He dropped flat and listened to the babbling conversation of the rebels and the quiet rustling as the grenades flew through the jungle. He counted to himself, and at three the first of the grenades exploded. The sudden noise cut through the jungle. The animals reacted to it, screaming in fear.

There was a series of explosions then. Dirt and debris

erupted upward. As it began to fall back Martinez was up on his knees, firing at the rebels.

Someone shouted, "There!" and the rebels whirled, shooting into the jungle. Bullets whipped through the vegetation, slicing it into bits.

"Get them!" yelled a rebel.

The enemy came up out of the jungle, firing and screaming. Martinez returned fire, his weapon on full auto. He emptied the magazine and dropped down to the jungle floor, trying to reload.

There was another series of detonations but these were different. It was the C-4 of the claymore mines firing in loud, flat bangs. The steel ball bearings sliced through the jungle, cutting the rebels off at the knees, or the waists, or the necks. The charges blew off arms and legs and shredded bodies. The enemy fell in heaps, blood turning the jungle floor crimson.

The attack broke as the rebels tried to get away. Martinez and the rest of the team were up again, firing at them. Men fell and died. The rebels threw away their weapons as they fled. Only a few fought back and they were cut down quickly.

In seconds it was over. The firing was sporadic and then single, well-spaced shots. Martinez got to his feet, took the empty magazine from his weapon, dropped it on the ground, and reloaded. He touched the safety with his thumb but didn't put it on.

"Chavez, you, Espinoza, Brown, and Gibson check the enemy."

"Yes, sir."

Martinez stepped around the trunk of a tree and leaned against it, surveying the damage. There had to be more than a hundred dead. A firefight that lasted less than a minute and they'd killed more than a hundred men. The smells of the dead and dying filled the air. The acrid stink of gunpower drifted on the light breeze. A few of the wounded were moaning, and one man was calling for his mother over and over.

Martinez looked down at the broken body of one of the rebels. White bone showed through a hole in his chest. His wide-open eyes stared up into the canopy over them, but they were milky and unseeing.

"Think we got Castillo," said Chavez, approaching.

"Where?"

"Over here. Can't be sure because of the damage to the face."

Martinez shrugged. "I'm not sure that it matters now. We broke this up. No support from here as the rebels move on the city."

"Yes, sir."

Martinez wanted to pick up the weapons and military equipment, but he didn't have sufficient manpower. He wanted to destroy them, but that would take too long. They'd have to leave them and hope that the jungle ruined them before anyone could find them, though he suspected that the locals would be all over the battlefield in a matter of hours.

"Let's get moving," said Martinez finally.

"Where?"

"Into Managua, toward the embassy. If nothing else, we can get a beer there."

"Yes, sir. Who gets the point?"

Martinez was about to give it to Chavez again but realized that it wasn't fair. "Let Brown have it."

"Yes, sir. Gladly." Chavez turned and raised his voice slightly. "Let's get going," he called.

From his vantage point on the roof of the embassy building Boyce could watch the almost empty streets. The sun had been up for more than two hours and still they were virtually deserted. That could only mean that everyone knew something was going to happen and was staying home to avoid it.

A marine captain, Louis Gavin, joined him and raised

his binoculars to his eyes. Grinning, he said, "It's too quiet. I don't like it."

Boyce saw that Gavin was smiling and let the comment pass. He pointed to the right, where the presidential palace stood, barely visible through the trees. "Looks calm enough."

"Radio reports of some military units moving," said Gavin, "but no reports of fighting."

"Next couple of hours could be critical."

"There!" Gavin pointed down one of the main streets.

Boyce turned and saw movement. He studied it and then said, "Looks like a tank."

"Going to help or attack?"

"That's the question." Boyce picked up the handset of the field phone, spun the crank, and then said, "We've got movement about a mile away. Doesn't seem to be coming in our direction."

Then, almost as if to make a liar of him, there was a loud boom and a moment later a round landed short of the embassy wall.

Boyce was on the field phone again. "Got one, two, three tanks coming up from the south. I don't see any accompanying infantry."

Below, a half-dozen marines ran to the wall, one of them carrying a LAW. He ripped the cotter pins from it, extended the tube, lifted the sights, and then popped up to peek over the wall. He dropped down as another shell exploded, still short of the embassy grounds.

Boyce turned slowly, surveying the city. He saw black smoke on the horizon and heard the distant boom of tanks or artillery and the rattle of machine-gun fire. "It's starting," he said.

"Where are your people?" asked Gavin.

"In the field."

The lead tank, now about half a klick away, fired again. The round hit the roof behind Boyce and Gavin. Both men dropped as the shell detonated.

"Getting close," said Gavin.

Boyce crawled to the edge of the roof and then used his binoculars. The tanks were closer, moving in line. Now Boyce could see them clearly without the glasses.

At that moment one of the marines near the wall stood, his feet spread and the LAW over his shoulder. He aimed at the tank and fired. The backblast of smoke and fire swept the ground, creating a whirlwind. The rocket leaped from the tube, flew straight, and struck the tank at the bottom of the turrent, exploding in a ball of bright orange. A plume of fire shot from the hatch. Black smoke billowed from the rear of the tank.

The marine had stood straight, watching the scene unfold. As the tank began to burn ferociously he tossed the empty, useless tube to the side and lifted his arms over his head like the boxer who had just scored a knockout. His friends slapped him on the back. He took half a dozen low-fives in celebration.

As soon as the lead tank was hit, the second and third reversed and began to back away, gaining speed. They kept going until they disappeared from sight.

"That was easy," said Gavin.

"It's not over yet," said Boyce.

NORTH OF THE TEXAS BORDER

Roving patrols along the river watched the fords and the banks opposite them. Companies in the various towns had been organized to support the local police and sheriff's departments, and outposts were located on all the high points where they could see into Mexico. Men in civilian clothes, in civilian cars, cruised the roads inside Mexico, searching for signs that something was being planned.

Reisman stood in a tent, the flaps up to catch the morning breeze, and watched as the radio operators, sitting at flimsy tables with the controls on them, worked. For a makeshift radio shack, thrown up in less than thirty minutes, it was impressive, including the satellite link that was run from a van parked next to the tent.

Pointing to a map spread on one of the tables, the officer next to Reisman said, "We've got the whole division deployed, spread out, and I think we've got the border sealed. No one gets past without us seeing."

Reisman nodded and then walked to the front of the tent, where he could look out and see Mexico. Without turning, he asked, "Are you sure that something is going to happen?"

"No, sir," said the officer. "It's the impression of the intelligence people that they'll want to get even."

"But nothing concrete."

"No, sir."

"So we've deployed an entire division, costing the taxpayer hundreds of thousands of dollars. . . ."

"Well, sir, I'm not sure about the cost. Had we not moved down here, had we gone on maneuvers at Fort Hood, it would have still cost money, but here we're getting practical experience and performing a service."

"Good answer," said Reisman, grinning. He turned away from the front.

"You have to remember that we've had one of our patrols attacked."

"But there is no reason to believe that the Mexican government had anything to do with it."

"Tensions have been growing since the defeat of the free-trade pact."

"Lot of American jobs went south, anyway."

"So," said the officer, "we patrol the border, trying to intercept raiders."

"What's the policy on illegal immigrants?"

"We follow the guidelines established by the State Department, the Immigration Service and the Department of the Army. We take illegals into custody and they are returned to the point of departure."

Reisman took a deep breath and exhaled audibly. "I'm afraid that there isn't much of a story here."

"You're welcome to join one of the patrols if you'd like. Six or eight hours down on the banks of the river."

"I don't think so."

"Up to you."

"When can I get back to San Antonio?" Reisman asked.

"Later this afternoon. We'll be running back and forth. You can catch a ride then."

"Thanks."

The heavy beat of the helicopter blades finally broke through the fog in his mind and Frankowski lifted a hand to block the sun. He rolled over in the bottom of the waterlogged raft, put a hand on the side, and forced himself to his knees. He tried to spot the chopper, but the sunlight was too bright and it seemed the helicopter was hidden in the brightness.

He fumbled for the survival radio that was floating in the water at the bottom of the raft. He picked it up, pointed the antenna at the helicopter, but said nothing into it.

The helicopter, like a giant bird of prey, circled the raft and then began to hover. The rotor wash whipped at the surface of the sea, flipping up the spray.

Frankowski rocked back on his heels and watched as the pilot maneuvered so that he was looking down at the raft. Frankowski raised a hand, waved once, and then closed his eyes.

There was a splash to the left as one of the crewmen jumped the twenty feet from the rear of the chopper to the water. As the chopper backed off, climbing to a hundred feet or more, the crewman swam to the raft. He popped his head over the top and asked, "You Frankowski?"

"Yeah."

"We're here to get you out."

"One of my wingmen is down in Cuba. You get anything from him?"

"There're a bunch of people down all the hell over the place. I don't know who's where or what's going on."

"You got here fast."

"You were in the water." He hitched a thumb. "You're far enough from Cuba, it's no problem, though we still have fighter protection."

Frankowski looked up into the bright blue sky. He could see the flashes from the wings as a couple of fighters orbited overhead. They were looking for the Cubans, ready to swoop down if the enemy showed himself.

"If you're not hurt, I'll get the chopper back and we'll get you out of here."

"I'm fine. Few cuts and bruises from bailing out, but I wasn't wounded."

"Okay." The man let go of the side of the raft, kicked once, and then began treading water. He waved a hand and the helicopter came back in.

Now it hovered directly overhead. The boom of the winch was swung out and the harness was lowered. The man in the water caught it and pushed it toward Frankowski. "Slip that over your head."

Frankowski did as he was told, pushing his arms up through the harness. He grabbed the cable and looked up at the helicopter. One of the crewmen was crouched in the cargo-compartment door, looking down. He held a thumb up and Frankowski felt a jerk on the cable.

The helicopter lifted slightly and Frankowski came up out of the water. He dangled at the end of the cable, twisting and then rising toward the chopper. After a moment the crewman in the cargo compartment reached out and grabbed the cable, pulling it toward him. Frankowski used a foot, hooked the edge of the chopper, and pulled. As the cable stopped, Frankowski pulled himself in.

They unhooked him quickly and then the chopper descended until it was only inches above the surface of the water. The crewman there grabbed the cable and the harness and was lifted quickly into the back of the helicopter. The instant he was in, the chopper began a rapid climb as it turned toward the north.

Frankowski sat dazed for a moment, his wet uniform dripping on the deck. One of the crewmen crouched in front of him, looked up into his eyes, and asked, "Are you injured?" He gave Frankowski a blanket.

"What?"

"Are you injured?"

Frankowski stared and then shook his head. "I'm okay. I'm fine."

"You sure?"

"My flight is gone. All of them. Gone."

"Call sign?"

Frankowski looked at the man as if he was crazy but said, "Strides."

"Any parachutes?"

"Maybe. One. I don't know." Frankowski pulled the blanket around his shoulders.

"There are other SAR forces out. If any of your people are up on guard, we'll get them."

"Blew up," said Frankowski. "Watched the airplanes blow up. Gone."

"Yes, sir . . . We'll be back in the States in about an hour. Is there anything that I can get you?"

"No. Thanks."

Although he had been listening closely, and had been watching the signs as they moved through the jungle, Martinez spotted no evidence of a pursuit. They had ambushed a superior force and inflicted so much damage so quickly that the survivors weren't inclined to fight back: they were busy thanking God they had gotten clear and were running for their lives. In an hour or two they'd realize that they had been defeated and would start worrying about being the survivors, but at the moment they didn't care.

Martinez and his men worked their way through the jungle, crossed a stream quickly, and then avoided a wider river. They found a bridge and staked it out, but when they saw no evidence that the enemy held it, and that there was no traffic, they used it. As soon as they were across, they disappeared into the jungle again, with no sign that the enemy had seen them.

They reached the outskirts of Managua. Around them were the shanties constructed by those who had migrated to the city but who didn't have the money to buy their way into one of the better sections. They built shelter from whatever was available: scraps of plywood, cardboard, corrugated tin, and mud. A stench like an open sewer hung over the place. Fires burned near some of the shelters, the smoke hanging above the fires, not moving. People in ragged clothes and kids without clothes stood around watching and waiting.

As they passed, Chavez shook his head. He stared into the vacant eyes of the kids, who didn't flock around the soldiers as children did in a hundred other places. No one said anything. They stayed back, afraid to call attention to themselves.

Brown had stopped at the far edge of the shantytown. From that vantage point he could look up into the heart of the city with its high-rise hotels, penthouse apartments, and ornate offices. A helicopter dived through the clouds, hovered over one of the high rises, and then settled to the top of it.

Martinez moved to the front of the patrol. Brown pointed and said, "Looks peaceful enough."

Looking to the right, Martinez spotted a black column of smoke. "Got a big fire over there."

"No sounds of firing," said Brown.

"None that reach us," said Martinez.

Chavez approached and asked, "How much longer?"

Martinez shrugged. "We get to the embassy and we're home free. Chopper out of there and back to Panama."

"Then let's do it," said Chavez.

Martinez turned to study the master sergeant. "What's your problem?"

"We're standing here, sight-seeing, in front of a bunch of potentially hostile strangers."

"They're no threat," said Martinez.

"Let's just get out of here," said Chavez.

"Brown," said Martinez. "You've still got the point. Let's move it out."

"Yes, sir."

They left the shantytown, crossed a muddy street, and then followed a paved street toward the center of town. They spread out now, the interval between the men larger than it had been in the jungle. They watched the ground, the houses and buildings, the cars and trucks, and the people circulating, searching for the rebels.

They reached a major intersection and stopped. Brown crouched, looked at the oncoming traffic, at the buses and cars and trucks, at the bicycles and pedestrians, and shook his head. He waited for Martinez. "Sir, I'm beginning to worry about this. Someone fires at us and we're going to be screwed. We can't shoot back without taking out a bunch of civilians."

"Yeah," said Martinez. "Espinoza, why don't you whistle up some transport for us."

"Yeah," he said. "I wondered when we were going to give up on the walking." He moved off to string his antenna.

To Chavez Martinez said, "Let's get a loose perimeter set. We'll wait right here."

"Yes, sir."

Martinez stood for a moment, his back against the stone wall of a building. It felt strange to be on patrol in a modern city that seemed to be at peace. The civilians, used to seeing armed soldiers on the streets, ignored the Americans. They moved around them, going about their business.

Espinoza walked over, grinning. "They said to grab a taxi or two and motor on up to the embassy."

Martinez couldn't help but laugh. "Now that's an anticlimatic end to a patrol. Walk into the city and climb into a cab."

"They'll send a truck for us in a little while. Situation around the embassy is unstable, but Boyce said—"

"Colonel Boyce is there?"

"Yes, sir. Said that he thought the rebellion was collapsing, and if we'd be patient, he'd get to us."

Martinez looked at a small market across the street. A kid stood near a huge tub filled with bottles of Coke and what looked to be a hunk of an iceberg. "This is the strangest patrol that I've ever been on."

"We stay here?" asked Espinoza.

"We'll stay here," said Martinez. "Have the trucks pick us up as quickly as possible."

"Yes, sir."

"And get us an ETA."

"Yes, sir."

As Espinoza worked to arrange the transport Davis asked, "We get some Cokes?"

"Go ahead. But watch your back and bring me one, too."

"Yes, sir."

"Now what?" Chavez asked.

"We wait for the trucks."

NORTH OF THE TEXAS BORDER

There were more headlights bouncing across the prairie in Mexico than anyone had ever seen. Reisman, standing on a hilltop with a pair of binoculars to his eyes, listened to the soldiers around him. They had been patrolling the area, had been watching the movements of the Mexicans for several weeks, and now they were concerned.

"I make it fifteen vehicles," said one of the sergeants.

"Sixteen."

"Fifteen. Count them again."

Reisman counted and decided that the sergeant was right. Fifteen. He couldn't tell much about them except that they looked like passenger cars or pickup trucks and not military vehicles.

"Coming right at us," said the sergeant.

"It doesn't seem that they're going to waver. They're heading for the only place to ford the river."

"Damn it," said the sergeant, "I wish they'd just stay home." He lowered his binoculars. "You going to be accompanying us, Mr. Reisman?"

"You going down there to stop them?"

"Intercept them, yes. Turn them back before they cross onto American soil."

Reisman held his binoculars to his eyes, watching the bobbing lights. "Can't blame them after what happened."

"Diplomats," said the sergeant, "are supposed to handle these problems. The Mexicans aren't supposed to invade our country."

"Regardless of the provocation?" asked Reisman, lowering his binoculars. In the dim light thrown out by the lantern in the radio tent, he could see the sergeant's name was Reynolds.

"No provocation for invading the U.S.," said Reynolds. "None whatsoever."

"They're not wavering."

"Right. Burrows, get the rest of the platoon ready and let Captain Liemback know that they're coming."

"Right, Sarge."

"You don't have to go down with us," said Reynolds. "You'll be able to see everything from right up here."

"Not the same," said Reisman.

Reynolds pulled his 9mm pistol from the holster. He held it out, butt first. "You going to want this?"

Reisman looked at it. The implication of taking it was startling. He would move from an observer to a participant. Journalists were supposed to observe, though there were some notable exceptions. Walter Cronkite, landing with the airborne soldiers during Operation Market-Garden, inadvertently put on an officer's helmet and had soldiers following him. Others had made a name for themselves as participants. Robin Moore became a trusted member of A detachments in Vietnam, though he was only supposed to be reporting on them.

Reisman reached out finally and took the pistol. He looked at the safety and then put the pistol in his pocket. "Thanks."

"You know how to use it?"

"I know which end the bullets come out. Fourteen in the pistol if there's one in the chamber."

"There is."

"I don't plan on using it," said Reisman.

"Doesn't matter," said Reynolds.

Reisman laughed. "Nice to be ready for anything."

The captain approached, and as he did so Reynolds came to attention and saluted. "If we were under observation by the enemy, I wouldn't do that, sir."

"I appreciate that, Reynolds." He looked beyond the sergeant at the open ground on the other side of the border. "They're getting close."

"Yes, sir, and it doesn't seem that they're going to turn back."

Liemback looked at Reisman. "You going down with us?"

"If that's all right."

"Up to you," said Liemback. To Reynolds he said, "Let's get the men ready to move out. We'll set up in the trees with two squads, throw one out on the bank to let the Mexicans know we're there, and keep one back with the heavy weapons."

"We're ready."

Liemback stepped past the two men and stopped in the flap. "Alert Six that we're going down. I'll fire a red flare if the situation goes to shit. Green if they turn back."

"Yes, sir."

Turning, he said to Reynolds, "Let's hit it, Sarge."

Juan Guerrero was in the lead vehicle. He glanced at the side-view mirror on the passenger's side of the car and saw the lights of the vehicles behind him. Fifty men, armed with automatic rifles, a couple of grenade launchers, and pistols, ready to get even with the Americans for their raid. Guerrero, not being stupid, had decided to attack a bank. Let the raid pay for itself.

They drove up a short rise and stopped. Guerrero got out of the car and walked forward until he stood at the side of the headlight beams. He scanned the area on the other side of the river but could see nothing other than a single dim light on the top of a hill a kilometer or two beyond the river.

One of the men joined him. "The gringos are asleep. No one to oppose us."

Guerrero turned, clapped the man on the shoulder. "Then let's get to it before the gringos wake up."

"Yeah."

Guerrero returned to the car and climbed in. He pointed and said, "Let's go."

They drove down the slope, moving slowly. They reached a flat plain that led down to the river, rolled out, and stopped, the cars parking in a long line.

Guerrero got out again and half a dozen men joined him. He pointed at the center of the river and said, "Let's make sure that we can ford it."

One of the men waded out, feeling his way along. He got to the middle of it, where the water was barely knee-deep. He turned and waved, and then walked back to the bank.

"Let's do it," said Guerrero.

The men returned to their vehicles. Guerrero, in the passenger's seat, said, "Move it forward slowly, but remember we don't want to get stuck."

"Right."

They rolled down the bank and entered the river.

Reisman, standing in the trees next to a Humvee, watched as a squad of soldiers left their cover and spread out along the bank. They took what cover they could find, with the

squad leader centering himself on the bank in the path of
the oncoming vehicles.

"Now," Liemback said, "if we can convince them
that they should return home, everything will be fine."

"Sure."

Liemback raised a hand, putting it beside his mouth.
"On my command, turn on the main light."

"Yes, sir."

The vehicles in the water were churning their way
closer. The headlights on the lead vehicle bounced up and
down and finally illuminated one of the soldiers standing
on the bank. The car didn't slow or stop. It drove into the
shallow water near the bank and out of the river, then
stopped.

The soldier, standing, had his hand out trying to stop
the line of cars. Those behind the lead vehicle altered their
direction, fanning out to the right and left. One of them
bogged down in the river and the doors popped open with
the men piling out. They stood in the knee-deep water,
watching what was happening on the bank.

Men from other cars opened the doors and a couple
of them stood up, their weapons cradled in their arms.

The sergeant walked forward a few steps and said in
a loud, strong voice, "This is the territory of the United
States of America and you are entering it illegally. Turn
your vehicles around and return to the south side of the
border."

At that moment Liemback shouted, "Now!" The
searchlight snapped on, its beam focused on the cars directly in front of the sergeant.

The Mexicans raised their hands to shield their eyes,
but no one made a move to return to the cars. They stood,
unmoving and unspeaking.

"If you refuse to leave, you will be taken into custody. We do not want bloodshed but are prepared for that."

"You invaded our country first," shouted one man.

Another moved to the right, out of the beam of the
light, and dropped to his knees. He raised his weapon and

opened fire, the burst aimed at the light. His bullets snapped through the night air, thudding into the trees, the Humvees, and the ground near the light.

"Take them!" yelled the sergeant as he dived to the side.

The Mexicans fired first, the rounds tearing into the ground. Tracers flashed overhead.

Reisman stood for a moment, watching the beginning of the battle much like a man watching the beginning of a movie. He didn't move, letting the events swirl around him. There was a breaking of glass as the searchlight flared into brilliance and then burned out with an audible bang.

The soldiers around him ran to the edge of the trees and began to fire. They spread out, shooting at the muzzle flashes of the Mexicans.

The headlight of one car was hit and went out. Another was rocking on its worn-out springs under the impact of the rounds. There was a dull thump and then a grenade exploded near the front of another car. Steam hissed from the radiator.

A man was hit and fell into the water. Another began to scream. He broke from cover and ran toward the river. Bullets kicked up the water around him. He was hit once, nearly fell, and then was knocked from his feet.

Reisman, listening to the bullets swirling around him, decided that it was time to take cover. He crouched near a tree, a hand up on the bark.

"Two on the right," yelled an American.

Firing diverted and the two men moving along on the right were cut down. One rolled into the river, but the other dropped on dry ground, tried to crawl, and collapsed in the beams of the headlights.

There was a scream behind him. "I'm hit. *I'm hit!*"

"Medic coming."

The first of the Mexican cars began to move then. It pulled forward and then backed up. The driver spun the wheel and gunned the engine. The car leaped forward and nose-dived into the river. The rear wheels spun, digging it in deeper but not pushing it out. The rear window exploded and the taillights went out. There was a plume of flame as the gas from the leaking tank began to burn.

"Let them go," yelled Liemback.

"Fuck that. Kill them."

Another Mexican was hit. He tossed his rifle into the air and fell back into the river was a splash. A friend grabbed his shirt and pulled the injured man from the water. He threw down his own weapon and held his hands up, surrendering. It looked as if the fight was about over.

Guerrero had been surprised by the men on the American side of the river. He'd been surprised by the size of the force, and by the searchlight. The Americans had been where they had no right to be.

He didn't know who fired the first shot. Just that it came from one of his men. At that point he didn't care. The battle was on.

He jumped back and scrambled around, taking cover at the right rear of his car. He saw that the Americans had men on the shore in front of them, and to the right of them, in a line of trees that had concealed the searchlight.

As the firing increased he turned his attention on the light, shooting into the center of the beam. It flared and went out, leaving only a few headlights to illuminate the battlefield.

He called to the man on his right. "Concentrate on the men in front."

The pattern of firing changed, the majority of it directed at the front. But that from the side, into his line, increased, and a couple of men were hit. One fell screaming.

Guerrero realized that there was nothing he could do. The American force was superior to his. They held the high ground and the cover. They had the firepower.

Guerrero and his men were up against the river. They had no choices.

More of his men were hit. Someone tried to get away in one of the cars, but it hung up in the river. Flames spread from the rear of it, flickering on the water.

"Get out," said Guerrero suddenly. "It's time to get the hell out of here."

Another man was hit and fell into the water. Someone dragged him up onto the bank and then tried to surrender.

The car next to his started and began to back away. Guerrero leaped toward it, ripped open a rear door, and dived in. His cheek hit the knee of a man already inside the car.

They rocked to the right and then the left and there was a splash. The engine raced and water fountained, spraying the windows with mud.

"Go!" yelled someone. *"Go faster!"*

Guerrero twisted around and crawled up to look out the rear window. He could see men running along the bank of the river. Two of the cars were now in flames, and in the flickering light the scattered bodies of the wounded and the dead were visible.

The car lurched once, bounced high, and suddenly they were back on the Mexican side of the border. They slid to a stop and Guerrero opened the door, climbing out. The fight was over on the other side of the river. They hadn't penetrated more than ten meters into the United States.

A half dozen of the cars were able to get back across the river. The rest of them were scattered across the bank or in the water. A couple were burning.

Reisman climbed to his feet but didn't leave the cover of the trees. He was waiting for the soldiers to move. He turned, looked over his shoulder, and saw a couple of them getting ready.

Liemback said, "You wait here for a moment, Mr. Reisman."

"I'm going."

"No, sir. You wait and I'll let you know when you can leave here."

Reisman shrugged and nodded. "Sure."

The soldiers moved out, on line, sweeping toward the burning cars and dead enemy. A couple of men had moved down to the river's edge, where they could watch the men on the other side. They were the blocking force.

Liemback stood at the edge of the field, watching his men. They checked the bodies and picked up the weapons. They avoided the burning cars, afraid that the gas tanks were going to blow.

"Over here," yelled a man. He was crouched near the body of a Mexican. "Got a wounded man here."

The medic, his bag held in his left hand, ran over and knelt. He looked up and said, "We're going to need to evac this guy or he's going to die."

Reisman thought that the soldiers would drag their feet trying to get help. They'd just shot him, why rush to get him medical attention?

Liemback whirled and shouted, "Get a chopper in here."

"Yes, sir." There was a moment's hesitation and then: "Chopper's inbound in zero five."

Reisman left the trees then, walking out to the battlefield. There were a couple of bodies lying near a car. He looked down at them, surprised that he felt nothing. Here were two men who, minutes before, had been alive. Now they were dead and Reisman didn't feel a thing.

Liemback approached. He glanced down at the dead men and said, "Stupid. Should have known that they couldn't get away with it."

"Why?" asked Reisman.

"To get even. Just to get even."

TEXAS

Daniels cradled the phone and stared at the wall opposite him. He couldn't believe it. But Rider wouldn't be wrong about something like that. He stood up and walked to the door, opened it, and yelled, "Amos!"

"Yes, sir!"

"We got trouble coming. Rider was on the phone. Police are on the way."

"What the hell are we going to do?" asked Amos.

"We're not going to surrender to them," said Daniels. "We've important work to do here. The original members of the Texas Revolution didn't surrender, even when they knew it meant certain death. We can live up to that tradition."

Amos stood with his arms folded across his chest and

his feet spread. "I'm think it's time that we get the hell out of here."

"No," said Daniels. "This is our land. No reason for us to get out."

"Joseph," said Amos, using Daniels, "it's coming apart. The raid was a stupid idea . . . maybe not stupid, but we didn't execute it well."

"Going to desert?"

"I think it's time to fold our tent and get out." He wanted to say more but couldn't think of what.

"We've got thirty minutes. How many people are on the compound?"

"Maybe thirty."

"Then we man the blockhouse. We've got food enough for a month, a well for water, and all the ammunition we need."

"Christ, use your head. The people coming have nukes. They don't have to get close. We can call on maybe four hundred people. They can call on four hundred thousand. We don't have a prayer."

"Then get out." Daniels stood up. "Run."

Amos didn't move for a moment, and then grabbed the doorknob. He left without another word.

Daniels glanced around the office a final time. On the wall behind his desk was a color photo of the chapel at the Alamo. On another wall was a painting of the defeat of Santa Anna at San Jacinto. Brave men doing what had to be done. But Sam Houston had an army of eight hundred and Santa Anna was trapped against a river. His weapons were no better than Houston's.

"What can I do with thirty men and women against the might of the United States?"

With that he walked out, saw Rogers, and said, "Get everyone into the blockhouse."

"We gonna make a stand?"

"We're going to do what we can." Daniels looked down at the floor and knew that there was nothing he could do. The best would be a standoff with a negotiated settlement. That was absolutely the best.

Of course it wasn't surrender.

It was the only thing they could do. Negotiate for the best terms they could get.

Reisman was in one of the command vehicles with the radios squawking constantly and an officer giving instructions to everyone who would listen. Liemback sat next to him, his rifle clutched in his hand. He was wearing a desert-camouflaged helmet with the chin strap buckled.

"You're sure that these were the guys that raided into Mexico?"

"Who gives a fuck about that?" asked Liemback. "These are the assholes that gunned down our people."

"You sure about that?"

Liemback laughed. "There was a raid into Mexico a couple of hours before the shoot-out at the river crossing. We've tied them to the raid into Mexico. What do you think?"

"How many people are going in?"

"A company. Intelligence says that'll be enough."

Reisman twisted around and looked over his shoulder. The column was stretched out for about half a mile. Mostly desert-painted Humvees, but also a couple of armored fighting vehicles that would support the infantry if they needed it. It was more of an invasion than a police action to arrest criminals.

He turned around and settled into the seat. He glanced at the map and then back outside. "We're getting close. You think they know we're coming?"

"I would suspect they do."

"Right," said Reisman.

They pulled off the main road onto a gravel track, and then headed off across the desert. They smashed through a barbed-wire fence and climbed a gentle slope, stopping just short of the crest. Overhead there was a single helicopter, circling like a vulture over something about to die.

Reisman opened the door and got out. Standing in the hot Texas sun, one hand on the top of the vehicle, he couldn't see anything other than the top of the hill.

"One Jeep in first to see if they'll just come out," Liemback ordered.

"And if they don't?"

"We all go in."

Reisman nodded and watched as the helicopter dipped once, righted itself, and continued to orbit.

Over the radio in the back of the Jeep, he heard, "Be advised that the subjects have left the offices and barracks, heading for a single, concrete structure."

"Roger. You see any evidence of arms?"

"Negative, but they've got a full-blown rifle range down there."

"Roger."

"Got the Jeep coming up now."

Liemback said, "Let's go take a look."

Reisman thought the captain would get down and crawl up to the top of the crest, but he walked to it, standing there like a football coach on the sidelines. He reached around and pulled his binoculars from their case and lifted them to his eyes.

Reisman joined him and watched as the Jeep stopped in front of what looked to be the headquarters building. One man, dressed in desert camo, got out. He was supported by a police officer who walked forward, his hand on the butt of his pistol.

With the helicopter circling overhead, and a man standing in the rear of the Jeep behind the M-60 machine gun mounted there, the two men entered the building. A moment later they reappeared. Neither seemed to know what to do.

"Looks like the place is deserted," said Reisman.

"See the concrete blockhouse? They're in there."

The two men turned and started toward it. The dirt

around their feet erupted and a minute later the sound of
the firing drifted to Reisman on the hilltop.

"That tears it," said Liemback.

The men had stopped but didn't move. They waited,
but there was no more firing. They conferred and then
slowly backed toward the Jeep.

Liemback turned and waved a hand over his head.
"Okay, people, let's wind them up."

"What's going to happen now?"

"We go down there and convince them of the error of
their ways."

Inside the blockhouse Daniels, with his tiny band, watched
the approach of the Jeep. Rogers, standing next to him,
said, "One Jeep. Shit."

They watched it stop and then the men search the
headquarters. When they started for the blockhouse, Rogers asked, "What are you going to do?"

Lloyd Ladd was next to one of the machine guns
placed at a firing port. Daniels pointed to him and said,
"Give them a short burst low. Don't hit anyone."

"Yes, sir!" Ladd worked the bolt, aimed, and pulled
the trigger. The bunker was filled with the rattle of firing.
The expended shells hit the floor, bouncing. "They
stopped," said Ladd.

"Now we wait," said Daniels. "See what they do."

"They're getting out," said Ladd. "Heading back to
the Jeep. You want I should speed them on their way?"

"Nope," said Daniels. "Let them go."

Gannon, who was sitting at one of the tables, said,
"This is way out of hand. We didn't bargain for this."

"You want out now?" demanded Daniels. "You want
to go? Join that chickenshit Amos?"

"He showed good sense," said Gannon quietly.

Daniels whirled, stormed across the floor, and
slammed a hand to the table. "The only way, *the only way*
that we're going to get out of this is to stick together. They

break us apart and they'll chop us up easily. One at a time."

Gannon sat quietly, staring up at Daniels, her eyes locked on his. He looked away first, turning toward Ladd.

Rogers said, "Somebody's comin'."

Daniels glanced back at Gannon and then walked toward the firing port.

"Two, three . . . looks like a company-size push coming at us. Armored vehicles and maybe two hundred men," said Rogers.

"Nobody panic. Advantages are to us. They can't just level the place. Let's get set. Man the weapons but no one fires until I give the order."

The line of vehicles rolled down the slight hill and stopped two hundred yards from the blockhouse. One platoon broke off and headed to the south, another to the north, so that they had it effectively surrounded. After five minutes the engines were cut and the only sound was the pop of rotor blades as the helicopter hung in the air about two thousand feet above the target.

Reisman, along with the rest of the soldiers, exited the vehicles and spread out. Some of them crouched behind the Humvees or the APCs while others found cover in depressions of the terrain or rocks and bushes scattered across the hillside.

"Now what?" asked Reisman.

"We wait to see what happens next."

The Jeep reappeared and drove toward the blockhouse. The military man got out, lifted a bullhorn to his lips, and said, "You in there. You are all in violation of various local, state, and federal laws. You will surrender your weapons and come out with your hands up."

"You really think that will work?" Reisman asked Liemback.

"Hell, got to try. We storm the place and there is going to be hell to pay."

The officer stood in front of the blockhouse, the bullhorn at his side, watching. He kept his attention focused on the building.

"Standoff," said Reisman.

"Advantage to us," said Liemback. "They can't get out, but we can. They have limited supplies, but we have unlimited resources."

A soldier appeared. "Sir, I've identified the power cables into that place and can cut them at any time."

"Thank you, Sergeant."

"Works only if they don't have their own generation capability," said Reisman.

"Which means a gasoline or diesel generator and finite resources."

The man with the bullhorn said, "You have five minutes to come out."

"And then what?" asked Reisman.

"That's the question I hope they're not asking inside that blockhouse."

"Our choices are fairly limited," said Gannon. She hadn't moved from the table. "We can surrender or die."

Daniels looked at her. "Then we die. Here and now for what we believe."

"Oh bullshit. Believe that we can do something by pretending to be soldiers. We're nothing. Just a bunch of jerks who play soldier."

"That your attitude?" snapped Daniels. "Then get out now."

Gannon stood up, looked at the others, and then dropped back into the chair. "I'm going to stay."

"Then keep your mouth shut."

"Yes, *sir*!" she said sarcastically.

The man with the bullhorn started speaking again. Daniels looked at Gannon, at the firing port, and then back to Gannon. He ignored the man outside. "Are you with us?"

"I said that I was."

Daniels walked back to the firing port and looked out: at the man with the bullhorn standing fifty feet away, at the Jeep behind him, and then at the soldiers on the hill behind the Jeep.

Rogers said, "I believe that we are rightly and truly fucked here."

"We got five minutes to decide," said Ladd.

But Daniels didn't hear it. Instead he was seeing William Barrett Travis standing on the parapet of the Alamo as a Mexican soldier demanded the surrender of the men in the old mission. Travis, with a single shot from the fort's cannon, launched the siege that went down in history.

"Give him another burst," said Daniels, "but don't hit anyone."

"How about I should flatten the tires of that there Jeep?" asked Ladd.

Daniels considered it and then said, "No. Just chase them away."

Ladd turned his weapon slightly, the barrel aimed at the ground in front of the officer. He pulled the trigger and let fly; the ground near the officer's feet erupted and then he grabbed his belly and fell.

"Shit."

"What happened."

"Ricochet," said Ladd. "Had to be a ricochet."

The two men remaining in the Jeep leaped from it, ran forward, and grabbed the wounded officer, dragging him back. They lifted him into the rear of the Jeep and then climbed in. One man spun the wheel, and the Jeep rocketed off in a cloud of dust.

"Now the shit is going to hit the fan," said Daniels. He was secretly pleased.

Reisman couldn't believe that they would shoot anyone. That would escalate the confrontation.

As soon as the wounded man and the Jeep were clear of the area, Liemback yelled, "Fire!"

The whole company opened up. Machine guns, automatic rifles, and even the grenade launchers using high-explosive shells. The bullets bounced off the concrete sides of the blockhouse in little puffs of dust. Pockmarks appeared around the firing ports and the steel door. Someone began shooting at the cluster of antennae on the roof, knocking them down. There was a loud explosion to the right as the engineers cut the outside power into the blockhouse.

There was return fire. A rattling of automatic weapons. The rounds hit the Humvees, the rocks, and the ground. They bounced up and disappeared into the sky. They erupted in clouds of dust, obscuring the enemy blockhouse.

Reisman, crouched behind a Humvee, watched the battle. Smoke and dust partially hid the target. The sound of firing filled the air, drowning out the drumming beat of the helicopter overhead. For a moment he wished he was a broadcast journalist, because the firefight would make for good television. And then he was glad that he wasn't, because he could tell the real story without pictures getting in the way of the facts.

For ten minutes there was no other sound. Just the hammering of weapons as the soldiers tried to knock down the blockhouse with small arms.

And then Liemback was shouting, "Cease fire. Cease fire. Cease fire."

Slowly, one by one, the men and women stopped shooting until there was only the sporadic rattle of weapons from the blockhouse. And then that firing, too, stopped.

Damage had been done to the structure. Huge chunks of concrete had been knocked from it, exposing the reinforcing rods. They hadn't penetrated the walls yet, but they would soon.

Liemback was on the radio, talking to his boss in the chopper above them.

When he emerged from the Humvee, Reisman asked, "What now?"

"We wait."

"Sir," said the RTO. "Colonel's on the horn again."

Liemback returned to the radio, spoke softly. He emerged an instant later, his face a mask of rage. "Carlisle just died."

"Oh shit."

"That's it for them," said Liemback. "They want to play by the rules of war, then we'll play by those rules and reduce that bunker of theirs to rubble."

Daniels ducked instinctively as the first of the rounds hit the walls of the blockhouse. Then it seemed as if all the mean kids in the neighborhood were hammering on it with ballpeen hammers. There were massive concussions as the grenades detonated against the walls. Dust filled the air, making it hard to breathe.

"Shoot back," he called. "Shoot to kill."

But when he stepped to his firing port, there wasn't anyone to shoot at. The soldiers had taken cover and were pouring a steady stream of deadly fire down into the blockhouse. Standing to the side, aiming out to the right, Daniels fired. He aimed at one of the vehicles, trying to break the headlights and flatten the tires.

The interior of the blockhouse began to warm rapidly, the air-conditioning unable to compensate for the heat being generated by the bodies and the firing and the sun beating down from overhead. There was a single crash and the air-conditioning wound down and stopped.

"What the hell?" asked Gannon.

"They destroyed the power lines in," shouted Daniels. "We've auxiliary."

"Not to run the air-conditioning," said Rogers. He sat

on the floor, his back to the wall. He held his rifle in both hands but made no move to get up to fire it.

Ladd was firing and laughing, spraying the area like a kid with a squirt gun. He stepped in front of the firing port and was hit once in the center of the chest. He dropped his weapon and fell back, flat. Blood stained his shirt and began to pool under him.

"Help him," yelled Daniels.

Gannon leaped forward and then crouched near the body. She reached out, touched it, and then drew her hand back. She didn't need to try to find a pulse. The hole was over the heart and there was too much blood.

She stood up and was hit in the back, pitching forward, landing on her face. She struggled to get to her feet but couldn't do it, and collapsed, facedown.

Rogers stared at the two bodies and all the blood. Suddenly he didn't want to be there and wondered why he had allowed Daniels to get them all into the blockhouse. He should have gotten out with Amos. Amos had known the score and had recognized the sinking ship.

Another of the men was hit. He clapped a hand to his shoulder and sat down hard, blood flowing down his side to stain his trousers and the floor near him.

Daniels and a few others continued to shoot, putting out rounds. The weapons hammered, the noise reverberating from the concrete walls. And now the interior of the blockhouse was filled with dust and smoke and the odor of cordite. It was oppressive, and Rogers knew that they wouldn't be able to survive much longer. Especially now that it seemed that the army was going to blow the blockhouse down bit by bit rather than sit them out.

"Let's pack it in," he said quietly, but Daniels didn't hear. "It's over," he said, his voice louder. He stood, clutching his weapon in his hands, his face drained of blood. It was obvious that he was frightened.

From outside the firing began to taper. Rogers put a hand back against the wall and pushed himself to his feet.

He held his rifle loosely in one hand. "Joe, it's over. We can't last in here."

At that moment another of the men was hit. He screamed once and fell to his side. He didn't move. A second later another man was hit. He died without a sound, his body hitting the floor like a fat sack of yesterday's garbage.

"Joe!"

Outside, the Army had stopped shooting. The only firing was coming from the blockhouse, but it was sporadic, as if the soldiers no longer believed in the cause.

"Joe!"

Daniels whirled, his weapon pointed at Rogers. "What do you want, coward?"

"Joe. It's over. There is nothing we can do. They have us outnumbered, outgunned, and surrounded."

"Travis didn't quit."

"Travis had nearly two hundred men and the hope for help. We've got nothing and we're being whittled down."

"Then quit," said Daniels.

"All right," said Rogers. "I will."

Before he could move, Daniels growled, "You go for the door and I'll kill you."

There was a shot then and blood splattered the wall near Daniels. He looked down at the hole in his chest and then at the man who had fired. "You too, Whitney." There was a surprised look on his face. He didn't believe, couldn't believe, that his men would mutiny. He touched the hole, saw the blood on his fingers, and fell to his knees and then to his face.

"Man was crazy," said Garnett.

Rogers nodded. "Let's get out of here before anyone else gets killed."

GUANTANAMO, CUBA

Ramey stood amid the smoking ruins of the base, surveying the damage. Several buildings had been burned, vehicles had been wrecked, and equipment destroyed. The bodies of the dead were still strewn over the landscape. Marines had stripped them of their weapons and had searched for the wounded so that medical aid could be offered. American dead and wounded had been removed as quickly as possible.

He walked along one of the rubble-covered roads, looking down at the expended brass from the firefights. It was funny, the things seen after a battle. Ramey noticed the brass, reminding him of the hours on the rifle range or on the assault course.

Jenkins came around a corner. "Ah, Captain. We've got the pickets posted with the rest of the company relaxing near one of the dining halls. Cooks are making sure that the marines are well fed."

"Anybody have any beer?"

"No, sir. Got one of the NCOs watching the beer. Figured we'd hand it out after seventeen hundred tonight."

"Good."

"Wilson and Philips are dead, but the rest of the wounded should survive. Twelve of them, in the hospital. None to be evacced until tomorrow."

"We'll want to get over to see them this afternoon," said Ramey.

"What the hell do you think they were trying to do?"

"Take Guantanamo away from us. Show the world that we can still be beaten. With Castro dead, there's talk that Cuba isn't very strong. Their soldiers are out of Angola, their economy is in a shambles, and there's still a struggle to take over. Guess they wanted to show the rest of Latin America they were still tough."

Jenkins looked at the destruction and shook his head. "They didn't make it."

"The question is," said Ramey, "did they inflict enough damage to make them look good. They can't claim that they threw us out, because the evidence shows they didn't. Can they convince the rest of Latin America that they hurt us?"

"Doesn't really look like it."

Now Ramey laughed. "But we did call in the Eighteenth Airborne Corps."

"Who didn't get here until the battle was won."

"Hey, don't tell them that. It'll irritate them. Besides, I think we'd have been in deep trouble if they hadn't arrived. It was close enough that the Cubans might have committed some additional troops to push them over. This way they knew they were beaten and got the hell out."

"Then maybe I should buy some of those paratroopers a beer," said Jenkins.

"I think that's a very good idea. But this afternoon, after someone else takes over for us on the perimeter."

"Yes, sir."

•   •   •

Martinez, still wearing jungle fatigues, but clean ones with fresh creases, sat in a small conference room with Chavez and Alvarez, Boyce and Lombard. They were waiting for General Keaton.

"I think we can write the end on that chapter," said Boyce. "That broke the back of the rebels."

"That democratic government is more than a little shaky," said Martinez.

"That explains why we're probably going to go back in to finish the original mission. Help the people establish a strong base and teach them a little about civilization."

"Hell of a thing for the army to be doing," said Chavez.

"But, Sergeant," said Boyce, "if we can make the government strong, then we don't have to fight there again."

"Yes, sir," said Chavez. "I was just making a little joke. Apparently is wasn't very funny."

Boyce ignored that. "The Special Forces concept is to teach the people to protect themselves so that they're not at the mercy of a man with a gun. They will be able to defend themselves. And if we can move them into the twentieth century, then our job is easier."

Chavez realized that he had set Boyce off on one of his favorite lectures, the role of a modern army in the preservation and expansion of civilization, and there was no way to stop him.

Chavez leaned close to Martinez. "Sorry, Captain."

But then the door opened and Keaton walked in. He was beaming at everyone, and as the men moved to rise he waved at them. "Keep your seats, gentlemen." He dropped into another one and asked, "Do we stand on ceremony?"

"No, General," said Boyce. "Special Forces believes in getting the job done."

Still grinning, Keaton said, "Fine. Lieutenant?"

Keaton's aide set a small box in front of Martinez. On the top it said *Silver Star*.

"What's this?"

"As a general, I have the authority to grant certain awards myself. I know what you and your men did in Nicaragua, based on what Colonel Boyce told me, based on the intelligence reports that came from the rebels, and based on what happened in a matter of hours. Given that, and the fact that a planned coup was destroyed by your actions, I think the award is more than justified."

"I concur," said Boyce.

"But there were others there," said Martinez.

"Sometimes the commander gets the credit," said Keaton. "Often he gets the blame. But this isn't one of those times. Lieutenant."

The aide set boxes in front of Alvarez and Chavez. Both held Silver Stars.

"The debate was," said Keaton, "should everyone get a Silver Star or should those outside the command structure receive Bronze Stars for valor. Colonel Boyce explained the Special Forces to me, suggesting that it was more of a team effort than one man leading. Because of that, everyone will receive the higher award."

Martinez reached out and touched the box. "It's nice to be recognized."

"You and your men did a hell of a job. Had you not hit that unit when you did, the fight in Managua would have been longer, tougher, and cost more lives."

"And the situation has now stabilized so that we have no real worries in the area," said Boyce.

"One thing we do know," said Keaton, "is that you got the revolution's leader. He was among the dead that you left when you hit the rebels."

"The party," said Boyce, "starts at seventeen hundred, and I'm buying the first round."

"And I have the second," said Keaton.

·   ·   ·

There wasn't a brass band waiting for him when he finally returned to his home station. As the plane touched down and rolled along the taxiways, Frankowski couldn't see anything unusual on the ramp or near the operations building. A single man, dressed in dark green fatigues, walked from a parked car into the closest door.

The plane lurched to a stop and all the sound around it ceased. In the quiet Frankowski could hear the pilots talking in the cockpit. The loadmaster opened one of the troop doors, pulling it in and lifting it up, out of the way. Sunlight and hot moist air poured in.

Frankowski walked forward, held up a hand to shade his eyes, and then climbed down onto the tarmac. He glanced at the operations building, surprised that Marie wasn't there to meet him.

He felt let down. When Marie had returned from her ordeal in Saudi Arabia, there had been the brass bands, speeches, and crowds welcoming her and her friends. It seemed to him that at the very least, they could have had Marie come out.

"You okay, Major?" asked the loadmaster.

Frankowski turned and nodded. "Yeah. Thanks for your help."

"Sure, Major. Sorry about what happened back there. You did a hell of a job."

"You get any word on Spelman or Hobbs?"

"No, sir. Not a word."

"Thanks again." Frankowski turned and walked toward the operations building, wishing there had been a Jeep to pick him up.

When he opened the door, the interior erupted. A trumpet blared, people cheered, and fistfuls of confetti were thrown at him. He ducked under some of it.

"What the hell?"

Marie launched herself at him. She wrapped her arms and legs around him, planted kisses on his face. She didn't speak to him at all.

Frankowski staggered under Marie's weight. But he

didn't care. He was home with her, and with his friends and fellow pilots.

She whispered in his ear. "Now I know what you went through."

"But I'm home."

"Yeah. I think it's time that we found other careers."

Before he could respond, the squadron commander, Hahn, had pushed through the crowd. As Frankowski disengaged himself Hahn said, "Welcome home, Major. I know that it won't make up for the trials, or the loss of your wingmen, but I have put you in for the Air Force Cross. I don't think it'll be downgraded."

"Thank you, Colonel."

She was sitting up in bed, looking pale, almost frail. Her blond hair was stringy, needed to be washed, and there was the bulk of a bandage creating a lumpy look to the stiff hospital gown. But the tubes had been removed and the IV was gone. As Reisman entered she smiled weakly.

"Do I know you?"

"Not really," said Reisman. "I was here right after you were brought in. Then I ran south with the rest of your unit to watch them . . . what? Get even?"

"Even?"

"Guess you don't know all that much. We found the people who shot you and killed the sergeant. They've been taken care of."

"Arrested?"

"A few. Most were killed in a shoot-out with a company from your division."

"Good."

Reisman moved forward slightly and wished that he'd thought to bring flowers or a card or something. He didn't know why he'd come. He didn't know her, had only seen her the one time. Still, he felt an attraction for her. A brave woman, gunned down while doing her job. A gutsy woman who wasn't whining about the circumstances, but who worried more about getting even with the bad guys.

Reisman looked around uncomfortably, wondering what to say next. He should be getting quotes for a story, but he didn't want to press her about that. "How long will you be here?" he asked inanely.

"Don't know. Couple more days and then home to rest."

Reisman took a shot. "When you're up to it, I'd like to buy you a dinner."

"Why?"

"Why not?"

She closed her eyes briefly, reopened them, and asked, "What is it you do?"

"I'm a reporter."

"Oh. Well, I'm not sure that I care to talk to you anymore. Thank you for stopping in."

Reisman laughed. "I'm on your side here. I saw the end of the operation against the ... survivalists, I guess you'd call them. I'd like to know the truth of what started it."

She remained quiet for nearly a minute, the only sounds coming from the hallway and another room, where there was the low buzz of conversation. Finally she said, "Could be a while."

"Fine with me," said Reisman.

"I'm very tired," she said.

Before Reisman could respond, her eyes had closed again and she was asleep. He grinned at her and then left the room, pulling the door closed behind him. As he walked down the hall he didn't understand his sudden feeling of elation.

ABOUT THE AUTHOR

Capt. Kevin D. Randle, USAFR, has had a long military career in two branches of the armed forces. He flew helicopters for the army during the Vietnam War, serving with the 116th and 187th Assault Helicopter Companies at Cu Chi in 1968–69. While in Vietnam, he was decorated with the Silver Star, the Distinguished Flying Cross, the Army Commendation Medal for Valor, and forty-one Air Medals. Upon his return to the U.S., he graduated from the University of Iowa, and went on to serve twelve years as an intelligence officer in the Air Force. He is the author of numerous articles and books, and contributed significantly to the VIETNAM: GROUND ZERO series by Eric Helm, and WINGS OVER NAM by Cat Branigan. He currently lives with his wife, Debbie, in Cedar Rapids, Iowa.

In the late twentieth century, a series of stunning geopolitical changes destabilizes a dozen major governments around the globe, swiftly pitching the armies of every nation into true world warfare. With the new age of killing technology, there is no neutral zone—no respite in this nightmare epic of a world at war.

GLOBAL WAR: DAWN OF CONFLICT

by Capt. Kevin D. Randle, USAFR

Flashpoint: China. Japanese and American saboteurs hit the Chinese coast to instigate revolution.

Flashpoint: Saudi Arabia. The royal family goes through a bloody power struggle, led by Soviet "advisers."

Flashpoint: Colombia. Elite American forces encounter Cuban military bases in a strike against drug cartels.

Flashpoint: Cuba. Soviet and American troops face off during the last days of the tottering Castro regime.

Flashpoint: Iran. Iran and Iraq gear up again for war—but another country is pulling the strings.

Battle on seven continents,
A world afire...
